The Janus Pope

What if the Pope were a pawn of the KGB?

In a secret room deep in the Kremlin, a bizarre and sinister plot is being hatched – to kidnap the Pope and replace him with his own brother, a fanatical Communist agent. The terror spreads – from Moscow to the Oval Office to the Vatican's inner sanctum – and builds to a high-voltage climax on Easter Sunday as the world awaits the blessing of . . . the Janus Pope.

The
Janus Pope

George Marton

W. H. Allen · London
A Howard & Wyndham Company
1980

Printed and bound in Great Britain by
W & J Mackay Limited, Chatham, Kent
for the Publishers, W. H. Allen & Co. Ltd,
44 Hill Street, London W1X 8LB

ISBN 0 491 02911 X

I

They smoked their pipes in silence. Three middle-
aged scholarly individuals, very tweedy, very British.
Three Harris Tweed jackets, one brown, one gray, and
one heather. Three pipes stuffed with three different
brands of tobacco—Three Nuns in the pipe of gray-
jacket, Baby's Bottom in that of heather-jacket, and
Dunhill's 74 in that of brown-jacket.

The headlines pronounced the thumbnail résumé
of the state of the world—the American presidential-
election campaign, the unrest in Poland, political upheaval in Yugoslavia, effervescence in the Middle East,
and senseless killings in Ireland. The larger main fea-
ture announced the impending first free elections in
South Africa.

The gray light coming from the clerestory windows,
which had been installed by a mad Georgian architect,
fell on a calendar on the white wall, which showed this
to be the fourteenth day of August, and on the clocks,
which pointed to the time as 9:00 A.M. in Los Angeles,
5:00 P.M. in London, noon in New York, and 7:00
P.M. in Moscow. Against the wall stood a huge television set made in Japan.

Outside the gray, ugly building dusk was setting.
The sound of the chimes of the Saint Demetrius
Church cut clearly through the crisp, cold autumnal

air. When the chimes stopped, the deep baritone of
the Kremlin bells could be heard from the distance.

These mid-August days were defined in Occidental
calendars as summer, but, in the Cyrillic timetable of
Moscow, they spelled early fall. The men and women
returning from their jobs were heavily clad. They hastened home to their samovars.

The sidewalk in front of the gray building was
empty. Four black cars stood beside the main entrance. The four fur-hatted drivers leaned against the
black Ziv, smoking their long yellow cigarettes and
having a friendly chat. There were no pedestrians;
whenever anyone reached the curb in front of the
building, he crossed to the other side of the street:
there was no sign forbidding them to walk in front of
the building, but their instinct would not allow it. No
one knew what went on in that building. There was
no inscription, no sign on it. The lodgers of the nearby
apartment houses knew that it was "government." The
cars in front of it, dark in color, big Zivs and Mosk-
witches, all had xG plates. Frequently, small delivery
trucks could be seen bringing groceries from the lux-
ury food stores reserved for the elite. Not all the visitors or employees of the building, which the locals referred to as "the Box" seemed to be Russians. Men
and women went in wearing what the people on the
street thought to be Western European clothing. They
even saw Hindus and black Africans enter the Box.

The three men listened to the Kremlin bells. The
tallest of them, lean and bald, looked at the gray-
haired man sitting behind the desk. He had put the
newspaper down and removed his glasses. Ronald Colvin, the bald-headed one, said, "You know, Alan,
whenever you listen to those bells, you have a nostalgic
look on your face. Would you like to hear Big Ben?"

Alan Houndsworth smiled. "After twenty years?

Nostalgic? For what? You mean the sepia clichés? The railway station, the steam engine, the rain, the priest in the raincoat waiting for his niece? Or English food cooked in mutton fat? The shabby old Rolls-Royces with seedy stockbrokers waiting for the recovery of the pound sterling? Balderdash."

The youngest of the three, a portly redhead, intervened, almost absentmindedly: "Are zakuski better than roast beef? Or snow and ice? Fact is, we didn't make this move here for the food or climate." He stopped and looked at the clock on the wall. "How much time do we have?"

Houndsworth checked his wristwatch with the wall clock. He liked precision. He answered Cholmondley's question: "Roughly ten minutes, Tom. The convention started in Los Angeles about half an hour ago. We can switch that Japanese marvel on any time. Maximus put two special satellites in for us."

"Do you think it is going to be Patrick Donovan?" Colvin asked.

"I hope so."

"Is there such a difference between him and Browne?" Cholmondley's raised eyebrows underlined his skepticism.

"A great difference," Houndsworth said, and the two men looked at him with attention. It was clear that he was "the Boss." "Donovan is a pathetic, pathological pacifist. If he is elected, we will be able to maneuver easily in some fields."

"How can we help get him elected?"

"Maximus wants to leak the Osipov Papers to the press."

"Through the Poles as usual?" Colvin asked.

"That's right. He thinks it will discredit the incumbent."

"You seem to have doubt," Cholmondley said.

"I don't like the idea of making a man an underdog over there. The Americans have a weakness for underdogs. Still we probably have to do it."

"Browne seems to be so popular. You don't think he has a chance?" Tom Cholmondley asked.

"Browne is a turncoat. A Republican turned Democrat. That makes him a traitor in many eyes."

Colvin said with a bitter smile, "And, as we know, nobody loves traitors."

Houndsworth shrugged. "Talleyrand said that treason is a question of timing."

As if dreaming, Cholmondley looked up at the ceiling. "So, if our timing is proper, someday we may become heroes. Not only on this side." He shook the dream off and asked, "Can we turn the thing on?"

Houndsworth nodded and pressed the button. The sound erupted like an explosion. "God!" Cholmondley quickly turned the sound down.

The picture they saw was that of a fantastic, oversized circus. Everything was loud, overloud. The colors, the sounds, the movements were gigantic, boisterous, chaotic. A speaker on an elevated platform raised his gavel, grabbed the microphone. The thunderous sound of the applause intermingled with the bellowing of bullhorns. The man on the platform began his speech, and the amplifier made it almost comprehensible. He said something that sounded like, "The great and beautiful state of Nevada . . ." The people in the immense hall paid no attention to the speaker; it seemed as if they could not hear him at all. The crowd could be described as heterogeneous, a euphemism that understated the reality. Young men in blue denims with short hair and long hair and ponytail hairdos; old men with cowboy hats and sailor hats and yarmulkes and top hats; young girls in bikinilike dresses reduced to a minimum, young girls in slacks, young

girls in long white evening dresses; fat middle-aged ladies with half-bared bosoms, Afro hairdos for the
whites, foot-wide Florentine hats for the blacks; men
in Madison Avenue gray flannels and button-down
shirts, jostling men in gold shining fabric with red and
yellow sun-visor caps, two obese black men engaged in
a sandwich-eating contest, a man in a sombrero with
the big sign TEXAS on it, waving a lasso above his
head; a tall handsome woman dressed, unpredictably,
in the red uniform of the Canadian Mounted Police
and carrying a poster with the inscription JUSTICE FOR
ABYSSINIA on it. The cries "We want Pat!" were
drowned by the bullhorns of the opposition. The
whole image exuded power, youth, optimism. It was
cheap, vulgar, and exhilarating. A Barnum and Bailey
circus of confidence in the future, of firm belief in
America.

It was a relief when the deafening noise stopped. A
deep, resonant voice extolled the virtues of a shiny red
Japanese automobile. His laudation was underlined by
derogatory comparisons with its competitors, a new
trend in advertising.

"Can I turn off this rubbish?" Cholmondley asked.

"Not off, just down. I am interested," said Houndsworth.

"Interested?" Ronny asked.

"Advertising, publicity, commercials, are all an integral part of their daily life. A life we have to study.
Know thy enemy. Advertising of Japanese cars can
have political importance."

Eager to learn, Cholmondley asked, "May I ask
how?"

Always ready to teach, Houndsworth stuffed his
pipe, leaned back in his chair and said, "If a Republican President is elected, there might be no importation
of foreign cars. The Republican party is traditionally

for protectve import restrictions. If the Japanese can't
sell cars to the United States, they might reconsider
their ties with them. *Quod erat demonstrandum.*"

"So why don't we push for the Republican side?"
Cholmondley asked.

"Because both Maximus and I think that we should,
as you so vulgarly put it, *push* Patrick Donovan. You
know how important South Africa is for us. If Donovan is elected, he will put into effect his pacifist aims.
Which means that he will stay out of South Africa,
where only two personalities have a commanding impact on the population—the American President and,
God help us, the Pope. I will tell you more, but first
let's get back to the convention."

Cholmondley turned up the sound. The noise
seemed to shake the room. The background was the
same, but there was a new speaker on the platform.

"Turn it off, please, Tom. Give us a rest. I asked
our good Uzbek cook to make us his famous Irish
stew. It will be past midnight before we hear any results of the voting. Gives us time to eat and discuss
things leisurely." He picked up the phone and ordered
dinner to be served.

The waiters rolled in a trolley with food and drinks
and set up three folding tables. Houndsworth took out
a bottle of whiskey from his desk and filled three
glasses. "Cheers," he said.

"I need cheering. That rah-rah stuff depressed me,"
Colvin said. "Stupidity on such a large scale always de-
presses me. Even in the potential enemy."

Houndsworth shook his head. "They are not stupid.
'*Les Americains sont* "childish," ' to quote André
Gide. It's a childish circus of a young and virile people. To let off steam. Don't be fooled by it. It is meaningless. Just a big loud show."

"You say, don't be fooled by it," Cholmondley said.

"But are these clowns fooled into thinking that they have a say or can determine who leads the country?"

"They are. After all, they have the vote. And they have their problems. We have a guided, realistic public opinion. They haven't. They still suffer from the Vietnam-Watergate syndrome. Do we suffer from our setbacks in Czechoslovakia or Hungary? Or the Greek and Portuguese elections? Nobody thinks of these anymore. Not the man on the street nor even the Politburo. And they? Just last week, our esteemed enemy, General Holt of the CIA, quoted Montesquieu again: 'A free government, that is a government constantly subject to agitation, cannot last if it is not capable of being corrected by its own law.' Can you imagine a government constantly subject to agitation?"

"Hardly. I am curious to know whether these cowboys we saw had an influence on what they used to call 'détente' a few years ago," Colvin said.

"Détente . . ." Houndsworth mused. "A dead word. Do you know that in the French original it has two meanings—not only the lessening of tension but also to pull the trigger?"

Colvin smiled. His puckish round naughty-boy face showed pleasure and contentment. "I like it. A good definition," he said. "And I like this stew, too. I wonder who taught our Uzbek to make Irish stew."

Houndsworth admitted modestly, "I did."

Cholmondley looked at him. "The eternal teacher," he said. "When we first met in Oxford, I hate to say how many years ago, Ronny and I decided that you were the one to make the grade to professor. Maybe even to dean. And you haven't changed."

"I guess none of us has—not much. Only we are getting older. And the local climate is getting through to us."

Both men looked at him. The words did not mean

much, but the way Houndsworth said them, slowly in
his deep baritone voice, carried a hidden meaning.
Houndsworth went back to the desk and pressed the
button. The servants entered instantly. "Clear the tables," Houndsworth ordered, and he stuffed his pipe.
He touched the top of the desk with his index finger.
"Full of dust," he said. "I don't know why they don't
clean the place properly."

"Security. Nobody is supposed to enter this room.
We made our choice between hygiene and security. We
opted for the latter," Cholmondley said.

Houndsworth was amused. "*Security*," he said. "An
obsolete word. With our new Enigma II and their Ul-
tra 78, we know what happens in Washington before
they know, and vice versa. Want to know what General Holt is having for lunch?"

"Frankly, no," Cholmondley said. "And I don't
think he gives a damn whether you eat zakuski."

"Let's try this Georgian cognac. Maximus gave me
the bottle with his compliments." He poured three
generous portions into the snifters.

Colvin looked into his glass. He thought of what
Houndsworth had just said. Houndsworth never made
idle conversation. Cautiously, he said, "Nice cognac.
Did Maximus give any other compliments?"

Houndsworth's face showed his pleasure at Colvin's
fast reaction. He sighed, "Alas, no. He is not enrap-
tured with our latest activities."

As if talking to himself, Cholmondley said, barely au-
dibly, "Gratitude has its own statute of limitations.
How long should one be grateful for past deeds?"

Houndsworth began pacing up and down. The two
men settled back in their chairs, waiting for the lecture.

"Gratitude. Romantic nonsense. In opposition to
realpolitik. Face it—we are getting a little stale, prag-

matic, which is understandable. The secret service is an office, part of the bureaucracy. We were not hired as apparatchiks. Good Marxists here are a dime a dozen. But at Oxford, we were boy scouts, adventurers, men of fantastic ideas."

"They put dampers on us as you know," Cholmondley said.

"That was under the 'détente' period. The dampers are off."

"Does this mean . . ." Colvin started, but Houndsworth interrupted.

"Let me explain. And relax. This will take time and concentration. More cognac?"

He poured the brandy into the snifters and started his lecture, speaking slowly, like a real Oxford dean.

It was getting colder in the room in spite of the central heating. The sky, visible through the skylight windows, was darkening. No stars, just billowing black clouds full of Siberian moisture.

Cholmondley looked at his friend standing now in front of the desk. His *friend*, in the best classic meaning of the word. Yes, Colvin was a dear friend too, but not in the same league as Alan. His relationship to Ronald Colvin was deepened by some sexual feelings, and improbably, their friendship had outlasted the emigration, the intrigues of the secret service, the triumphs and setbacks. Perhaps his ties to Ronald needed this mutual sexual attraction. With Alan no physical involvement was necessary. It was a friendship pure and lasting, built on solid ground.

They had not acquired any new friends in Moscow. When they had talked about this, Alan had said, "Friendship is not like cut flowers; it needs roots."

By looking at the fine Celtic face of his friend, Cholmondly tried to guess his troubled thoughts. He wished he could be of help. He would do anything to

take over some of Alan's problems. His head slightly
bent, the weight of this troubled world on his shoulders, Houndsworth reached for a second pipe on the
desk. Cholmondley tried to remember when he had
first noticed Alan's stooped posture. Was it a way of
keeping, literally, a low profile due to their clandes-
tine profession? Or had it started when Pollux was
killed? Or was it the constant menace and burden of
Castor's unbridled misdeeds? Problems with one's off-
spring should be limited to vice-presidents of a bourgeois society—they don't belong to ours, he thought.

Houndsworth continued, "I have to outline our own
shortcomings as compared to the activities of our esteemed colleagues of the CIA. Our service is perfectly
organized, especially in such vital areas as West Germany, Canada, the United States, and, recently, in
South and West Africa. Our network is impressive,
both in quality and quantity. They collect good hard
facts, but they lack imagination."

Colvin asked, "You mean covert political actions?"

"Yes. The CIA is not better organized in the information field, but I cannot help admiring them for
their action in Chile and the elimination of Trujillo
and Lumumba."

"They failed with Castro," said Cholmondley.

Houndsworth shrugged. "That was too bad. Would
have saved us some headaches. Like Angola, which in
the long run backfired, as you know. The KGB very
seldom undertook such highly effective operations.
Not because we are so honest or so controlled. We simply lack the fantasy for it. I don't have to draw any
pictures. Our scientists have the imagination and capacity to send Gagarin into space, explore Mars and
the moon, and build an almost usable supersonic
plane. But we still can't buy shoestrings or color film

in Moscow, and I'm tired of removing the windshield wipers every time I leave my car on the street."

Colvin nodded. "It's all true."

Cholmondley shook his head. "Can we have more of that good Georgian brandy? Not bad at all. Not as smooth as Hine or Courvoisier, but mellower than Metaxa."

Houndsworth refilled the snifters. "One more word about secret services before I get to my main theme. We all know, of course, that ours is excellent, almost equaled by the CIA. But do you know which one is the best?"

Almost in unison Cholmondley and Colvin said, "Israel."

Houndsworth smiled. "Almost right," he said. "The top dog is the Vatican."

Four eyebrows were raised. Again, in one voice, they asked, "The Vatican?"

"Yes, the Vatican. And for obvious reasons. Think of the millions of Roman Catholics dispersed around the world confessing to their priests. They are not spying. They are only reporting on the state and mood of their diocese to the Vatican. Do you know that between October 1939 and April 1940, the Vatican sent out a warning called 'Case Yellow' of an imminent attack on Holland and Belgium? Do you remember that in 1942 Menzies figured out that the Vatican could be used to filter back spy reports to the enemy? Menzies let Pope Pius the Twelfth know through Sir d'Arcy Osborne that the invasion of France would take place in the Cherbourg peninsula and not in the Normandy, where we planned it. It worked. Like all of Menzies's schemes." His face took on a dreamy expression. "His enemies called him a witless, upperclass snob. He died on May 29, 1968. Sir Steward Graham Menzies.

Bridges Court, Luckington, Wilshire. Knight Commander of the Bath, Commander of St. Michel and St.
George. Major General Menzies."

Colvin had to smile. "Come back to Russia, Alan.
We're not in England, and we're living in the eighties,
not the forties. Although it is true, to misquote Bos-
well, if I thought the world was coming to an end, I
would move to Russia, because everything happens
there fifty years later."

Houndsworth shook his dream off. He said, "We'll
try to make things happen today—not in fifty years.
The present state of the world calls for astute, intelligent, and daring action. We are, or will be, if Donovan
is elected, in a state of synchronicity."

Where does he dig these words up? Cholmondley
thought. I must check this one in the Oxford. As if
reading his thoughts, Houndsworth continued.

"Simultaneous events. Coeval. The American presidential election, the South African elections, the set-
tling of accounts in France, Italy, and Spain. The con-
stellation was never more favorable for us. The
slightest push will tilt the balance to our side. With
the amateurish hesitations of their State Department,
South Africa will fall like a ripe plum. In France, Italy, Spain, and Portugal, or if you wish, in all the
Latin countries, Communists have now Cabinet rank.
But they are not yet the government. I think we can
correct that."

"What about the effervescence in Poland?" Colvin
asked.

Houndsworth shrugged. "Not our bailiwick," he
said. "Comrade Karpov is paid for that."

"And the Near East?" Cholmondley wanted to know.

With a deep sigh, Houndsworth said, "Look,
friends, Jews are expendable. They always were. In the

last war, when the Hungarian and Romanian governments started armistice negotiations with us, we leaked the news through the London *Times*. The Germans sent in five armored divisions to quell the peace overtures, and the SS killed four hundred thousand Jews. But we had five panzer divisions less to face in the Normandy. It was the right decision. And Kissinger, God bless his soul, said on October 26, 1973, during the Yom Kippur War, 'We must end the hostilities in a manner that would enable us to make a major contribution to removing the conditions that have produced four wars.' Even a nonastute reader deduced that Kissinger wanted a limited Israeli defeat in order to make peace. And the best way was to withhold arms from Israel as long as politically possible. Yes, the Jews are expendable and the Arabs fickle. A brush fire in the Middle East is easy to start and just as easy to extinguish. For the moment we will discard this problem."

Houndsworth sat down at the desk. The two men waited for the imminent announcement of a forthcoming operation. Only the hissing sound of the heater was audible. The sound was a gesture of apology for the minimal amount of heat coming out of the radiator.

Finally, Cholmondley's curiosity overcame his discretion. He said, "Okay, chum, Poland and Israel are not our problems. Tell us what is."

"Everything depends on whether Donovan gets elected. Tom, please turn on the television. Perhaps the voting has started."

Cholmondley turned on the button. The noise was not so deafening now, and the meeting seemed better organized. The camera focused on a big man wearing a red-visored hat. He said, "The great and sovereign state of Alabama casts its vote for the future President

of the United States, Patrick Donovan!" The applause
was thunderous. Colvin took a writing pad and a pencil from the desk.

"Check one, Alabama."

"It starts auspiciously," Houndsworth said. "Let's
hope it continues."

II

"I'm sure that Alan doesn't mind this. But, old man, let's face it—this is the ugliest room in the world." The square room was really ugly: an olive-green linoleum floor, neon lights, a ceiling shaped like the top of a Quonset hut, a gray steel table with a swivel chair behind it, and two steel chairs facing it—not even a portrait of Lenin on the wall.

Colvin nodded agreement. "It's like a descent into Hades. How many floors under street level are we?"

"Four. I wonder whether the Duke of Wellington's war room was more comfortable?"

"It probably was. He had it somewhat easier. Napoleon did not use electronic devices to monitor the duke's conversations."

"I'm sure Alan has valid reasons for moving us down here," Colvin said. "We made the entire building of the American embassy radioactive with our listening devices, and now they have reciprocated in this one. Seemingly, we can't trust our scramblers anymore."

"And we pay for our privacy with this . . ." Cholmondley made a sweeping gesture.

The padded door opened and the armed guard ushered in Alan Houndsworth. "Sorry, men, that I kept you waiting. But I have important news for you." He went to the table, put down the heavy folder on it, and sat down.

In the moment of calm before the storm, all three men stuffed their pipes. So soothing for the nerves. Houndsworth looked at his two friends and said, "I am going to start with an anodine cliché. I have never doubted your convictions, your loyalty, and your ability to keep a secret. What I have to tell you, however, is an unusual top secret. It will be known only to four—ourselves and Maximus. Of course, those carrying out our orders will know of it, but not all. I want it clearly understood that no one, no relative, no lover, no member of the party, not one single member of the Politburo is to know of the plan or any detail of it. If I did not need your brainpower and cooperation I would not tell you about the project, either. Is this clear?"

Both Cholmondley and Colvin nodded.

Houndsworth leaned back in his chair. "We are going to kidnap the Pope and replace him with a Communist."

Cholmondley and Colvin sat rigidly, not breathing. They did not trust their ears. Cholmondley was not sure that he had heard correctly. He asked, "Kidnap the Pope and replace him with one of ours?"

"Yes. His brother, the dean of the faculty of philosophy in Bologna, the number two man in the Italian Communist Party."

"Professor Giulio Monticelli," Colvin said.

"He resembles his brother a great deal, but a few minor retouches will be necessary."

"Will he cooperate?" Cholmondley asked.

"Monticelli has not yet been briefed. He will be brought back here and properly persuaded. I have no doubt that he will agree. Don't forget, he is the most reliable pillar of our party—the only real party, the one here in Moscow. The Italian party now firmly believes in their own independence. Baroque nonsense. If communism is to survive, all parties in the world must be guided and ruled by Moscow. Monticelli plays our game by pretending that he is for this new independence. And as you know, nobody hates the Church and the Pope, his own brother, more than Giulio Monticelli. Yes, he will cooperate."

All three concentrated on their thoughts. Cholmondley broke the silence.

"I can see the possibilities, but I am sure you have more concrete ideas. What is the prime reason for kidnapping the Pope?"

"Remember—synchronicity. The Catholic countries are ripe, overripe. Some minimal help coming from the sacrosanct mouth of His Holiness the Pope might tilt the scale in our favor. Our men in the Vatican will consolidate all our power. We'll have more influence over more people through the Vatican than through scores, even hundreds, of pockets of the party throughout the world." He stood up and wiped his face with his handkerchief.

"God, it's hot and stuffy here."

Colvin shrugged. "It sure is. Isn't it strange that they can build a good scrambler but their air conditioners stink?"

Houndsworth continued, "I have been thinking of this plan a long time, but I did not want to put it into operation unless Donovan was elected President of the United States. Now we can start immediately."

"Why is Donovan necessary?" Cholmondley asked. "Where does he fit in?"

"He and the Pope are old friends," Houndsworth said. "The Pope has an enormous influence on Donovan. And the Pope is due in the United States sometime in January or February."

"And that's why we have a deadline, It must be *our* Pope who makes that visit."

He knew the answer but he still had to ask the question. "Who is going to be in charge of the field operation?" Cholmondley asked.

The answer came as expected. Very quietly, almost inaudibly. "Castor," Houndsworth said.

Cholmondley did not look at Colvin. He knew they both had the same thoughts.

"Is he an irrevocable choice?" he asked.

"Let me put it this way. He would be my final choice. But let's discuss this fully. I want your advice."

"Does the plan include physical violence and termination of opposing elements?" Colvin asked.

"I don't foresee any," Houndsworth said. "At least, I hope there won't be any."

"You don't intend to kill the Pope, do you?" Cholmondley was anxious to know.

"Definitely not. The person of the Pope is negotiable, an asset to be kept for eventualities. He will be taken to our safe house, the Galenium in Switzerland."

Cholmondley continued, "And you think that Castor is the man for the job? As you say, a nonviolent job."

Houndsworth shrugged. Perhaps not too convincingly, he said, "I think I can restrain him. I want to believe I can."

"Did you consider Petrov for this?" Colvin asked.

"I did. He is too conspicuous, too tall, too Slav. We can change his flaxen hair but not his cheekbones. And his English is tolerable, but he has no Italian. Castor's Italian is perfect."

"Languages are not his problem," Cholmondley said. He added, "And he certainly does not look like a Slav. A typical Celtic face."

Houndsworth managed a smile. "Since he *is* my son, he is entitled to a Celtic face."

"What about using Boniface?" Colvin asked.

"I don't think Italians are right for this. The matter is too sensitive. I thought of Lefeiulle, but he had trouble in Milan in connection with the Feltrinelli case."

Cholmondley stepped closer to the desk. He said, "Now, Alan, don't think we are being purposely negative. I trust Castor is able to hold a secret and can carry out difficult missions, just like you did. The question is whether he can really be restrained from violence."

"I repeat that I am sure I can restrain him," Houndsworth said.

Colvin straightened up and decided to speak up. "Look, Alan—try to understand my misgivings. I don't mind dealing with agents who carry out missions for the love of money. They are the safest. Or some of our best agents who act out of conviction—political, even religious conviction. Castor is not interested in money or in socialism."

Houndsworth interrupted. "He hates capitalism," he said.

Colvin would not be sidetracked. "Who doesn't? Anarchists, Maoists, even liberals hate capitalism. That does not make him a reliable Communist."

Houndsworth agreed. "You said that you preferred agents who work for money. What we must have is an agent who will carry out my instructions to the letter. Castor will do just that. Put him down in your books as a greedy bastard who works for money."

Cholmondley intervened. "We are not interested in his motivations. Only in his actions. But we know from experience that he seems to thrive on killings and brutal violence. I am willing to believe that you can control him, but you still take a certain risk."

"A calculated risk. I would not dare to entrust anyone else with this operation."

"Well, this is pure Kafka," Colvin said. "Have you considered the consequences if the project misfires?"

"I have. For foreign consumption we must have a waterproof cover. This is why I need the Korean File. Did you get it, Tom?"

Cholmondley opened his briefcase. "They wouldn't let me take the original out of Pugatchev Square. Here are the Photostats." He handed them to Houndsworth.

Colvin was both intrigued and irritated by the secret byplay inside the secret service. "Will somebody tell me what it's all about?" he asked.

"Certainly," Houndsworth said. "A crazy story. Six months ago three mad Koreans who wanted to kidnap the Pope and hold the Church up for money and political blackmail crashed their plane on our side of Mount Ararat. I still don't know whether they died or whether we're keeping them on ice in Siberia. Did you find anything on them, Tom?"

"Not a thing. Nobody seems to know."

"Unimportant," Houndsworth said. "What is important is that through a Korean priest they made a thorough survey of the Vatican and the Pope's habits. They had architectural plans, photographs—everything. We kept their papers and never announced the plane crash. If, as you said, something should go wrong—and I am sure it will not—we will leak this file to the world press. The Koreans will be blamed."

"Ingenious," Colvin admitted. "You said we have very little time. Here is my last question: Where is Castor?"

"Castor is in Moscow. I haven't seen him yet. He'll be here tomorrow."

"Well, we both wish you luck if 'luck' doesn't collide with dialectical history. By the way, have you selected a code name for this adventure?"

Houndsworth smiled. "I have. Operation Holy See."

III

Houndsworth had spent a sleepless night. Not even the sleeping pills from Professor Stakinin had helped. He did not look forward to the meeting with his son Castor.

He scrutinized the present position. His operative word for this "soul searching" was *scrutiny*, not *analysis*. *Analysis* was a good Greek word, degraded and distorted by the pupils of the great Jewish prophet Freud. The new opiate of Western bourgeoisie, replacing the old and cheap confession. He hated psychoanalysis and was happy in his hatred. It was good to hate. It kept the adrenals going.

Scrutinize. Thesis, synthesis, antithesis. He used Castor's talents and vices for valid political reasons. Castor was very useful, and it was Houndsworth's duty, as one of the high priests in the hierarchy of the Politburo, to employ the best available man for this difficult job.

He had a further reason for choosing Castor. He secretly hoped that Castor would destroy himself. He could not carry this out himself, but the impulse was there quite frequently.

In truth, Houndsworth was deadly afraid of his son. He shudderingly recalled Castor's report of the killing of forty-six passengers at the Athens airport, among them eleven children. His hands still covered with their blood, he examined the debriefing file casually and with no sign of emotion, with no pride, not even a cold cynical smile. A robot made of ice. After the meeting, Cholmondley, never mincing words, called Castor a "rat excrement."

Houndsworth did not feel any responsibility or remorse toward the two boys who were twins. Cholmondley had christened them Castor and Pollux, not for mythological reasons, but because the two names went well together. The names stuck. Pollux had been killed by some CIA hirelings in a shoot-out in Athens, but Castor remained Castor. Houndsworth had paid for their schooling, including a short term in Oxford. The boys became school dropouts in spite of very high IQ tests. From British schoolboys, they evolved into KGB assassins, in which neither Houndsworth nor his wife had any hand. Alison Houndsworth had refused to join her husband in Russia, although the British Foreign Office would have granted her an exit visa.

Alison had wanted her two boys to be decent British gentlemen and had changed their names legally to no avail. The boys, perhaps somewhat ostracized, somewhat impressed by the adventure of their renegade traitor father, just vanished from Oxford one day. When they showed up in Moscow some twelve years later, via Chile and Iraq, they were well-formed, well-trained, physically perfect terrorists. The thin veneer of Marxism was window dressing, meaningless.

Houndsworth tried to educate them. He sent the two undisciplined anarchists to the Vinohrady School to learn Marxist philosophy and dialectical history. He had no more success than their mother. They quit school and were trained in weaponry and electronic communications.

Castor loved assignments that took him out of Russia, preferably to South and Central America, where

he met up again with his cronies of the gang once
headed by the infamous terrorist Carlos.

Houndsworth's pipe tasted bitter when he recalled
the telegram he had sent to Castor in Bombay inform-
ing him of his mother's death. The cabled reply the
next day said, ACKNOWLEDGED. CASTOR.

Castor flew in the previous night from Caracas. The
Tupulov of the Cairo–Moscow run was late and he
spent the night at the Intourist Hotel at the airport.

He did not look forward to his meeting with "the
Boss" (he never called his father anything but "the
Boss"). Of course, there was always the hope for some
important assignment, but why was the old man so
long-winded? Why did everything have to be explained, described, emphasized to be of great political
importance to the party and the workers of the world?
Who the hell cared for the workers of the world?
What Castor wanted was clear, precise, and short instructions, without any of the ideological nonsense.

He shaved and looked into the mirror. He did not
like what he saw. His green eyes had deep shadows under them, for which he blamed Conchita. The long
Celtic face was all right and so was his strong crop of
dark blond hair, but his color was awful. Greenish
white. No time in Caracas for a little sunbathing. Oh,
well, he shrugged, he wasn't entering a beauty contest.

He put on a flannel suit made in London but pur-
chased in Caracas, a white shirt, and a striped tie. The
Boss did not approve of open-neck shirts and blue denims.

He shared a cab with a middle-aged couple from
Turkestan. At Red Square he continued on foot to the
Box. A guard escorted him to "the Dungeons."

Houndsworth, smoking his pipe, sat on a steel chair

behind the small table. On seeing Castor, he managed to twist his mouth into a semblance of a smile. Mechanically he stood up and mechanically he extended his hand. Castor took it and said, "Hello, Boss."

"Good morning, John," Houndsworth said. "How was Caracas?"

Castor shrugged. "As always. You called me back so we couldn't complete the standard job."

Houndsworth nodded. "How is Felipe?"

"The same."

The same, Houndsworth thought. A great conversationalist. Will he volunteer anything if I keep quiet? Let's try. He knocked his pipe against the ashtray.

Castor scanned the room and looked at the ceiling. Unexpectedly, he started talking. "You moved to the cellar—are you expecting an air raid?"

"No. The new listening device, 'the Puzzle,' frightens our experts. We don't know how effective our scramblers are against it."

Castor shrugged. "All they can monitor is conversation. Words. No radar yet to record our thoughts."

I wish I had that radar, Houndsworth thought. To find out what goes on in his head.

"How was your flight?" he asked.

"Fine. What are your orders?"

Orders. Instructions. Facts. Okay, Houndsworth thought, let's start. He opened the folder on the desk.

"You will fly tomorrow to Rome via Stockholm and Scandinavian Airlines. A Swedish passport in the name of Jorgen Johanssen is in the folder. You will go to the Eden Hotel, where Robles will be waiting for you. One day in Rome, mostly to have a look at the Vatican. After that Robles will drive you to Bologna. You will have two days to familiarize yourself with the topography of the University of Bologna faculty of philosophy. You will arrange for a personal meeting, alone, with Professor Giulio Monticelli and hand him this letter."

From the folder he took out a long yellow envelope and showed it to Castor. He put the letter back into the folder.

"Okay," Castor said.

"I must add that the letter is written by Maximus, and it is an invitation to Monticelli to fly with you to Moscow."

"When?"

"Immediately. Monticelli must pack a suitcase while you wait in his apartment. Robles will drive you. In an official embassy car. Diplomatic immunity. Robles will drive you back to Rome to the airport directly to the waiting Tupulov. After takeoff, you will receive further instructions from Flight Captain Orlow."

Castor looked at the ceiling while digesting the instructions. "Okay," he said, and stretched his hand for the folder.

Houndsworth stopped him. "Wait a minute. I must emphasize that no violence of any kind is permitted in this operation. This is a major job with which we entrust you, and of great vital interest for our country."

Here we go, Castor thought. Here comes the lecture. Vital for our country and all the workers and peasants of the world. He suppressed a sigh.

As if reading his thoughts, Houndsworth fastened his eyes on Castor's. "I will not burden you with more detail on further procedure. This will be a step deal, and the less you know, the safer we both are. I repeat—no violence, no brutality. You will manage to see Monticelli alone, without brutalizing or killing anyone. You understand?"

"Clear enough. What are your instructions in case Monticelli refuses to fly with me to Russia?"

"I don't think he will refuse. Not after reading Maximus's letter."

Castor was not satisfied. "Suppose that he says no. What do I do then?"

Houndsworth leaned on the table and sank his face into his palms. This was the stickiest part of the assignment.

"We must have Monticelli here. Imperative. But we cannot harm him. In the strictest emergency, and if there is no other way, you will have to use the syringe. I repeat—only if there is no other alternative. It must be done as gently as possible. Monticelli is a great man, and we need him, hale and hearty."

"I understand. Anything special for me to do at the Vatican?"

"Acquaint yourself with the entire layout. Entrances, exits, balconies. If you have time, look at all the buildings within a distance of no more than two kilometers and with a good view of St. Peter's Square. But only if there is enough time. This is for some future, but as-yet-indefinite, plans."

"When I get back to Moscow, do I report to you?"

"Yes. I will be in touch with you on your flight as soon as you reach Russian air space."

"Anything else?"

"No. That's all. Happy landing."

IV

Three students watched the television set in the *mensa academica* of the University of Bologna. With them sat Professor Giulio Monticelli, their teacher of theological philosophy. The picture they saw was in black-and-white. The university could not afford the still-expensive color set.

The four faces showed curiosity blended with undisguised mistrust. The teacher's visage added unbridled hatred to his contempt.

The deep, melodious voice of the commentator carried respect, awe, and religious fervor, as he described the immense crowd waiting at the Piazza del Vaticano for the appearance of the Pope.

The deep rumbling of the mass turned into a roar as the Pope appeared on the balcony. Flanked by four cardinals, he began the hand movements blessing the crowd. The loudspeakers carried the sound of the Latin words.

Monticelli had three options. He could stop the show by pressing a button, he could smash the set, or he could turn his head away and concentrate on his own thoughts. He longed for direct action, but discipline was stronger. He obliterated the present—students, television set, the Pope—and thought of his past.

When had he started to hate him? Probably at that Christmas when Marco, who would one day be known as Pope Clemens, had been five years old and he was four. Aunt Clara had bought a fine ivory crucifix for Marco. All he received were some stale chocolate-covered almonds. He had thrown them down the toilet.

He thought of the Pope. His Holiness the Pope, the monstrous symbol of Roman Catholic voodoo and deception. The Pope he hated so much. The Pope who was his brother.

The crucifix had only been the beginning. All the presents went to Marco. The Monticellis were too poor to be able to pamper the nine boys. Marco got everything. The small electrical-appliance shop of Papa Monticelli did not yield enough lire to provide all nine boys with a decent education. The money from the sale of light bulbs, flashlights, and electric shavers was used for the schooling of Marco. The overtime work in repairing fuses and crossing wires so that the poor could have free electricity from the Municipio took care of the groceries. Their only common education was in repairing small electrical appliances, but even at that, Monticelli remembered with bitterness, Clemens had been better than his brothers.

The hatred had built in him through the years until it became an obsession. Their fistfights ended by the intervention of their father, who inexorably sided with Marco. When, in an uncontrollable rage of his choleric temper, Giulio went for Marco's chest with the kitchen knife, Papa Monticelli beat him badly and ordered him to leave their home. It was only his mother's intervention that rescinded the order. Perhaps he should have left then and not years later, when Clemens had been accepted as a pupil at the Collegio Papio. Even at this moment he remembered properly stealing both his father's gold watch, a present from the cardinal, and his youngest brother's bicycle. He left Livorno at midnight and rode north all night. Always at night and always toward the north. He stopped in Bergamo, not far from the Swiss border, and found work in an electrical-appliance shop. He read classic literature and studied, mostly at night.

On his eighteenth birthday he became a member of the Italian Communist party. He fought in the Second World War against the Nazis with the Communist underground. It was easy to join the party in Bergamo. The mayor was Communist, and so were the trade unions, the schoolteachers, and the small merchants. Even Sergio, the owner of the appliance shop where he worked, was a Communist, although he made good money selling gadgets to the eager-buying Italians. Giulio liked big, boisterous, wine-loving Sergio, but he could not understand how a Socialist could remain a religious Roman Catholic. His own fanatic devotion to the party was only partly due to the class struggle and the dictatorship of the proletariat. He cared less about destroying the establishment and the economic system; he wanted mostly to destroy the Church.

For his fight against the Vatican he needed more cerebral ammunition. When he realized this was not obtainable in Bergamo, he moved to Bologna. The unexpected windfall of a "purse" facilitated the move. He received this money from a lawyer who told him that the gift came from a rich, anonymous benefactor, and he accepted it gratefully, without giving it too much thought. When this gesture was repeated in Bologna, he also didn't allow himself to question it. He continued his study. His vituperous hatred of organized religion, personified by his brother's involvement with and success in the church hierarchy, increased.

The University of Bologna, one of the oldest in Italy, was famous for its faculty of theological studies. Because of the large majority of Communist voters, the faculty became the focal point of anticlerical studies.

Giulio's zeal and total devotion to the cause helped him in his rapid rise to assistant professor, full professor, and then dean in three years. He also rose constantly in the party hierarchy to the place of "Numero Due." He studied and knew the mechanism of operations of the Vatican better than any cardinal and perhaps better than his brother, the Pope himself. He knew every line every heretic had written about the Church, from Joseph of Arimathea to the schism, from the Jansenists to Hus to Martin Luther. He wallowed in all the dirt filtered down through the centuries about the Holy See, and he enjoyed quoting the Renaissance gossip of homosexual popes and the poisonous dinners of the Borgia heads of the Church.

His obsessive dream, the destruction of the Vatican, was so overwhelmingly strong that he would not allow himself to consider a life apart from his compulsion, including a serious love affair with any woman. He had his small and pleasant adventures, mostly with admiring female students, and this satisfied him. He chuckled when he thought of his own career and that of his brother, the parallel of their careers. The Monticelli boys had risen rapidly in the hierarchy of their professions. He was now dean of the University of Bologna and his sanctimonious brother was the Pope. Clemens, certainly, was not tempted by women; he had never been interested in the opposite sex. His love was reserved exclusively for the Holy Virgin. The thought made Giulio slightly nauseous.

His lecture classes on the vicissitudes of the Vatican were crowded. He spoke well, and his passionate hatred for the subject made them more popular. He was perhaps less liked by the pragmatic leaders of the Italian Communist party, who navigated the danger-

ous waters of religion against religion, Marxism versus
Roman Catholicism. There had been a moment when
Berliguer, the head of the party, thought Giulio a dangerous fanatic and that he should be "muzzled," and
he suspected him of more loyalty to the Soviet leadership than to the Italian.

With great relief Monticelli noticed that the students had shut off the television set. He stood up and
went out for a stroll.

V

It was early in the morning. When Kenyere looked at his wristwatch he saw it was only 6:35. He did not mind. He loved the early-morning hours, and he often felt the urge to say a prayer of thanks when he sniffed the bracing air and looked east to the rising sun. He was not very good at saying prayers anymore, not for many years. He contented himself with this feeling of gratitude to no one in particular for being alive.

He opened the screen door of his home. It was not much of a home—more like a shack than a Roman villa. But it was just what he wanted. A hut among many other huts, among his children. The Bantus, the Kaffirs, the Nassus were all his children. He loved them with the same deep passion he had felt for them when he taught school in the suburbs of Joburg.

Kenyere opened his arms wide and inhaled the breeze coming from the Indian Ocean, a big ocean, which linked his Africa to Asia, a body of water that carried the vessels of communication and commerce between continents. He loved the sea and frowned when he realized that his thoughts of that sea were disturbed now by the dangers emanating from it. He dismissed the thought and went back to the house.

His round-faced, rotund wife, Nata, standing at the table, poured coffee from a huge earthenware pot. Kenyere went around her and sat down. With his left

hand he reached for the milk, and with his right, he
patted the firm and impressive backside of his wife.
The morning routine always sent electric tingles
through his fingers, down his spine to his groin. In
spite of his sixty-two years, he liked the sensation and
was proud of it.

Nata placed the big bowls of porridge in front of
him. Kenyere took a big portion of the red one the
Dutch liked and not the gray one the Anglos ate.
Frankly, Kenyere always felt a little ashamed of this
compromise. He disliked the Boers and had a secret
admiration for the Anglos. However, he knew that a
politician's life was filled with compromises.

Such a compromise existed in his feeling of commu-
nity, of understanding, for the American people. He
had spent two years and two months in the United
States, invited by that scholarly historian, the secretary
of state. He liked many things about America and succeeded in building his own image of the United States.
He knew this was distorted but he did not care. His
America consisted of blacks, Italians, Puerto Ricans,
and Jews. No Wasps among them. For him, mixing
and conversing with "cold whites" was impossible.
The   cold whites were the Boers, the Germans, the
British, the Scandinavians. And, the Russians. Especially the Russians, who, in his imagination, were en-
crusted with Siberian ice and snow. It was true that
the Russians tried much more than the others to be
friendly with him and his party, but Kenyere did not
trust them. "Do you know that you are a bizarre kind
of a racist?" his friend Professor Kenney of the University of Joburg once asked him. Yes, that's what he was:
a bizarre racist.

He stiffened when he heard the hissing sound, followed by a thud. His neck went rigid, his eyes riveted
upon the door, his ears sharpened. Silence. Relaxed, he

got up, smiling contemptuously at his unnecessary alarm at the daily routine—the newspaper boy dropping the paper on the porch of the house. He opened the door and picked up the paper.

There was not much in it for him. The usual diatribes of his own party, the African National Council, ANC for short, supposed to be an umbrella organization respected by all blacks in Africa, fighting against the ANU and APC, both Communist oriented. His friend, Bishop Kwa, had written an excellent editorial, but to what use? The ANC had the words, and good words they were, but the others had the guns. Kenyere did not like guns, and he never wavered in his hope and conviction that unity amongst the blacks could be achieved without the use of firearms.

When he saw on the second page the picture of Donovan, the man who was most likely to be elected President of the United States, he crossed the fingers of both hands. The incumbent at the White House was a useless nonentity, and there was always hope in a new man, in fresh ideas. He did not want to admit to himself his fears of Donovan. His enemies called him a "morbid pacifist." Pacifist to what degree? Would he help when help was needed? How could Kenyere inform this new President that Nadbaning, the mighty leader of the APC, would not only kill all the whites he could lay his hands on, but that first he would massacre all the non-Zulu tribes. This was not a guess; he was certain of it. He still had a few devoted friends who, at the risk of their lives, infiltrated the APC ranks and gave him very accurate reports of the leader's intentions. Last month, one of these, Zeli, who attended the APC meetings in spite of his eighty-five years, had been found strangled in his bed. How did they find out about Zeli? How many spies did "they" have in the ANC ranks?

He suspected that Nadbaning, who paid lip service to Marx and Lenin, knew next to nothing about socialism. But he knew the value of Russian gold and Soviet Kalishnikov machine guns. He, Kenyere, knew a great deal about "imported communism." It had not worked in Angola and it would not work in West Africa. Not in this climate and not with "his" peaceful, primitive, and gentle blacks. He had his own conception of real African democracy.

And that democracy was terror. African democracy was a sham. Yes, his people had a real chance to live peacefully and well, now that the hated apartheid was ending. Apartheid, an ideology (if you wanted to call it that) that could be traced back to the Calvinist beliefs of the early Dutch settlers. They held that God's will demanded separation of the races. But in practice, this became an excuse for an economical system benefiting the whites, who used and exploited cheap black labor for all menial and backbreaking jobs. Kenyere thought of all those well-meaning reformers who ended up creating more chauvinism and race hatred than progressive philosophy—Calvin, Muhammad, Luther.

He opened the drawer of his rough-hewn wooden desk and took out a sheet of note paper. He did not need his glasses to read it; he knew it by heart. It was a letter he had written many months before. It started with "Dear Mr. President," and he was waiting to send it to Washington if Donovan got elected.

VI

They crossed the Bridge of Saint Angelo to the castle. The weather was fine, more springy than wintry. Small playful white clouds chased each other, unveiling the blue sky in ragged patterns.

Castor's stride was purposeful. His eyes darted from the street to the building and to the crowd surging toward St. Peter's Square. Occasionally he glanced at his escort, Robles, who seemed to be enjoying himself. Robles, the swarthy Cuban "gorilla," whose first name nobody knew. Or was Robles his first name? Castor was aware of the Cuban's hungry eyes as he stared at all the females. He breathed heavily, his huge chest expanding. His body oozed dirty and ever-ready machismo.

The Street of Conciliation took them to St. Peter's Square. The immense crowd seemed to wave in the wind like a field of wheat. Over the heads of the multitude the slender obelisk raised a warning finger, assisted by the jets of water in the fountains. Bernini's colonnades embraced the square like two open arms, which lead to the Dome of the Basilica.

The impact of it all, the crescendo of the bells in the immense cupola, the imperial grandeur of the marble figures, and the overwhelming abundance of the columns had their effect on Robles, but all he would ven-

ture to remark was, "Why do they call this a square? It
is round."

Castor did not answer. He was busily noting all the
details as they slowly pushed their way in the direction
of the papal apartments. He saw buses of all sizes and
from all the countries of Europe, the private cars, even
a few horse carriages. On his right, there was the motley, disciplined mob of tourists, priests, peddlers offer-
ing small boxes of rosaries, workers in their blue denims, bank managers in double-breasted dark suits, fat
Sicilian ladies with huge breasts, slender girls in loden
overcoats.

The gentle breeze from the Alban hills carried the
dying-out sound of the noon bells. With the ebbing
tinkle, the murmuring of the crowd sank lower. As all
faces turned to the balcony of the papal apartments,
the sounds suddenly stopped completely.

On the fourth floor of the palace a door opened and
Pope Clemens appeared, dressed in white and flanked
by four cardinals. The Pope, in spite of his age,
seemed to be physically strong. His face had a warm,
congenial expression, and his eyes were young and perceptive. There was a mildness with an underlying
strength. Humility, which commands respect. When he
raised his hands in blessing, the crowd reacted by gen-
uflecting and by crossing themselves.

Castor had his small field glasses forcused on the
Pope when he felt a poking in his ribs.

Robles whispered, "When in Rome, do as the Romans do. Cross yourself while the Pope bestows his
blessing."

"Some blessing. Empty slogans, translated into
thirty-six languages."

"Like we do in the Kremlin."

"Yeah, but we do it only once a year. On the first of
May. They do it every Sunday, not to mention those

endless holidays." He added, with his cynical smile, "Matter of fact, holidays are the real working days for these cats. Preaching the same drivel from thousands of pulpits."

The amplifiers carried Pope Clemens's words: ". . . for the Lord is your refuge and your fortress. No evil shall befall you because He has given His angels charge over you, to protect you in all your ways . . ."

Robles was amused. He said, " 'Angels to protect you'—damned good slogan. We could learn from them."

"Learn what? This driveling nonsense?"

"The word believes it because it is senseless!"

Castor pointed at the Pope with his chin. "He does not believe it. Look at the face of that hypocrite."

"Don't you underestimate them. Even Khrushchev said some nice words about the Pope. With good reason. The Church carries a lot of power."

"What kind of power? Stalin, who was a lot smarter than Khrushchev, asked how many armored divisions these clowns have."

The Pope's words continued: ". . . therefore we shall not seek to know who is right and who is wrong, but, according to God's will, we shall seek peace, understanding, and unity . . ."

Robles whispered, "Unity. He is using our slogan."

Castor shrugged. "They have been using it for two thousand years. Not very successfully."

Pope Clemens was concluding his address: ". . . and blessed be the Lord who created heaven and earth . . ."

Castor added, "In six days, but rested on the seventh. Union rules."

The black crowlike figures started to disperse slowly. "Let's get the hell out of here." Robles started to walk away.

"Wait a second," Castor stopped him. "I have to look at something." He turned and stared at the buildings on the north side of the Tiber. Not satisfied, he raised his field glasses and looked northeast.

Across the Tiber, facing the Piazza del Popolo, he saw the newly built apartment houses on a hill. He lowered his glasses and said to Robles, "The Monte Pincio. That's it. Let's pay it a visit."

VII

It was past three o'clock in the morning on this fifth day of November, and they were exhausted, all three of them. They held half-empty glasses of champagne in their tired hands and smiled wearily at each other.

Patrick Donovan, tall, dark-skinned, and handsome, sat on the chintz-covered couch, his hand in that of his wife, Gladys. His rolled-up sleeves displayed muscular arms, and his fifty years were scarcely evident. She wore a loose-fitting houserobe that did not disguise a slim figure. Facing them across the low coffee table with a champagne bucket on it, Phyllis was sprawled in an overstuffed armchair.

Donovan pressed the remote-control button and turned off the television. "Enough of that," he said. "The battle is won."

"And you are the winner, Mr. President," Gladys added. "I still can't believe it."

"You've got to believe it," Phyllis said. "The sonofabitch just conceded."

"Watch your language, Phyllis. You are the Crown Princess now," Gladys said.

"Some Crown Princess," Phyllis shrugged. "You can't inherit the presidency. Presidents' daughters disappear into limbo, never to be heard of again."

Donovan raised an admonishing finger. "Gladys is

right. We'll have to be careful what we say. The eyes
of millions—"

Gladys interrupted. "I know, Pat, I know. Muzzle
me. No more free talk about women's lib, about easing
divorce proceedings and taxing bachelors. I will be
prudently brave."

"And what about me?" asked Phyllis. "What's my
life going to be like with so many restrictions?"

"*Prudence* is the operative word," Donovan said.
"Tennis is okay. But watch it with the guys, my darling daughter. Flirting can be a dangerous sport for
the President's daughter."

"Pat, the poor kid is a twenty-one-year-old divorcée.
She can't be a nun. She needs a man. She's a woman."

"A man, yes—but be careful what kind."

Phyllis squinted at her father. She picked up her
horn-rimmed spectacles and put them on. Her languid,
feline femininity was not dispelled by them. She said,
"What are the chances of meeting eligible bachelors at
the White House? I've scanned the members of your
Cabinet. They are either over fifty or wildly unattractive. Did you select them to scare me off?"

"Frankly, I had other reasons. Cheers!" Donovan
lifted his glass.

They sat in silence for a moment. The atmosphere
was relaxed, warm. Gladys patted her husband's arm.

"You'll have to watch your language, too."

Surprised, Donovan looked at her. "My language?"

"Yes, yours. People will tire of your conversations
with God. Religion is fine, but too much religion can
be an awful bore."

"I am not aware—" Donovan was interrupted by
Phyllis.

"But we are."

Nothing could spoil Donovan's good mood. He
lifted his glass. "I swear by God Almighty that I will

not use His name more often than absolutely necessary."

They all laughed. Donovan's belief in God and
strong religious convictions were his anchor, his stabil-
ity. Gladys and Phyllis were less emotional about their
beliefs and often ribbed him.

They all smiled and drank their champagne.

Gladys sighed happily. "Before we go to bed, let's
have a stroll in the garden. Just the two of us."

"Let's." Donovan got up. "Just the two of us and
fourteen agents of the secret service. Good night
Crowned Princess."

"Good night, Mr. President," said Phyllis.

VIII

The University of Bologna, in the majestic Palazzo Foggi of the sixteenth century, seemed an absurd anachronism towering above a shouting, hysterical mass of students carrying predictable slogans on their posters. They shouted these phrases as they marched. They seemed evenly divided—half of them for the Democratic Christians, the other for *comunismo*. The fury was mostly vocal, the sporadic fistfights not very convincing. They had loud resonant Italian voices. The sound was deafening.

Robles had driven the stately Ziv limousine of the Russian embassy from Rome to Bologna in just over two hours and had parked the car on a side street next to the square. He leaned over the steering wheel and said to Castor, "How in hell can you get in there?"

Castor shrugged. "I'll manage. This is nothing compared to the University of Caracas. You wait here until I get back."

He circled the seething mass of demonstrators and made his way to the main door of the university. A student obligingly guided him to the entrance of the huge amphitheater, which was overcrowded with eager listeners. Castor squeezed himself into the back row. He craned his neck to get a clear view of Professor Giulio Monticelli standing on the elevated platform. He was surprised to see that in spite of a gray moustache, Monticelli's face resembled that of the Pope. He looked vigorous and youthful for a man in his late fifties. He spoke with the dedicated, almost fanatical conviction of a teacher who knew how to captivate an audience of young students. A late twentieth-century Savonarola, Castor thought, as he became fascinated by the lure of Monticelli's diction. Here, surely, was a man who could sway people's opinion.

For a moment the lecturer paused and listened to the sounds coming from the street.

"They are loud, aren't they? Are they shouting to convince themselves? The loudness might ease their consciences if they have any. Because they are fake. They are fighting communism under a counterfeit flag—under the Christian Democrat flag. They are neither Christians nor Democrats. They are Fascist hirelings."

He stopped for the thunderous applause, then continued: "And who is the supporter and financier of fascism in Italy? The Roman Catholic Church. The Church that regained its independence by a pact with Mussolini. They pay lip service to an understanding with the working class, then turn their backs on any approach for such an understanding. When that great man, Marchais, pleaded in Paris for a unity between Christians and Socialists, the Vatican said, 'No. We believe in heaven and they don't.' They want to sell us the theory that the first Communist was Christ, not Marx. The same Christ whom they destroy and despise. They are constantly borrowing Marxist doctrines, giving them a religious tint, and presenting them as the original. Just listen to this announcement."

He picked up the sheet from the pulpit and put on his reading glasses. " 'It is clear that the hiring of labor and the conduct of trade are in the hands of a small

number of rich men able to impose upon the laboring
poor a yoke little better than tyranny . . .' "

He listened to the murmur of curiosity or incredu-
lity of the audience for a moment and then continued:
"Familiar words, aren't they? Can you guess who said
them? Marx? Engels? Lenin? No, my comrades, I am
quoting verbatim from a papal encyclical."

Again, for a moment, he stopped to enjoy his success. He is good, Castor thought. I understand why
they selected him in Moscow for whatever job they
need him for.

Monticelli went on. "The Pope himself must admit
that the Church cannot remain blind to the pressing
problems of the computer age. To avoid their proper
commitments, they use pious words, corrupt ecclesiasti-
cal language to obscure, rather than reveal, the truth.
Yet language alone, no matter how subtle the seman-
tics, no matter how obfuscating, cannot hide the fact
that the charitable Church is a ruthless tyranny. Their
sacrosanct dogma imposes on their subjects a cruel discipline, prescribing not only their actions and
thoughts, but even their behavior in bed."

Listening to the applause, Castor thought, here
comes the abortion issue.

Monticelli raised his voice. "And who enforces these
inhuman rules of sexual conduct? A bachelor. A celi-
bate. The Pope! Claiming to be the one and only re-
cipient of Divine Revelation. The Keeper of the Key
given to him by the man from Galilee, who did not
even know he was a Christian. The man who fought
hierarchy, orthodoxy, priestly jurisdiction, and who, if
he came back to earth today, would be shocked to find
himself represented by an institution dominated by
the same enemy he had been fighting. A high priest
called the Pope and a group of Pharisees called the
cardinals."

He paused for a moment to sip some water from the glass on the pulpit. "They are supposed to be the princes of the Church. But they are only money changers, like the ones Jesus drove out of the Temple. Their main interest is in the collection of riches. They are subservient to any secular power. They always pay ther dues to Caesar. They use God's name to bless the poor, but they do not ask His help to feed them."

A bell sounded the end of the lecture. Monticelli picked up the papers on the pulpit. "This will be all for today. See you tomorrow."

After a burst of applause the students started to leave. Castor remained seated. He watched two students approach Monticelli with notebooks in hand. Monticelli opened the books, nodded, and initialed one of them. The two students left by the center aisle.

Monticelli must have felt the impact of Castor's piercing eyes. He looked up at him and asked, "Are you waiting for someone?"

Castor stood up. "Yes," he announced. "You."

Monticelli shrugged. "Well, I am here."

Castor slowly descended the slanting aisle and stopped in front of Monticelli. He reached into his breast pocket and brought out the envelope.

"I have a letter for you. From Moscow."

Monticelli took the envelope but did not open it. He looked at Castor and said, "You are Castor."

Castor nodded. Houndsworth must have gotten word to the professor.

Monticelli took a small penknife from his pocket and started to open the envelope. "Do you mind?" he asked.

"Please," Castor said.

Monticelli read intently, his lips repeating the words silently. When he reached the bottom of the page, he reread it again. He folded the letter and

placed it on the pulpit. He repeated one word aloud:
". . . immediately."

He looked startled and puzzled. "Have you read this?" He indicated the letter.

"No."

"But you know what's in it?"

"The main item. And I know who signed it."

"When do you expect my answer?"

"Now. Immediately."

Startled and irritated, Monticelli said, "*Immediately* is not a favorite word in my vocabulary. I need time to think."

"How long will it take you to think?"

I am not sure that I like this character, Monticelli thought. Be that as it may, he is Maximus's envoy and must have very important reasons for his request. Or rather his order.

He tried to relax. "Let me take you to lunch to my favorite *taverna* just around the corner. With the espresso, you will have my answer."

"Fine," Castor said. "Give me the address. I have a friend waiting for me outside. I'll tell him to wait."

"Via Ugo Bassi, Number Four. Just around the corner."

"I'll meet you there in five minutes."

When Castor stepped inside the small Taverna degli Angeli, he could not find the professor. The room was crowded. A small, very obese man stepped up to him and asked, "Signor Castor?" When he nodded, the man signaled him to follow. He ducked under a low archway and saw Monticelli sitting at a small table in a room that was barely larger than the table.

Monticelli pointed at the chair facing him. "We have privacy here."

Castor sat down and picked up the menu.

"Don't look at that," Monticelli stopped him. "Tell

me what you like. The spaghetti is homemade and the *coda di rospo* comes straight from the Adriatic. Fresh, not frozen."

"I'll settle for a plate of spaghetti," Castor said.

"Bolognese, of course," Monticelli added.

"Of course."

Monticelli ordered, along with a bottle of the house red Tuscany wine. "This is real first-rate Tuscany," he said. "Not like the Chianti that is sold each year in quantities four times more than the amount that is harvested."

The fat gnome of a waiter brought the steaming plates of spaghetti, and they started to eat.

"I am not a great conversationalist at table," Monticelli said.

"Nor am I."

"What I have to say, I say at political meetings and at the university."

Castor nodded. They ate in silence.

Monticelli ordered the coffee and finished the wine. He took the envelope out of his pocket and placed it on the table.

"Immediately. This means that I must go home, pack my suitcase, and go with you. Where?"

"Rome. We have a car waiting for us. In Rome the plane will be ready."

Monticelli leaned back in his chair. "Signor Castor," he said, "I will go with you. I have waited all my life, worked all my life, to strike at the Vatican." He paused, thoughts of his brother flashed through his mind. "Yes, I've waited a long time."

The cabin of the Tupulov plane was especially roomy for its three lone passengers. Castor proved the extent to which he was a man of few words. On the two-hour drive from Bologna to Leonardo da Vinci

Airport in Rome, he hadn't uttered more than ten
words—either to Monticelli or Robles.

Monticelli tried to sleep on the plane but could not.
He decided to read and reached into his carryall for
the Teilhard de Chardin book of essays. Occasionally,
he took a sip of the iced vodka and accompanied it
with a generous portion of caviar.

"When do we expect to land?" he asked Castor.

Castor looked at his wristwatch. "We will be in Russian air space in about a half an hour. I'll find out
from the pilot."

When he returned to his seat next to Monticelli, his
face was inscrutable. Monticelli looked at him, and
Castor answered the unasked question with a laconic,
"Soon."

Forty-seven minutes later Castor walked up to the
cockpit and signaled Robles to follow. A few seconds
later they both reappeared carrying three folded parachutes.

Monticelli had noticed the change in the pitch of
the engines. They were losing altitude and seemed to
be circling a fluffy mass of dense black clouds.

"Are we landing?" he asked and started to fasten his
seat belt.

"Don't do that," Castor said sharply, and handed a
parachute to Monticelli. "We have engine trouble.
We're going to bail out."

Incredulous, Monticelli repeated, "Bail out?"

"Yes. Sorry about that. Nothing new to you, though.
As a major in the Italian Resistance, you learned how
to use parachutes." He started to put on and fasten his
own gear.

"That was a hundred years ago. I was a little
younger. I am not sure I can handle this."

Castor helped him put on the parachute. "It is like
swimming. Once you learn, you never forget." Castor

inspected Monticelli's parachute and tested the belt buckle. "Fine," he said. He pointed at the cord in front. "This is what you pull."

Forgotten memories popped up from the computer in Monticelli's brain. "I know," he said.

The plane was circling now under the clouds at an altitude of four thousand feet. Monticelli looked down at the green fields scattered among forests and a serpentine river. Let's hope I can land on those meadows, he thought.

A buzzer sounded. Robles opened the center emergency door and said, "Ready."

Castor nodded. "I go first. You follow me." He went to the open door, steadying himself on the backs of the seats. He did not hesitate for a moment. He jumped.

Monticelli forced himself. Hesitation and delay would be fatal. He groped his way to the open door, closed his eyes and jumped.

The rush of cold air hit him with a fierce impact. He opened his eyes and pulled the cord, bracing himself against the sudden pull of the air brakes.

He was falling slowly in the total silence of the bracing air when he heard the deafening sound of an explosion. Twisting his head, he looked up to the right and saw the Tupulov disintegrating in midair.

IX

The room was almost dark. The small night lamp could not penetrate the tenebrous shadows.

Houndsworth sat astride a steel chair and waited. He could barely see the bed, the white bundle in it, and the other figure near it. His sense of smell tried to break down the chemical composition of hospital odors—linoleum, disinfectant, bedsheets, electric wiring. Or was it the smell of viscera, of dry blood? Or just the smell of death?

The sound of his own voice startled him in the stillness of the room. He said, "Jabotinsky, can we have more light?"

The figure answered, "Five minutes, Comrade Houndsworth. His eyes are very sensitive. We had to make some incisions near them. I gave him a pain killer."

Five minutes—not an eternity, Houndsworth thought. Will it work? Will he perform as he agreed to? Two weeks of intensive persuasion, conversation, discussion. Finally, the man had given in after a long session at the Kremlin. For the man, this should be the fulfillment of a dream. Why had it taken so long to get his final consent? Stage fright? Were there hidden bourgeois objections in his brain?

Dr. Jabotinsky groped his way to the window and pulled up the blinds. Houndsworth squinted. In the strong sunlight he saw the palm trees swaying in the breeze. The sea, a silver pancake, was freckled with white sailboats. He turned back to the bed. The beauty of nature did not interest him.

He stood up and looked at the man on the bed. "Now?" he asked the doctor, who nodded.

The doctor, with his sensitive professional hands, very slowly, very carefully, unwound the bandage. The man on the bed started to moan and move his head from right to left. The doctor propped him up into a sitting position. The man whetted his lips with his tongue and said, "*Acqua!*"

"*Subito.*" Houndsworth went to the nightstand, poured some water from the pitcher, and held it to the man's mouth.

The man drank it all and said, "*Grazie.*" He added for Houndsworth's sake, a nonliteral English translation, "God damn it! It hurts."

Houndsworth found this funny. "Sorry about the pain. It will soon go away. But, my friend, cursing is not permissible from now on."

"You said this was a free country. Well, let's get it over with. Where is the mirror? I feel naked without my moustache."

"Yes," Houndsworth said. "The mirror, please, Doctor."

Dr. Jabotinsky fetched a hand mirror from the bathroom. Houndsworth stepped up to the man. "You look handsome, Giulio," he said.

"I looked better with my moustache. Do you have a picture of His Holiness?"

Houndsworth opened his briefcase and took out a large photograph. "Here he is."

"Not bad. All Monticelli men are handsome."

"You just committed the sin of vanity, Guilio."

"Speaking of sin, what do I do when the devil tempts my carnal desires?"

"The devil has no access to the Vatican."

"I know. However, there were a few well-known exceptions under the Borgias."

"Don't worry, Giulio. You'll have some free moments. Your brother has a laudable habit of leaving the Vatican, incognito, so to say, to visit the needy, thus giving the Italian secret police nightmares."

"Fine. I shall visit the needy when the devil raises his ugly head. I will be the needy."

Doctor Jabotinsky had been listening in the background. "Do you need me here?" he asked.

"No. Thank you, Doctor." Houndsworth followed Dr. Jabotinsky to the door. Castor sat in a chair in the corridor.

"Anything special you want, Giulio?"

"Spaghetti Bolognese and good red Italian wine. And Sophia Loren."

"I am afraid she is in the middle of a picture. But I sent for your favorite wine and taught the hospital cook myself how to make spaghetti."

"Good. When are you flying me to Rome?"

"Not right away. Castor is flying there tomorrow to check on the Pope's exact schedule and movements for his visits to the poor. The *sampetrini*."

Monticelli was not happy. "Castor, always Castor. Why? Don't you have someone else?"

"In fact, Giulio, we haven't. He is the best. And I am sure you will get along with him. His is a purely mechanical job. Think of the mechanics who install intricate electronic devices without knowing the first thing about Newton. Which reminds me—I need a little technical help from you, too."

He took several sheets of paper from his case with

Photostat copies of the Pope's signature. "You will have to practice signing his name."

"That won't be too difficult," Monticelli said, after looking at the handwriting. "We counterfeited many false signatures in the Resistance. I'm an old hand at this."

"All right. I'll leave you now. You'll have all you want from spaghetti to books. The doctor said you should try to sleep. And dream. The dream of fulfillment. A Marxist Pope in the Vatican."

Monticelli shrugged. "It is *your* dream. I am only a tool."

"But what a tool! The best brains of the Italian Communist party. And a true, eighteen-carat Monticelli. You will have fun with all those stupid bishops and cardinals. And—you will be shaking the hand of the President of the United States!"

"You are making all this sound really unattractive, Alan. Well, I'll take your advice and get some sleep. I'll start practicing His Holiness's signature when I awaken."

Houndsworth closed the door and stepped out into the long, neon-lighted corridor. The guard was still there but Castor was gone.

When Dr. Jabotinsky left the hospital he was so sure he was being followed that he didn't bother to look back. He knew that Castor, whose face by now was familiar, was following him.

The moment that he had been selected to perform this face operation, he knew he would be shadowed. He had performed such operations before for the KGB, but this was a special job. Jabotinsky was an intelligent and perceptive man. He had tried to foresee the consequences—though his options were limited. He had thought of smuggling out a letter in Hebrew to his brother in Elath, Israel, but soon realized the impossibility. He knew he would be shadowed from the moment of this assignment. The letter lay on his desk. He did not care anymore whether they found it or not. But he did send his wife, Ruth, to her parents in Kiev. He told her nothing. When they questioned her later—as they would—they would find nothing.

And he had taken a cyanide capsule from the hospital pharmacy. He had placed it into an upper cavity in his mouth.

He drove out from the parking lot in his Moskovitch and saw Castor's black Volga swing in behind him.

On his way home he thought for a moment of the reasons they had selected him for the job. Yes, he was an excellent plastic surgeon, but there were others. He knew the main reason had been his application for an exit visa to Israel—which he would never see.

Before inserting the skeleton key to the apartment, Castor pressed down the knob and was surprised to see that the door was open.

Jabotinsky, still in his overcoat and hat, sat behind the desk. Castor reached for his gun when he noticed the macabre, frozen smile on Jabotinsky's face.

"Comrade Jabotinsky." He held the gun in front of him. There was no reaction. Slowly he stepped forward, aiming the gun at Jabotinsky's head. When he reached the desk, he leaned across and touched the doctor's head with the barrel. As the muzzle made contact with Jabotinsky's forehead, his head slowly bent forward and touched the desk.

Castor put the revolver on the table and felt Jabotinsky's pulse.

"The sonofabitch is dead," he muttered to himself, and began to search the apartment.

X

The Pontiff sat behind the massive walnut Renaissance desk in his private study; the two cardinals faced him on red-velvet-upholstered armchairs.

The large room was ascetically furnished. The walls were whitewashed, and the artificial lighting came from ornamental recesses in the ceiling. A reading lamp on the desk was not lit. On the wall behind the desk hung a large worm-eaten wooden crucifix. On the opposite wall was a wide, colored map, on which small flags were pinned, indicating the location of all the Roman Catholic centers in the world.

The Pope's face showed a worried expression. This morning's conference about the affairs of the Church did not please him.

He looked at the two cardinals facing him—Giovanni Petrarca, secretary of state, very Italian, very urbane, very olive-skinned, with a slight speech impediment; Massimo Poncini, the Prefect of the Congregation for the Propagation of Faith, gray-haired, lean and tall, with a strong Roman nose. Vatican gossip (and how rife the Vatican was with gossip!) bandied around the rumor that Poncini had some Jewish ancestry.

The Pope spoke. "Every move I make, my brothers, is censored and somehow obstructed. The Church placed me in this position of absolute power, and the cardinals do everything in their power to limit it. When history passes its verdict on me—as you know, nobody escapes the judgment of history—what will it say? Who am I? A Byzantine relic of ancient Occidental and Eastern history, the guardian of Capitalism, a stumbling block to socialism. I would prefer a different *epithethon ornans* for myself."

Cardinal Petrarca tried to put in a word of consolation. "Your Holiness," he said, "our own power is very limited in this special case. We did not obstruct any of your instructions for Africa. The obstruction is in the situation itself."

"It is our fault," the Pope said. He stood up and went to the map on the east wall. "We failed. Instead of following the methods of St. Francis Xavier, we did not train and establish a native clergy. We are regarded as a foreign body, as representatives of unloved Western Europe. The natives think of our nuns and priests as a Roman Peace Corps—nice people to take gifts from and even nice to listen to. But foreign, always foreign, ad infinitum. Only a native clergy, native nuns, blacks, could have made a real impact in Africa. I know that we are trying to correct this now. I am afraid it is too little and too late."

The deep lines in Petrarca's face, the burning fire in his black eyes, showed anxiety and concern—almost anger. He said, "Holiness, we have carried out all your instructions as far as possible. As I must repeat, the opposition does not come from us; it comes from local conditions. We ran into it from all quarters, some unexpected."

"From where?" the Pope asked.

"Well, it could be foreseen from Marxist-oriented groups, but we had a lot of flak from the Protestants, too."

Flak—a strange word, the Pope thought. He must

have picked it up with the Resistance during the war.

"You will have more information on this, Holiness, when Bishop Kwa arrives," Petrarca continued. "I believe he is due soon, even before your departure for the United States."

For a moment the Pope remained silent. Finally, shaking his head, he said, "We will continue tomorrow. Go with God."

He went back to his desk and pressed a bell. From a dark-red Florentine leather folder, he extracted some letters as the Maestro di Camera entered, bowing deeply.

"How are you this morning, Alessandro?" the Pope inquired. "Is your back still bothering you? It should be better now that the rains have ceased."

"It is better, thank you, Your Holiness. You have seen your mail?"

"I haven't read it yet. You know how difficult it is for me to read in this harsh light. And I have tried the little lamp that just arrived. It does not work."

"But Your Holiness, it is a present from the cardinal of Boston. He sent it to you expressly so that you would have a good reading light. I don't—"

The Pope interrupted him. "Alessandro, my friend in Boston overlooked the fact that the current there is one-ten volts while ours is two-twenty."

"Surely one of our electricians can convert it."

"I don't need an electrician. You forget that I am the son of an electrician. I learned the trade when I was five years old. Look . . ." he pointed to a screw on the bottom of the small lamp. "All I need is a screwdriver. See?"

"I will get you one, Holiness."

"No, Alessandro. Just go to my bedroom, open the drawer on my nightstand, and bring me my own that is there."

"Immediately, Your Holiness."

"And Alessandro," the Pope called after him, "unscrew the bulb in my night lamp and bring it along."

The lamp was fixed so easily by the Pope's expert technique that Alessandro cried out, "Bravo," then, frightened by his own impudence, he added, "Please excuse me, Your Holiness."

The Pope began to read the mail. The first letter produced laughter. "This is from an eight-year-old boy. He asks my advice. He wants to know whether he should become the Pope or a policeman."

"A difficult choice, Your Holiness."

"Not really. A question of being the master or the victim of discipline. I shall advise him to become a policeman."

The Pope finished reading—then returned to the third letter from the top.

"This is from Father Anselmus, an old priest who has one wish before he dies. To receive a personal blessing from the Pope."

Alert and disturbed, the chamberlain looked at the Pope, who was getting up from his seat.

"A personal blessing? Your Holiness is not going to see him?"

His voice firm and clear, the Pope said, "A request I can't deny."

The chamberlain did not concede. This was a game, a daily routine that had to be played out. Perhaps one day he might even win.

"May I remind Your Holiness that the Civil Governor's Office warned us over and over again that your frequent unannounced walks among the people are a constant security risk."

Pope Clemens shrugged. "So it was for Jesus. Yet he did walk among the people." He turned toward the door and added, "And so will I."

The chamberlain turned his palms out in despair. "I will pray for Your Holiness's safety."

At the door, the Pope said, "No one will hurt me. I am the shepherd of Rome, and I am afraid for my sheep. Have Carlo pick me up with the small car at the Angelic Gate."

XI

The black Fiat wound its way slowly in and out of the narrow Roman streets. *Alleys* would have been a more appropriate name. The driver, Carlo, drove with great care, his alert eyes flickering to right and left.

Pope Clemens sat contentedly in the rear, a smile on his benign face. He enjoyed these private visits to his "flock." It was good to have contact with the parishioners and to be of some spiritual value, and it was good to get away from the "office" for a while. The Pope had seen the green Alfa Romeo swing out of the parking space at the Angelic Gate and get in line behind the Fiat. He recognized the face of one of the uniformed men in the Alfa, that of Colleone, his officially assigned "guardian angel."

The green car stayed forty feet behind them in the narrow alley. The Pope turned, and with a slight shrug, he said to Carlo, "My church won't leave me alone. Uniformed angels are guarding me, and I suspect that instead of wings, they have pistols under their arms."

Carlo did not turn his head when he answered the Pope. "This is a very poor neighborhood, Your Holiness."

"That's why I am here. The rich don't seem to need my assistance."

Carlo slowed the car down to look at the house numbers. He stopped. "This is the address, Holiness. Via Carpaccio Seventeen. What a dirty house."

As he stepped out of the car, the Pope said he had not come here for hygienic reasons.

Carlo walked to the flaky wooden door. There was no name or sign on it. To the right of the door hung a copper pull covered with green patina. Carlo pulled it, and a screechy tinkle could be heard.

One of the uniformed men stepped out of the Alfa and walked up to the Pope. "Your Holiness," he said and bowed.

"You again, Colleone?" the Pope said. "Can I ever get rid of you?"

All smiles on his fat boyish face, Colleone said, "I am just doing my duty, Your Holiness. Good pay, too. For the sake of your safety, may I enter first?"

"What do you expect to find in there? Hired assassins of the infidels? Are you a Catholic, Colleone?"

"Of course, Your Holiness."

"Then you must believe in my Higher Protector. You must know that I do not need human body-guards. You remain outside and wait."

The door opened slowly with a creaking noise. A tall man, all dressed in black, stood in the doorway. He bowed deeply. "Your Holiness," he said.

In a mildly protesting voice, the Pope said, "Not Holiness. Just a reverend father visiting a fellow priest."

The man in black opened the door fully and stepped back, letting the Pope enter. The door closed behind them, with the eyes of the security men and Carlo riveted on it.

The Pope stopped in the small entrance hall lit by a naked bulb. The man in black, almost resembling a

in his turtleneck sweater and dark silk suit,
d again and said, "Our prayers are answered. The
last wish of Father Anselmus is fulfilled."

"Are you a friend of his?" the Pope asked.

The man, whose name was Castor, answered, "I take
care of him."

"God will reward you for this, my son."

"Your presence here is my reward."

"Where is Father Anselmus?"

"This way, Your Holiness."

The Pope followed Castor up the curving narrow
staircase. They reached a corridor, also dimly lit by
one yellow bulb. Castor opened the first door to their
right and ushered in the Pope.

The small room was almost barren. A candle cast its
shadow on a bed and on the prostrate figure of a man
in it. With slow, measured steps, the Pope approached
the bedside and said, "Father Anselmus?"

He leaned over to touch the man's forehead. A
slight noise caused him to turn back, as he felt an iron
grip on his shoulders. This was his last conscious memory before the chloroform, coming from the handkerchief pressed on his face, took effect. The man holding
the handkerchief let the Pope's body slowly slide down
to the floor.

Castor's voice commanded, "Light," and Robles
pushed the button.

The moment the light came on, Monticelli stood up
from the bed. He looked down at the unconscious
body of the Pope. "Sorry, Your Holiness," he said.

With no loss of time or movement, Robles and Castor lifted up the Pope and placed him on the bed. Castor snapped his fingers, and Robles handed him the
syringe. Castor pulled up the Pope's sleeve and in-
serted the needle into his vein.

Robles looked down at the Pope's body. "I don't know," he said. "I'd feel safer if I could just knock him on the head."

"You're an idiot," Castor said. "He is out cold. And we are not to harm him. He is negotiable."

"Negotiable?" Monticelli asked.

"Yes. That's what the Boss said. Come on, we have no time."

He looked at Monticelli and nodded approvingly. "You look good. Just like the real thing. May I kiss your hand, Your Holiness?" he asked smirkingly. "Let's go," he added, and turned to Robles. "You wait here."

He led the way down the staircase and into the hallway. "There are two security men waiting out there. And your driver."

Monticelli said, "His name is Carlo."

"Yes. And don't worry. From now on, you are the Pope. Marxist, but the Pope." He opened the door.

Monticelli stepped out. He could almost hear the sigh of relief coming from three bodies.

"Everything all right, Your Holiness?" Carlo asked.

"Yes, Carlo. Let us go home."

Carlo opened the door for him, and Monticelli stepped into the car. He saw the servicemen getting into theirs. He was on his way to the Vatican.

XII

It was almost dusk when they reached the foothills. They turned off the freeway at the road sign MENDRI-SIO. It was now over eight hours since they had left Rome. Robles drove the Cadillac ambulance very carefully, neither too fast nor too slowly. They stopped only once at a gas station. Castor occasionally looked through the peephole at the man lying on a stretcher inside the ambulance.

"Keep your eyes on the road," Castor snapped when he noticed Robles's glance at the half-empty Chianti bottle next to him on the seat. "Tonight you'll get all the booze you want."

Robles shrugged and stuffed part of a thick sandwich into his mouth with his right hand. "Nothing but ham and cheese." This was not a reproach; merely a statement of fact.

They had no trouble at the border. All their papers were in meticulous order, meticulously forged. The Swiss border guards were used to ambulances crossing the border. When the sergeant of the guard read the description of the inmate of the car as a "psychiatric case," he said to his corporal, "A fancy psychiatric sanatorium if you have the money. If you haven't, the loony bin."

The road became narrow and curvy. The roadbed deteriorated from concrete to macadam to dirt, a solid, whitewashed, alpine dirt. Small patches of ground fog disappeared as they climbed higher. The air was much cooler now.

When they saw the sign GALENIUM, they turned off to the right. "Three minutes," Castor said.

They drove through a forest of spruce and hemlock, almost in darkness, which dissipated when they emerged from the woods. At the far end of an emerald meadow they saw the "chateau." The building was a copy of a medieval castle, having been constructed in the late nineteenth century, with crenellated walls and round turrets. It suited the talents of Professor Gregory Lebedev, who was well-known and controversial with his psychiatric theories. He experimented not only with all the Freudian and Jungian couch-confession routines, but alternated Rorschach tests with electroshock treatments. One of his adversaries in London accused him of indecision between the "compress and the computer."

"Gee," said Robles, surprised. "It's pretty."

"A God-awful monstrosity." Castor made a disgruntled sound in which he put all his hatred against this rich man's asylum and all of Switzerland, for him a small, mercenary country, the embodiment of bourgeois safety and comfort.

Abruptly they came to the opening in the twelve-foot fence, a shiny, rust-resistant Swiss fence. The gate was closed, and a large-lettered sign warned the wayward tourist in the four languages of the country— Italian, French, German, and English—not to continue any farther. One of two guards approached the car. Castor lowered the window and held a pink slip under his nose. The guard nodded and signaled the other man in the booth. *"Sofort,"* he said in German. The man in the booth put the receiver down and pushed a button. The barrier rose. Robles drove the

car to the back entrance where two tall men in white
were waiting. They picked up the stretcher and took
the man on it inside.

Both Castor and Robles followed the man. The
door behind them closed slowly and silently. They
walked on a deep-blue runner covering a shiny parquet floor down a long corridor, past high, numbered
white doors with brass knobs. Everything was spotlessly clean. Dark, uninspired oil paintings hung on
the walls, works of minor Dutch artists. There was a
strong scent of pine oil mixed with the antiseptic odor
of cleaning fluid, a trademark of the best hotels. The
fluorescent lights in the ceiling were a brutal contrast
to the baroque appointments.

Lebedev was standing in the middle of the high-
ceilinged room. The windows were closed, the shutters
fastened. A brass Polish chandelier hung from the ceiling, all of its six bulbs lit. Still, the light in the room
was opaque, due to either the high ceiling or the weak
bulbs. Everything in the room was unusually high. A
dark Florentine credenza, another dark oil painting of
a nobleman trying to eat a hunt breakfast among his
yapping dogs. Near the wall stood a Renaissance bed
with carved posters. The two male nurses put the man
on the stretcher carefully in it.

The greetings between the three men, after the departure of the nurses, were at best semicordial. This
was a business meeting, not a family reunion. The language they spoke was Russian.

"All set?" Castor asked.

Lebedev nodded. "As instructed."

"You know about his food?"

Lebedev's smile was openly sarcastic. "Let us not
forget that I am also a doctor. A reputable doctor."

Castor had no time for banter. "Is the wire fence
electrified?"

"I don't think so. It is not my department. Ask Schweiker."

"I will. How many 'legitimates' do you have now?"

"Twenty-two. Mostly Germans." He added, "West Germans. And a few Italians."

"You had better be especially careful of Italians. See that he has no contact with them, not even with the servants. And very important—under no conditions shave him. Let him grow his beard."

"Any special instructions about reading matter, sharp pointed objects, et cetera, in the room?"

"None. Use your own judgment. He can read what he wants. No newspapers, though. As for sharp objects—don't worry. He is an old weak man under sedation. He won't harm anybody—certainly not himself." Now it was Castor's turn to smile. "He is not only a good Christian; he is the Pope."

"Will you spend the night here?"

"No. We have to get back to Rome. We'll sleep either in Florence or Parma. Please send Schweiker to the radio room. Is Fedja there?"

"Yes. Anything else?"

Castor turned to go. He was concentrating on his radio report to Houndsworth. What had he said about the Pope? He is "negotiable."

He turned back to Lebedev. "Doctor, this old man is a very valuable asset. He has to be kept in good condition. Please see to it that he gets the best of food. Wine, too. And invent some distractions."

"Distractions? That won't be easy. I cannot send him down to the lake, nor take him mountain climbing. I hope I can find some books in our library that are not on the Vatican's forbidden list."

Castor shrugged. Intellectual problems were always a bore. "I am sure you will do your best. Come, Robles."

Schweiker came into the Operations Room from the adjoining ex-kitchen, which now housed the radio equipment. He stood at attention and clicked his heels. Even his bushy eyebrows seemed to stiffen. He spoke fluent Russian with an East German accent, but Castor preferred speaking German.

"I want details of our security here," he said to him.

The computer in Schweiker's head rattled off the salient items: radar registered all cars approaching on the road, guards posted at every entrance of the castle, and on the perimeter.

"Is the fence electrified?" asked Castor.

Schweiker hesitated for a moment before saying yes. The slight hesitation did not escape Castor.

"What's wrong with the fence, Schweiker?"

"It is not the fence. It is our electricity. The prima donna who owned this castle was a little stingy. She did not want to pay for the county electricity. We are not attached to the main line. We create our own electricity here. Gasoline engines."

"And what is wrong with that?"

"If the motor is overloaded, the fuse goes, and we get temporary shortages. You know, *Kurzschluss*."

"Why the hell don't you see that we get the juice from the county then?"

"We don't like questions. They will ask how is it that we consume so much electricity. We don't want to explain about the radio, the radar, the fence. You know the Swiss and their curiosity."

"I still would prefer to be wired to the main line. Perhaps the embassy can help. I will call them tomorrow. Now, put me through to Moscow on the yellow line."

XIII

Donovan was an early riser. After his morning tea at six, his shave and shower, he put on his clothing except for his necktie and went to the small breakfast room to read the morning papers. A note pad and a red pencil lay on the table next to his armchair, for him to note any items of interest.

The headlines were not all bad. The government of Portugal had averted an abortive rightist take-over, and the rate of serious crime in the United States was dropping. And the Near East was relatively calm. So was Northern Ireland. The excitement about the forthcoming elections in South Africa was mounting—this item rated a red-pencil mark by the President.

The main headline, both in *The New York Times* and *The Washington Post,* dealt with the plane crash in Russia, north of Odessa, where, among others, Professor Giulio Monticelli, the Numero Due of the Italian Communist party, had been killed. Late last night Donovan had received the news from General Holt of the CIA, who had asked for an appointment this morning.

Donovan did not quite understand the urgency of Holt's call. After all, this was a matter of concern mainly for the Italian Communist party, with some possible tangential interest to the Russians, but not, or probably not, to the United States. The Italians had enough talent in the party to replace one Monticelli. Donovan was mistrustful of the CIA's tendency of making mountains out of molehills. In fact, he never felt quite comfortable with the idea of the CIA. It had only begun to live down its nefarious Chilean past. The organization had fallen into such disrepute that responsible government officials had suggested a change of name.

Donovan looked at the mimeographed sheet with the agenda for this morning's meetings in the Oval Office and picked up the financial section of the newspapers. He had almost finished when he noticed the black maid, Betty, noiselessly putting the tray down on the breakfast table, laid for three.

"Good morning, Mr. President," Betty said.

"Good morning, Betty. How is your tooth?"

"It's okay, Mr. President. I think it's only nerves."

"Nerves? Why should a healthy girl like you have nerves?"

"Nobody seems to know, Mr. President. Nerves are created equal; they hit the rich and the poor, the young and the old. Good morning, Mrs. President. Good morning, Miss Phyllis."

The two women were wearing their dressing gowns and looked attractive in spite of the early hour. Donovan folded his papers, went to the table and greeted them. "Good morning, my pets."

Gladys leaned over and kissed him on the forehead. "How are we doing?" she asked.

Donovan smiled. "I haven't reached the social page with the important news yet."

"Darling, stop putting me down. You know I'm not interested in that," Gladys objected.

He patted her hand. "I know. You're my conscience and my best advisor. My, this coffee is good. You see, love, you had no reason to mistrust the cuisine here."

Both Gladys and Phyllis laughed, while Betty discreetly joined them.

"What's so funny?" Donovan asked.

"Daddy," Phyllis explained, "Mother called Mr. Spitzner at the A&P in Holbrook and asked for a huge shipment of his own brand of coffee. The coffee that you always liked in Holbrook."

"That explains the mystery," Donovan said. "Too bad we are not in England. Spitzner, as a purveyor to the Crown, could paint the Royal Emblem on his shop."

"With the Hanoverian slogan *'ich diene'*," Phyllis added.

Gladys wanted to know, "What does that mean?"

"I serve," Phyllis said.

"I like that," Donovan said. "I could use it myself."

"Go easy on the eggs, Pat," Gladys said. "Mind your cholesterol."

"Cholesterol? I haven't got any. Maybe I could use some." He helped himself to one more fried egg and another piece of buttered toast. He turned to Phyllis. "What are you up to today?"

"Tennis at the club. Singles in the morning, then a lesson, and doubles after lunch. You know, my backhand is really improving. Yesterday, when Bob and Mary had match point, I smashed a backhand drive straight between them. They lost the set."

Gladys looked at her. "You know, there are certain items of conversation that should be banned in good society. Such as tennis, golf, bridge, or stamp collecting."

Donovan added, "Or lovemaking. By the way, pet, anything new? Any available bachelors at the club?"

"Only one. He is sixty-eight. But there is always hope."

A red-uniformed sergeant of the Marines entered the room and saluted in their best drill tradition.

"All ready in the Oval Office, Sir," he announced.

Donovan folded his napkin and got up. "I will be there in a moment." He turned toward the bedroom to pick up his necktie. "Good-bye, sweet princesses," he said. "See you later."

XIV

Monticelli had arrived safely in the Pope's private study. Carlo had driven the car to the back entrance. Monticelli descended and answered the salute of the papal guards with what he thought was a dignified nod and benedictional hand wave. Inside the Vatican, a friar was waiting for him. Monticelli automatically followed him until they reached the study.

He recognized instantly the chamberlain, standing near the desk in the study. How accurate the descriptions, the details, the topography were in the Korean File, which he had studied so carefully in Yalta! The chamberlain. The Maestro di Camera. Alessandro.

Clearly relieved and happy to see the Pope, the chamberlain said, "Your Holiness is back, thank heavens. I trust that all went well."

Do I call him Alessandro? Probably yes. Clemens always had a condescending nature.

"Yes, Alessandro," Monticelli said, watching the chamberlain's face. No reaction. "I even received a gift," he continued, and put the small transistor radio down on the table. He kept the small leather-bound Bible in his hand.

"A radio? Is the Zenith not functioning?"

"It does. But one should be humble enough to accept small presents."

"I have prepared the list of the reporters for the

press conference tomorrow, Your Holiness." He pointed
at the folder on the desk.

"I will have a look at it later. I am a little tired and
still have Vespers and Compline to finish."

"As you wish, Your Holiness. I think Sister Agatha
has prepared your supper." He bowed deeply and left.

Sister Agatha. This was new and unexpected. The
Korean File was two years old, and no Sister Agatha
was mentioned in it. Well, surprises like this had to
be expected. He said, "*Avanti*," when he heard the
knock on the door, and Sister Agatha entered, carrying
a tray. Monticelli sat down at the armchair behind the
desk and opened the small black Bible. Slowly, he
raised his head a little to observe the sister.

Sister Agatha was tall, angular, severe. The almost-
total absence of eyebrows was compensated by an
abundant moustache.

"Your supper, Your Holiness. Your Holiness's favorite fish, grilled *coda di rospo*. It was flown in from
Ravenna today. I thought for a change you might prefer to drink some Falerno with it."

"Thank you, Sister," Monticelli said. How can I tell
her that I hate fish and that Falerno is too sweet even
for a dessert wine?

"Will that be all, Your Holiness?"

"Yes, Sister Agatha. Good night."

The meal, with some good Bel Paese cheese and a
hard green apple was not a total loss. When he had
finished, Monticelli walked over to the door leading
to the bedroom, a large square baroque bedroom with
a nice big square baroque bed in it, all made up. A
pair of very unpapal pajamas had been laid out for
him. On the night desk lay the Zenith radio. The
bookshelves had to be inspected instantly.

Of course, St. Thomas Aquinas. The Bible in all
languages. Deviationists like Calivin and Teilhard de

Chardin. And—Engels, Babeuf, Koestler, Renan. On
the bottom shelf were assembled a large paperback se-
lection of English and American murder mysteries.

The bathroom was functional, with neon lights and
an electric razor. Monticelli brushed his teeth and
made a note to order new toothbrushes. He put on the
papal pajamas, picked up the latest Helen MacInnes,
and went to bed. He was a fast reader and the book
was almost finished when he heard the midnight bells.
He reached for the small radio and turned it on.
Shortwave on number fifty-seven. He had prepared a
note pad and pencil and began making notes after the
signal, Handel's "Ave Maria." The religious text came
through clearly. After three minutes the station signed
off.

Monticelli opened his black Bible to Ecclesiastes,
page 3, and started to decipher the message. It said
that Pope Clemens had safely arrived at the destina-
tion in Switzerland.

Like all people with a bad conscience, Monticelli
slept extremely well. It was a smell of strong coffee
that woke him up. A man was pulling back the drapes.
He turned to him and said, "A very good morning,
Your Holiness."

His butler, Giorgio, Monticelli thought. "Good
morning," he said.

"I am sorry I could not be back last night, Your
Holiness. Another strike. The train was four hours
late. Shall I prepare your bath, Holiness?"

Monticelli nodded as he concentrated on the silver
tray containing coffee, orange juice, butter, jam, and
the small, golden brioches, which only the Venetians
bake properly, but these looked good.

His bath was prepared, and Giorgio had laid out the
ridiculous garb he was forced to wear. From this mo-

ment until the press conference, he went through all
the motions like a well-trained robot.

He stood in front of the altar at St. Peter's and
raised the chalice with his right hand—an impostor,
figuring the value of the gold chalice in today's lire.
As the five hundred red robes of the bishops leaned
forward simultaneously in genuflection, it resembled
a cascade. He thought, I am the Vicar of Christ by the
grace of not God, but the Politburo.

Back in his study he was greatly relieved to be alone
in a room. He felt a little exhausted and asked Giorgio
for a glass of red wine, risking raised eyebrows for the
deviation from routine. Giorgio was not surprised. He
approved of the Pope tippling a little. Monticelli did
not anticipate any trouble at the press conference.
Both as a politician and as a professor at the university, he knew how to handle the press. And he knew
that he was a good mimic. For many weeks he had
listened to the record of his brother's speeches and had
learned every trick, every intonation, even the occa-
sional lapses into their own village patois

Still, it was safer to see the new reporter, Jerome
Sutherland of *The New York Times*, whose name
headed the press list handed him last night by the
chamberlain. Short explanatory notes were written in
the margin, and Monticelli had learned that this was
Sutherland's first visit to Rome, that he was a liberal,
a Roman Catholic, and close to President Donovan.
He had asked to see the reporter privately, before the
press conference.

Sutherland entered the study and bowed deeply, but
made no attempt to kiss the Pope's hand. He was about
fifty years of age, tall, with a lean aquiline face. His
gray eyes peered inquisitively behind round, horn-
rimmed glasses.

"Welcome to Rome, Mr. Sutherland," Monticelli

said. "I wanted to see you before I meet the other reporters. I understand that you have the ear of President Donovan, and I have the greatest respect for your
excellent newspaper." He paused.

"It is a great honor to be received by Your Holiness."

"I am very cognizant of the power of the press generally, and *The New York Times* especially," continued Monticelli. "I have prepared for you a copy of the
statement I will make to the world press. I believe it is
self-explanatory. What I wanted to emphasize is that I
will do all I can, with the modest powers at my disposal, to assist President Donovan in his efforts to
preserve the peace. Our Church always preached the
blessings of peace, but, alas, did not always act with all
its might and influence against the powers of war."

"Do I understand Your Holiness correctly in stating
that the Church will fight more concretely and ener-
getically against the promoters of the apocalypse in all
parts of the world? The East as well as the West?"

"Yes. We have to fight for peace in the fierce spirit
of God's legion, the Jesuits. With words, deeds, influence, money."

Sutherland could not keep a certain skepticism out
of his voice. "Your Holiness, I am glad to see your positive, combative spirit for peace. The question is
whether it will work in the East as well as the West. I
am certain that your peace offensive will fall on eager
ears with my President and with all the peoples of the
West, including your own, in spite of several Communists in the government. But what weight will it
carry in Russia, Poland, or Hungary?"

Careful, Monticelli said to himself. Just the right
dose. Not too much. Not yet. "The Church cannot accept a political or geopolitical division of the world in
two parts. The good people of the East are God's chil-

dren, just like the people of the West. We cannot lower our own Iron Curtain and cut the world in two. We have to try harder to communicate with our flock in the East."

Sutherland was not convinced. "I hope and pray for your success, Your Holiness," he said.

"I am a bad host," Monticelli said. "May I offer you an *aperutivo?*" Not waiting for the answer he rang the bell. The chamberlain appeared instantly.

"Your Holiness?"

"Two Americanos, Alessandro. Or would you prefer some port or dry vermouth, Mr. Sutherland?"

"An Americano would be fine, Your Holiness."

Monticelli nodded, but Alessandro did not move. He looked at Monticelli. "Not your usual Soave, Your Holiness?"

A slight blunder, not too serious, Monticelli thought. "Americanos for a change," he said.

Over the drinks Monticelli handed Sutherland the copy of the press release and received from him a personal note from the President of the United States in which he welcomed with enthusiasm the Pope's forthcoming visit to the United States.

Immediately after Sutherland's departure, a friar appeared to lead Monticelli to the auditorium. He had quickly inspected his clothing, his manicured hands with the papal ring, his general appearance, and the tonal quality of his voice. He was ready.

He faced a crowd of well over a hundred reporters. He spied Sutherland in the first row and the familiar face of Pancaldi of the *Osservatore Romano*. He did not see anyone he knew of the Communist press.

"It is with utmost pleasure," he started slowly, "that we meet you, ladies and gentlemen of the press. We consider the media, and especially the daily press, as a supreme instrument for enhancing unity and amicable understanding in a world of growing antagonisms and hostility."

He waited for a moment for the approving murmurs, and acknowledged the friendly nods with a benevolent papal smile.

"The unity we are trying to achieve has been called by different names, such as *peaceful coexistence* or *détente*. This is the language of the diplomats, and we are not a diplomat. As you know, we will travel soon to the United States, but again, not as diplomats. We will travel like simple Catholic priests, paying a visit to our flock, our fellow Roman Catholics who constitute a forceful minority in the United States—a force that helped elect a President who is also a Catholic."

When he used the word *force*, he purposely pronounced it *forsa* in the manner of Clemens instead of *forza*.

"Our trip to America," he continued, "will not be for the propagation of any religious doctrines. It will be our first step of a pilgrimage around the globe to promote reconciliation and understanding between all the creeds and political credos of this world. We will be calling on all the peoples, regardless of their present ruling systems. Because we look at all political parties only in terms of their present and perhaps ephemeral social effect. To accomplish our goal of unity and peace, we will have to make changes in this Church and adapt it to the ending years of this century. We will create a new image of the Papacy and open the doors of the Vatican wide, both to the Right and to the Left . . ."

XV

Donovan sat down behind the desk in the Oval Office and reached for the buzzer. He stopped. He needed a moment to look around him. He loved the Oval Office and felt now very much at home in it.

At first a few things had disturbed him. The light was too bright, almost to the point of hurting his eyes—strict artificial neon lighting, which denuded faces and underlined every wrinkle. It irritated Donovan to see that the secretary of state had shaved too closely and that the broken front tooth of General Holt had not yet been repaired. Will the secretary of the navy notice the pimple on my chin and the bags under my eyes, he wondered. The white ceiling threw the light back down on his desk, the tables, the chairs, illuminating the large world globe on its stand.

In need of sympathy, Donovan turned his head and gazed at Harry Truman's sculptured head in a niche behind him. Harry would understand his feelings. He looked at the portraits of the other great men: Benjamin Franklin, whose incisive humor came through even in the mediocre Charles Willson Peale portrait; across the room on a pedestal was a full figure of Lincoln, a ramrod slenderness that could have served as a model for Giacometti; facing it, a portrait of Washington in an ill-fitting uniform. He had the smile of a sergeant. Perhaps he had not been the greatest of generals, but certainly he was a great man.

Patrick Donovan swiveled back the black leather chair and picked up the blue folders with the day's agenda from the low table beside him. Before getting to work he looked at the silver-framed photograph of Gladys and Phyllis taken on the front lawn in front of their house in Holbrook. He waved a greeting at it.

He consulted the large white pad with the presidential emblem on it. Number one on the agenda was the secretary of state. Donovan pressed the button.

Duncan Mulford entered. In his fifties, lean, immaculately dressed in a double-breasted black suit, he looked like a trustworthy banker, not so much of Wall Street as of Lloyd's of London.

His greeting, "Good morning, Mr. President," was cheerful.

"Good morning, Duncan. What's the good news?"

"Right, Sir. I'll start with the good news. The Soviets acknowledged a mistake they made and apologized."

"That's interesting. For what did they apologize?"

"A violation of the Helsinki Agreement. They admit to a technical violation concerning the dismantling of fifty old submarine missile launchers before testing new missile-firing submarines at sea."

"Why did they do this? I mean, why the apology?"

"In the first place, Mr. President, they know that we know. The secretary of the navy had a report from our submarine listening posts in the Baltic. The second reason is testing."

"Testing what?"

"They are testing you, Pat." Occasionally Mulford called his old friend by his first name.

"They are testing *me*?"

"Yes. Our Kremlinologists think that the Soviets want to gauge your reactions. They want to know whether you'll live up to the pacifist image they seem to have of you."

"Well, I won't disappoint them. I shall gracefully accept the apology and will admonish them not to repeat it. A repentant sinner is always popular." Donovan regretted the phrase instantly. Repentant sinner. How often had he been warned to avoid expressions that reeked of the Bible or the Gospel. Well, it was out.

"And what is the bad news, Duncan?"

"South Africa, Mr. President." Mulford pointed at the blue folder on the President's desk. "You may want to read the full briefing."

"I will," Donovan said. "Meanwhile, give me the main points."

Mulford sighed. "Pat, it is not a euphemism when I say that the situation is incomprehensible. So many factions, so many facets. The most important key issue is the forthcoming election in South Africa. The first really free election. But in connection with it, we have this acute trouble with Namibia."

"What kind of trouble? Namibia is now a free and independent state. Their own SWAPO, whatever that stands for, is in power. So why the trouble?"

"They claim that South Africa has an economic stranglehold on them, that South Africa has ceased to import Namibian goods and has not kept its promise to invest in the developing of Namibian industry."

"Is this true?"

"To a large extent it is."

"Strange. I mean the behavior of the South Africans, now that they have a number of blacks in their government. What can we do? Should we lean on South Africa?"

"It would be pointless before the election. What we can do is try to help Kenyere's moderates get elected. If Kenyere is elected, the Namibian situation will resolve itself peacefully."

Donovan looked searchingly at Mulford's face. "When you say we have to help Kenyere, you don't want to bring up the question of the Seventh Fleet again, do you?"

Mulford sighed deeply, and the lines of his face seemed to deepen. He said, "I am afraid I will, Mr. President."

Donovan went to the huge curtained windows, pulled back a corner of the heavy drape, and looked at the outside world. He returned to his desk and sat down.

"Duncan, you know my stand on this. I don't believe in gunboat diplomacy—waving the flag. The South Africans will have to decide their fate without the assistance of the Seventh Fleet."

"Mr. President, if we don't move in, the Soviet Indian Ocean Fleet of Admiral Rokosowski will help the South Africans decide their fate."

"And if we do move in, it will mean a direct confrontation with the Russians. This is what I want to avoid, absolutely and definitely—a confrontation with the Russians."

"Mr. President, if Kenyere is defeated, we can write off Africa. All of it."

"Look, my Cassandra friend, there must be other measures than the movements of fleets. You are not only a masterful diplomat, Duncan, you have a first-rate brain. Think of economic help, building of hospitals, universities. Think, please. I will do the same."

When Mulford left, the President opened the top drawer on the right side of his desk and took out his favorite Dunhill pipe. He cleaned it with a reamer and stuffed it with the tobacco from the jar on the desk.

He was tired of the constant pressure to send in reinforcements to South Africa. It's what had gotten them in trouble so many times in the past. And still the State Department was after him always to do something, do something. He was firmly convinced that the tenuous situation in South Africa had to be solved by the South Africans, even though it pained him to turn his back on Kenyere—a man he admired from a distance. He would hold firm. He looked at the list on the desk and picked up the white telephone.

"Fred, I want to switch the secretary of interior and treasury. I see that Mr. Kleinman wants to see me. Please ask Congreve to wait for a few minutes."

The meeting lasted over an hour, and Donovan was getting tired. Still, he had to see General Holt who had called last night for an urgent audience. From the Thermos he poured himself another cup of coffee and pushed the buzzer. General Rodney Holt with his shrewd poker face and his square athlete's shoulders, inspired the confidence that the CIA badly needed. The scandals were over but not forgotten, and the image of the CIA still needed all the bolstering it could get.

His stiff military stance snapped back into position after a quick bow. "Mr. President," he said.

"How are you, Rodney? What's the emergency?"

"The Monticelli air crash. I trust you read about it, Sir."

Donovan nodded. "Yes, I have. Bizarre, isn't it?"

"Very, Mr. President. We are puzzled by it."

"Well, to coin a phrase, it's not our funeral. The Italian Communist party surely has some replacements. Numero Tre will move up to Numero Due.

And the Russians can certainly replace the Tupulov with another one."

"The sudden death of Professor Monticelli might bring about some changes. The questions are, Who profits by it? and Who suffers from it? We don't understand that hasty departure of his for Russia."

"How do you know it was hasty?"

"Italian security reported to our bureau in Rome that a note was found on Monticelli's desk in his apartment in Bologna. I quote from it: 'I am leaving for Moscow. Call the university and tell them.' They also reported that Monticelli seems to have packed one small suitcase in great haste. He did not take his insulin medicine nor his vitamins along."

"Was the Tupulov on a scheduled flight?"

"No. An embassy car took Monticelli directly to the waiting plane at Leonardo da Vinci Airport. Two men were with him. One of them, dark blond, about twenty-eight years old, had lunch with him near the university."

"All this adds up to what, Rodney?"

"I wish we knew, Mr. President. We are on the threshold of quite a few important events—the elections in South Africa, the Pope's visit to the States, the decisive atomic disarmament conference in Geneva. Every move of the KGB must be watched on the eve of such interlocking historical happenings."

"Do you believe in metempsychosis, Rodney?"

General Holt's face did not redden when he said, "I don't know what that is, Mr. President."

"The interlocking of disjointed historical events. For example, Galileo was born on the day Michelangelo died. Never mind. Continue."

"I wish the three boys in the Kremlin would not think up such riddles for us."

"Who are the three boys?"

"The British defectors, Houndsworth, Cholmondley, and Colvin. They've come up with some wild schemes for the KGB."

"You think they have something to do with this Monticelli crash?"

"I feel it in my old spy bones, Sir. They have the necessary cunning and fertile imaginations. I wish we had that kind of fantasy."

"Why don't you hire someone with it for the department?"

"I don't know where to look. In the last world war we engaged Robert Sherwood and the British had Ian Fleming and Noel Coward. Most of the spy writers these days, like Deighton, Forsythe, and Le Carré, are British."

The President thought for a moment and then pressed the buzzer.

"Sergeant," he instructed the navy steward, "please go to my bedroom. On my nightstand there is a book with the word *Circle* in the title. Please bring it to me."

General Holt asked, "A book?"

"A spy story. Written by a Tom something. According to the blurb, he is young and a Rhodes scholar. He has unlimited fantasy and writes an intriguing story. If you agree with me, try recruiting him into the agency."

After the general's departure, the President looked up at the grandfather clock in the corner. He preferred this beautiful clock to his wristwatch. He knew that it had been made by John and Thomas Seymour in Boston in the early nineteenth century. The clock showed the time to be 1:45. He was glad to see the door open and the sergeant announce, "Your lunch is served, Mr. President."

XVI

The old man could never remember those first days. Was it the shock of the sedation that numbed his mind so completely? He knew that he was a captive of evil men. He had no idea of their aims, and he did not want to think of them. Never, not for one moment, did he have doubts about his own fate. He was safe because he was in God's hands. God always wins against the devil; good triumphs over evil. It was as simple as that. Faith was thinking with one's heart, and the Pope's heart was good and strong.

It took perhaps a full week for him to start thinking with his brains. He noticed first small items. The coffee was less strong than in Rome, the croissants were crisper. The bed sheets were made of the finest linen, the parquet floor could be used as a mirror. The bathroom fixtures were new and better made than those of the Vatican. The toilet bowl had the trademark sign, HELVETIA. When he was allowed to walk a little in the room, the first thing he inspected was the electrical installation. He took the bulb out of the lamp on the small table next to his bed and saw that the voltage showed 220.

His mind started to work on two separate problems: how to communicate with the outside world and ask for help, and how to escape without outside help.

He said his prayers with fervor and devotion and

never wavered in his conviction that his God would take care of him. Nevertheless, he intended to lend God a helping hand. He knew that he was in Switzerland, but this did not matter. The Swiss were God-fearing Christians, too.

He tried to make conversation with the two male nurses, but he received only monosyllabic answers in poor Italian. The ancient room maid was a trifle friendlier and her Italian better.

But the Pope took an intense loathing to Professor Lebedev, a monster of an automaton. He said the Lord's prayer fifty times after each visit of the doctor as penance for his thoughts, though Lebedev behaved correctly. He took the Pope's pulse, inquired about his appetite, and brought him all the books he wanted, though he wondered at the requests. Why Darwin's *Voyage of H.M.S. Beagle* or *The Life of Edison?*

It was on the ninth day of his captivity that the Pope had a glimpse of this hospital-prison and its inmates. He was reading by the window when the maid brought his afternoon tea. She left the door slightly ajar and walked across the room to the Pope when the alarm sounded. It was an unpleasant piercing sound, which shook the windows. The maid quickly put the tray down on the bed and ran to the door yelling, "Fire."

Very calmly, the Pope got up and walked out through the open door. By instinct he turned right and reached a glass partition, which he opened. So far, nobody had bothered him. Men were running in different directions, shouting in what seemed to be a Slavic language. When the Pope reached a large, well-furnished room, the noise and the shouting suddenly stopped.

The room looked English, like one of the better

clubs on Pall Mall. Deep leather fauteuils, low coffee tables, landscapes with horses and dogs on the wall.

"Welcome to the Club," said the fat man in the black leather armchair who held a tall glass in his hand. On the other side of the table sat a leaner gentleman with a monocle in his right eye. He also said, "Welcome," but with a proper English pronunciation in contrast to the fat man's Teutonic accent.

"Come join us," said the German. "Celebrate with us the end of this false fire alarm."

The Pope approached the table and looked at the two men. Something in his attitude made the men get up. The German said, "I am Leonid Brezhnev." The man with the monocle bowed imperceptibly and said, "Churchill. Winston." The Pope still looked at the two men and said nothing. Were they part of the plot?

The German asked, "May we have your name, please?"

Slowly, with cutting dignity, the Pope said, "I am Clemens. I am the Pope."

The announcement seemed to relax the tension. "Come, Pope, have a cognac with us." Both he and the Englishman sat down. "Please join us. And change that Pope bit. No Pope has a beard."

The Pope touched his face and felt the stubble. "Sorry—" he started to say when the German interrupted.

"Enough of the family joke. My real name is Guenther Schaerin. Tax fraud. Over fifty million marks. His name is Terence Fenton. *Devisenverbrechen.* You know, smuggle of currency. Ten million pounds. Now, what is your real name and racket? You look Italian. Did the building you constructed collapse?" He laughed, but stopped when the two male nurses entered the room, and without a sound, they

went to the Pope, took his arms and led him back to
his room.

Fake hospital for rich criminals, was the Pope's verdict. I must get out of here, he thought. The fire
alarm had given him some ideas.

When the maid came back with his tray of tea and
cakes, the true Pope asked, "What was that fire alarm
for?"

The maid shrugged. "They say it is our weak electricity. If the motor is overloaded, all kinds of things
happen. The lights go out, the alarm sounds."

Interesting, the Pope thought. He asked, "What is
the cause of the overload?"

The maid liked a little chat in Italian and was glad
to show off her knowledge. "It is mostly the water."

"The water?"

"Yes, we have our own well, but not enough water.
An electric pump gets the water to the bathrooms and
showers. If too much water is used, the machine gets
tired and quits. Then we have no light and no power."
She added, "So don't use the shower in the shower
room, please."

The Pope shut his eyes and let his sharp mind concentrate on his plan. First, turn on all the showers simultaneously, including his own private one. His
training as an electrician came in handy. With the
help of a knife from his food tray, he would cut the
electric wire on the nightstand lamp and insert it into
the wall bracket. This would cause a short circuit, and
the firm alarm, possibly activated by batteries, would
go off. The doors would be operated manually. It all
had to be done at night.

He waited for the right time. Some weeks passed;
then he was ready. When he reached the main gate, he
saw that the barrier was open. The lone guard at the
gate was yelling into the telephone.

Sliding noiselessly under the cover of the trees, the Pope carefully stepped out on the road. He knew it must be a long walk to the main road, a painful walk in his bedroom slippers, as his shoes had been locked away. The cold air did not bother him, despite the pajamas and dressing gown, which were not ideally suited for a night walk in the hills.

It took him an hour to reach the main road, which was sparsely traveled at that hour; a few private cars, but mostly trucks. By observing the license plates, the Pope noticed that the heavier trucks carried Italian license plates. He definitely needed an Italian truck or car.

He heard the heavy rumble even before he saw the three-ton truck and trailer. He placed himself in the middle of the road, waved his arms windmill-fashion, and yelled, "*Aiuto!*" The truck screeched to a stop.

The driver opened the door of the caboose and yelled, "Okay, you bastard of a lunatic, climb in."

The Pope sat down on the hard seat and leaned back. Slowly, his eyes still closed, the Pope said, "Thank you."

The driver continued to bawl him out. "Don't you know you can get killed like that, old man? Where you want to go?"

The Pope leaned his tired head back on the hard seat. With his eyes closed, he answered, "Roma."

Lieutenant Gambarotti, in charge of the Italian custom guards, felt compassion and pity for the old man warming himself in front of the small gas stove. His slippers were off, exposing bleeding feet. His half-open dressing gown showed some white pajamas. Was he a doctor or a nurse? There was something strangely compelling, almost biblical, in the bearded old man's face.

"I want to go to Rome," Clemens started to say, but the lieutenant stopped him.

"First, I will get you a *Corretto*—hot coffee with grappa in it. Will make you feel better. Read the paper here. I'll be back."

Clemens picked up the *Corriere della Sera*. There on the front page in bold type was an item about the Pope with *his* photograph.

Gambarotti was puzzled. Where had the old man gone? He put the coffee down on the table and made a phone call to Lieutenant Tschudi at Valle Potorno in Switzerland.

When the call came through, Gambarotti said, "Hans? Sorry to disturb you, but have any of the loonies escaped from Galenium today?"

"At least one. There was a fire there last night and the search is on with dogs. Are you interested?" said Hans.

"Mildly. An old bearded man came through, with an interesting face. I had a hunch he might be a Galenium inmate. While I was getting him some coffee, he skipped out."

"Well, he's probably a top criminal or maybe even Mafia. I'm glad he is out of Switzerland. See you Sunday."

XVII

When he saw the Pope's picture in the *Corriere della Sera*, Clemens knew that he had to flee. Flee from what? The Mafia? The kidnappers? The Communists? What kind of diabolical plot was being constructed against him? He knew that in the time spent in the Swiss asylum, nothing as drastic as the election of a new Pope could take place. They would continue the search for at least six months. Who would benefit by placing an impostor in the Vatican? In that split second he thought of his brother Giulio, killed in an air crash over Russia—more than two months ago.

Clemens quickly slipped out of the custom's office. He looked around for some form of transportation heading south. At this hour there were no private vehicles on his side of the custom's barrier. On the other side he saw a large diesel truck, and he heard the starter. He ran to it, waving frenetically, and yelled, "*Prego*, please."

The stout driver of the truck lowered his window. "What's the matter, Grandpa? Want a ride? Hop in," he yelled.

Clemens went to the left side of the truck, which, strangely, had a right-hand drive like some of the heavy ones in northern Italy. The car door opened and a child's voice said, "Come in."

Clumsily, Clemens clutched his dressing gown and,

holding on to his slippers by curling his toes, climbed into the cab. The driver put the car in gear, and the big truck jerked into motion with a bitterly complaining moan.

"Good evening, old man," the driver said. "Where are we going?"

"Good evening, and thank you for taking me," replied the Pope. "Where are you heading for?"

"Bologna. And you?"

"Roma."

The little boy, who must have been six, looked at the Pope with admiration. "Roma," he repeated. "That's far."

"Not so far from Bologna. Two hundred twenty-two kilometers."

The driver whistled in admiration of the Pope's accuracy. "Exact, old man. What is your name? Mine is Antonio."

"Giorgio," the Pope said.

The little boy looked down at the Pope's feet and said, "Why are you wearing slippers?"

Yes, why, the Pope thought. I can tell them that I am the Pope on a flight from some unknown danger. An idea started to form in his head.

The boy was waiting for an answer. He said, "Some bad men chased me out of my bed, and I had to flee as I am." He stroked the boy's head gently.

"Aren't you cold?" the boy asked.

"Yes. A little."

"I'll give us some heat." The driver pushed a button.

The boy wanted to know more. "What kind of bad men?"

"What kind?" the Pope said. "They had black beards. Perhaps they were the Mafia."

Antonio quickly made the sign of the cross. "Mamma mia, do not mention that word, please."

"Tell me stories about bad men," the boy pleaded.

"And make it a long one, Giorgio," the driver added. "We have a long way to Bologna. On this wet road it will take close to four hours."

"All right," Clemens agreed. "Once upon a time there was a man who lived on the border between Italy and Switzerland. I think his name was Beppone, and he was a carpenter."

"A good carpenter?"

"Yes. But business was not good. Beppo had a wife, Margherita, and two sons, Felice and Mauro."

"How old were they?" the boy asked. His father stopped him and said, "Let Giorgio tell the story. Don't interrupt him."

"It was just before Christmas, and Beppone wanted to spend the holidays at his little hut, high in the mountains, close to the Italian border. So Beppone and his family packed knapsacks on their backs and climbed higher and higher until they reached the hut. The weather turned cold, and Beppone went into the forest to pick some firewood. He even found a small Christmas tree. He made a nice fire in the open fireplace and wished he had presents to put under the tree. All they had brought with them was some dark bread and a large piece of not-very-fresh cheese."

"Gorgonzola?"

"No. I think it was more like provolone. They were just about to sit down and eat their meager supper when suddenly the door was pushed in and three bearded men entered the hut."

"Mafiosi?"

"Quiet, Diego," Antonio said.

"No, they were not Mafiosi. They were surprised to find the family there and wanted to know what they were doing in the hut. Beppone told them it was theirs and offered to share their skimpy meal. The men just laughed and said they had to push the wooden table in the center of the hut to one side. Under it a trapdoor was opened that led to the cellar. A few minutes later the men came back carrying heavy wooden crates."

"How many?"

"About five or six. And a large green plastic bag. They took the crates outside and put the plastic bag on the table. They said, 'Excuse the intrusion, please. Merry Christmas. What you find in this bag is yours.' They repeated, 'Merry Christmas' and left. Beppone opened the bag and took out a big ham, a large round cheese, a pound of butter, three packs of cigarettes, several bars of chocolate, and two half gallons of red wine. He and Margherita stared—they did not believe their eyes.

"Felice, the older of the boys, said, 'I know who they were. The tallest was Balthazar. They were the three Holy Kings."

Clemens shrugged. "Perhaps in a way they were. But in real life, they were smugglers retrieving their goods cached in the cellar of the hut. They paid their safekeeping fee to Beppone."

"Was he happy?"

"Yes, he was. And so was the whole family. Food, especially when you're hungry, can be very gratifying."

This gave Antonio an idea. "Old man, aren't you hungry?" he asked. His sympathetic brown Italian eyes turned toward the Pope, and a whiff of garlic was in the air.

Clemens was not too fond of garlic, but at this moment it smelled like manna. "Yes, I am," he said, "but I have no money."

Antonio laughed. "Well, I don't want to stop at the Maria Luigiana in Parma to eat turkey. We have had our meal and have some salami and bread left over. How about it?"

"That will be fine, thank you, Antonio."

"Diego, get the basket." The boy quickly did as he was told. "Please eat, Giorgio," he said, as he opened the basket.

The Pope took out the loaf of bread and the salami, and silently said a prayer over it.

Antonio mistook the lip movements and said, "Sorry, old man, I thought you had a knife." He extracted a long switchblade knife from his pocket and handed it to Clemens.

The Pope broke off a piece of bread and cut a thick slice off the salami. He started to eat, slowly, enjoying every bite.

"How will you get to Rome, Giorgio?" the driver asked. "It will be late when we get to Bologna. You won't get any transportation before morning."

Clemens had thought of that problem, too. If he could spend the night somewhere without freezing, he might, with luck, find a good Samaritan of a truck driver to take him to Rome. Automatically, he said, "God will help me."

Antonio found this funny. "I will help you, too, old man. I will stop at the truck depot and find out who is leaving for Rome in the morning. You can spend the night with us if you don't mind sleeping on a cot in the kitchen."

"That's very kind of you, Antonio. I cannot pay you, but I will say a special prayer for you when I get to Rome."

"That is better than money, Giorgio. I think God will listen to you."

The yellow beams of their headlights cut through the thick darkness. The dullness of the *autostrada* was occasionally relieved by blaring signs announcing an

eating place outside of Milano and the tollgates near
Parma. The boy was getting sleepy. Quietly, he let his
head slide over on the Pope's left shoulder. Clemens
liked the feeling of the warm head on his chest. Celi-
bacy had never bothered him, but he had often wished
for a son. As he looked down at Diego's head he remembered the boy he had blessed a year ago in Rome,
the blind son of an American senator. He wondered
what had become of him.

Antonio turned on the radio, softly, so as not to
awaken the boy. "Let's hear some music," he said.

A commentator's voice came on fast but articulate,
as all Italians in the dissemination of news. The Pope
listened anxiously. There was nothing new—the same
killings in Ireland, unrest in the Middle East, earth-
quakes in China. Why did the Chinese report earth-
quakes and the Russians not? The announcer spoke
about an airplane crash that had taken place near No-
vosibirsk three months before, news that the Russians
had kept secret until now. Was it Marxist-Leninist
dogma to broadcast only good news? The radio spoke
of unrest in South Africa on the eve of elections.

The last item was about the Pope. There was talk of
his United States trip. How will I ever be able to prove
that I am the Pope and he is an impostor?

"Soon." Antonio pointed at the sign that indicated
BOLOGNA, 12 KILOMETERS. He took the northern exit,
and the car rolled slowly now past gas stations and ga-
rages, ugly and dirty satellites geared to the service of
oil and gasoline-consuming monsters. Next to the
neon-lighted AGIP station was the entrance of the
truck depot. Antonio turned into the big yard.

When the truck stopped, a little squat man came
alongside carrying a flashlight. "Welcome home, Antonio," he said. "The car is ready. I'll take you home."

Antonio started to descend. "Wait a minute, Alberto. I have two passengers, Diego and a friend. Put them into your car and wait for me. I have to get to the office."

Clemens gently woke up the boy and said, "We are home." He climbed down slowly from the truck, followed by Diego. Alberto switched his flashlight on and led them over to his little Fiat. He opened the door, and the Pope and Diego squeezed themselves in. In a minute Antonio returned and stepped into the car. They drove first down a narrow side street lined with old buildings until they reached a wide main artery. The Pope could only read the letters CORSO . . .

Antonio turned around and said to the Pope, "All set. My friend, Luigi, will take you to Rome. You'll have to be here at six o'clock. I report at six thirty, so I'll bring you back to the depot. Alberto will pick us up."

The *corso*, a wide avenue, separated new high, functional buildings of repelling ugliness resembling military barracks. They had been constructed for the more successful proleteriat. Tall streetlights emitted weak amber, giving out light on the yellow and brown apartment buildings, which were already showing signs of decay. Alberto stopped the car, and Antonio proudly announced, "This is where I live."

Carefully, they walked up the three flights of railless stairs. Antonio opened the door at the end of the corridor and yelled, "Maddalena!"

A very pretty, very fat woman rushed out of the back room, quickly fastening the belt on her dressing gown. "Antonio, Diego!" she cried out happily.

She first gave them some bread and cheese in the kitchen, and then they moved the table to the wall and set up the cot for the Pope. He was grateful for his good fate, for these warm, friendly people. When the lights were switched off, he fell asleep immediately.

He woke at five with a chill. He was trembling and he knew that he had some fever. I hope I won't catch pneumonia, he thought. I *must* get to Rome—I must see the American ambassador. What was his name? Woolrich. Alexander Woolrich.

With the aid of the hot coffee brought by Maddalena, he felt that he would be able to make the trip.

Antonio came back carrying some overcoats and shoes. "See how these fit you," he said. "You can't go around like that."

Clemens obediently tried on the overcoats, and a black one, turning slightly green, was "possible." So was one pair of dark-brown canvas hiking shoes. Maddalena said, "Wait a minute," and returned with a pair of heavy wool socks.

"I cannot pay you now," the Pope said. "I can't even give you my address in Rome. But I will send you money after my arrival."

"Please, old man, I told you we don't want your money. Just send the stuff back when you are through with it. Our address is in the coat pocket. See?"

Luigi was waiting in his Saurer truck. He had the same kind eyes as Antonio and he obviously liked the same garlic sausages.

In Rome he stopped the truck at the south end of the Via Veneto. Trucks were not allowed on the street itself. The Pope thanked him. He was very tired and felt his pulse racing as he walked slowly up to the gate of the American embassy. Inside he was stopped by a Marine sergeant. Very politely, the sergeant asked, "Sir?"

The Pope stopped, drew himself up, and said in good English, "I want to see Ambassador Alexander Woolrich."

So much authority, so much power emanated from

the bearded face of the old man that, against his better
judgment, the sergeant, puzzled and intrigued, was
also impressed.

"What about, sir?" he asked.

The Pope was prepared for the question. "I have a
message for the ambassador about a present he received from Cardinal Doran of Boston. About an electric gadget."

The sergeant tried to remember the words. He decided to turn this over to higher authority. "Please sit
down here." He pointed to the leather couch. "I will
be right back."

After fifteen minutes of hierarchical procedure, the
message reached the ambassador. He was dictating a
letter to the secretary of state when Milford from the
Chancery interrupted him.

"An old bearded man," the ambassador repeated.
"And he says he has a message about an electric gadget
I brought from the cardinal of Boston. In fact, I did
bring such a gadget. Well, I am curious. Please show
the man in, but don't leave me alone with him."

He stood behind his Louis XI desk, but did not offer a chair to the Pope. He said, "You want to talk to
me about a gadget I brought from the cardinal in Boston? Can you describe it?"

"Yes, Mr. Ambassador," the Pope nodded. "It's a device that, when plugged into the wall outlet, will indicate the presence of smoke and thus give warning in
case of fire."

"That's right. How do you happen to know about
it?"

Without turning his head, the Pope said, "I am
afraid, Mr. Ambassador, the message I have for you is
very personal and only for you and no one else."

The ambassador hesitated for a second. His instinct
told him it would be all right. He turned to Milford

and asked him to leave the room. Then he asked his
visitor to be seated and resumed his chair behind the
desk.

"I will try to identify myself, Mr. Ambassador. The
last time I saw you was when you brought me President Donovan's letter of invitation to the White
House. However, that is inconclusive, as the Maestro
di Camera and my secretary of state were present. But
when you brought me the smoke detector from my
friend, Cardinal Doran of Boston, we were alone."

Completely baffled and lost, the ambassador forced
out the words, "You mean to say—" when he was interrupted.

"I am Pope Clemens," he said.

The authority, the sincerity, were evident. Still, the
ambassador's hand moved to the buzzer on the table.

"Please don't ring. Hear me out first. I am a harm-
less, completely normal old man," the Pope said.

The ambassador took his hand off the buzzer. He
kept his voice low and calm as he said, "Please explain. I saw the Pope myself after his return from the
States."

"You saw an impostor, Mr. Ambassador. I was kid-
napped by I don't know what group nine weeks ago
and incarcerated in an asylum in Switzerland."

"And who is the man who took your place?"

"I don't know, Mr. Ambassador, but I have suspicions that it is my brother Giulio Monticelli."

"You mean the man who died in a plane crash in
Russia?"

"If he died. Perhaps he did not."

The ambassador did not know how to react to this
phantasmagoria. His hand slid again toward the
buzzer.

The Pope said quickly, "When you gave me the
smoke detector, I told you that it would have to be

attached to a transformer to correct the difference in voltage from the American to the Italian. You paid me a compliment for being so knowledgeable—I think that was the word you used—*knowledgeable* about electrical appliances."

How would this man know about a private conversation I had with the Pope? the ambassador thought. "Yes, I remember. And I asked you about your opinion of the situation in Portugal."

"You did not, Mr. Ambassador. You gave me advice about food in the United States and warned me to be careful of what I ate after my return to Italy. I thought that strange, and you said that food in the United States was cellophane wrapped, while here the food is full of bacteria that the American digestive tract cannot handle."

Was it possible that this bearded old man in rags was in fact Pope Clemens? If his story was true, immediate action had to be taken. Call the State Department, warn the Italians, call in the CIA.

Very slowly, very hesitatingly, the ambassador asked, "You came directly to me after your flight from the asylum?" And he added, cautiously, "Your Holiness?"

"Yes. I don't like to say this, as an Italian, but I don't trust my fellow countrymen at this moment. If the fake Pope is my brother, he was Numero Due of the Communist party. I don't know how many members of the Italian party are involved in the scheme. I would like you and your country to grant me asylum until I can see more clearly. I—" A coughing spell interrupted him. The ambassador looked at the Pope's pale face, his burning eyes. He noticed that Clemens's hands were trembling.

"Are you all right, Your Holiness?" he asked.

Clemens felt his throat getting drier and his temperature mounting. He said, "I think I caught a cold last night."

"I will order some tea. We will get a room ready for you, and I will call the doctor who attends to the embassy personnel."

"Your Excellency, please give me your word of honor that you will not notify anybody of my presence here—not your secret service nor your President, no one for the time being."

The ambassador shrugged reluctantly. "This is not easy, but I will respect your wishes. I will tell my wife that you are an old friend and that I want her, personally, to make all the arrangements for your comfort. Meanwhile, Your Holiness, will you join me in a cup of tea?"

This time the Pope did not stop him from pressing the buzzer.

XVIII

There was nothing British or gentlemanly in the way Cholmondley banged the desk in his office. He was livid. Houndsworth tried to control his own mounting blood pressure, and Colvin angrily broke the stem of his pipe.

"Goddamn Schweiker," Cholmondley said. "How the hell did they let him escape? Damn it!" He banged the table again.

"It's partly our fault. There's always a grain of sand to reckon with. We should have known that he is trained in handling electrical appliances," Houndsworth said.

"I don't care whom we blame. We've got to find him. And take him back to Galenium, or, if that's not possible, he has to be killed. Under no conditions can we let him into the hands of the CIA," Cholmondley said.

"Have all our agents been contacted and given his description?" Colvin asked. "I wonder if he still has the beard?"

"Yes. I am waiting for Schweiker's call. He stayed on in Chiasso. Our man, Oldrati, thinks that damned Pope hitched a ride in a Fiat truck going to Bologna, and the driver is on his way back to Chiasso, where he will question him."

"Well, let us hope that we get some tangible news.

The man could not just completely vanish. He has to leave some traces."

The telephone rang and Cholmondley grabbed it.

When Antonio stopped at the border station in Chiasso, two men in raincoats and felt hats came up to his truck. "Antonio Arrigato?" questioned the taller one, the one with the Etruscan black beard.

Antonio nodded. The man held a cigarette case up to the door and said, "Cigarette?"

"No thanks," Antonio said. "I smoke only cigars."

The second man reached into his pocket and offered a box with small squat Swiss cigars. Antonio took one.

"Thanks. What can I do for you?"

"We would like to ask you about the old man you took with you to Bologna."

Antonio thought of Giorgio. So they knew about him. Was this one of the "black-bearded men" who had made him flee?

"What would you like to know?" he asked.

"Where did you leave him? Where did he go?" demanded the bearded one.

"Why do you want to know?" Antonio asked.

"He is a lunatic. A dangerous madman. He must go back to the asylum."

Antonio whistled. "A lunatic! I would have never guessed." They say he is a madman, he thought. That nice, sane acting, sweet old man. "He slept in my house. In the morning I took him to the depot where a private car was waiting for him. I think it was an Alfa. He said the car would take him down south. To Naples."

"Thank you, Mr. Arrigato." The tall man turned away and went to the pay telephone.

Naples, he thought. Houndsworth isn't going to like this. Naples was a port from where ships sailed to all parts of the world. And a good haven in which to hide—the famous needle in the haystack. First, he had to call Moscow and, after that, perhaps Naples, unless the boss would take over himself. Somehow, Schweiker suspected the elusive Pope would never be found.

XIX

Castor hated the small dark stuffy room assigned to him in the back wing of the embassy. He tried not to spend any time there. He was a field man, not an office clerk.

He threw himself into the chromium chair behind the desk and put his feet on it, American-fashion. He opened the desk drawer and found the last Havana cigar there. He picked it up, chewed the tip off, and was about to light it when he heard a knock on the door. He asked the intruder to come in, hoping he had a box of matches.

It was Brussilov of the Chancery. "This just came from M. Do you want us to unscramble it?"

"Isn't the scrambler working here?" Castor indicated the machine.

"I am afraid not, Comrade. Some short circuiting problem."

"Well, have it unscrambled and bring it back yourself. Who is in charge of decoding today?"

"Fedya."

"Okay. No copies. And Comrade Leonid—do you have a match?"

"Sorry, Comrade, I have only a lighter. May I?" He approached Castor, who took the lighter from his hand and looked at it.

"German?" he asked.

"No, Comrade. Czech copy of an Austrian model. Keep it for the moment. I'll be back with the text."

His cigar half finished, Castor put the unscrambled message on his desk and read:

"C. TO C. FIELD INSTRUCTIONS FOR WASHINGTON: PRIORITY, REPEAT, PRIORITY ESTABLISH HUMAN OR ELECTRONIC ACOUSTICAL CONTACT WITH WHITE HOUSE TO GAUGE IMPACT FORTHCOMING PAPAL VISIT. EXTREME PRECAUTION AND NONDETECTION IMPERATIVE. CHANCERY INSTRUCTIONS FOR ALL NECESSARY FUNDS TRANSMITTED SIMULTANEOUSLY TO THE V. IN TREASURY. REPEAT TOP PRIORITY. CONFIRMATION REQUESTED IMMEDIATELY. C."

Five minutes later Castor pushed the buzzer for Brussilov. "Sit here and take notes," Castor instructed and started dictating. "Personal habits of President and family, all activities outside the White House. Outside, did you get it?"

"Yes, comrade."

"If available without being noticed, I need the list of names of all civilian personnel working in the White House, with personal data. If any difficulties arise, stop the operation and report to me. Understood?"

"Yes, Comrade."

XX

" 'Open the doors of the Vatican wide both right and left.' I am quoting verbatim. 'Opening to the left.' 'Apertura a sinistra.' That's how the Communists penetrated the government in Rome."

General Holt sat in the Oval Office facing the President. The secretary of state sat in the armchair next to Holt.

Holt looked straight at the President's face searching for the effect of his devastating news. The effect was nil. Donovan did not look terrified, not even puzzled. Holt waited for the President to say something. Donovan seemed absorbed in doodling on the pad in front of him. Perhaps, he had not quite understood the implications.

"The language the Pope used is the language of socialism. He spoke of the uneven distribution of riches, of the necessary control of how the wealthy dispose of their fortunes."

Donovan was tempted to say So did Jesus Christ, but he refrained. He remembered his wife's admonition: When in Cabinet meetings try to forget the Gospel. Holt waited for Donovan's reaction. But it was Duncan Mulford who spoke up.

"General, the Pope is preparing a voyage to the United States, not to Moscow. To use military jargon, he is covering his flank by making a gesture to the Left."

Donovan looked gratefully at his secretary of state. A word of wisdom. He had selected Mulford because of that—think first and then speak. Mulford was of Swiss descent. Men like Mulford were needed against the bellicose saber rattlers of the Pentagon and the CIA.

Holt saw the look of approval on the President's face. Always, when in the face of more than one adversary, he felt his own irritation mounting.

"Well, Mr. Secretary, the Pope is not helping us with this new pro-Socialist attitude. The moment is not well chosen. The edgy situation in the Latin countries, the South African powder keg. The Pope's influence in South Africa is still very powerful, not only with the influential Roman Catholic minority but with all Christians. I wonder who has been influencing him lately—which of the newly elected cardinals from France or Portugal put that Marxist bug in his ears."

Donovan tried to ignore the irritation in Holt's voice. He said: "Let us not forget that the Pope is no diplomat working for our State Department. His diocese is the world, and some of his parishioners live in Socialist countries."

Holt spat out, "Do you trust the Pope, Sir?"

Do I trust the Pope? Careful, Donovan said to himself, we are on dangerous ground. Secularization. The Church versus the State. Render unto Caesar. Decisions sometimes difficult if one is Caesar oneself.

"As you know, I am a Roman Catholic, General. I am also President of the United States. The state takes precedence over my religion. I am not dogmatic, and I do not believe that the Pope is infallible, but certainly he's entitled to preach what he believes. What I hope and believe is that when it will come to backing us on vital decisions, the Pope will make the right ones."

The secretary of state looked at his watch and got up. "Is there anything else on the agenda, Mr. President?"

"No, Duncan. I thank you, gentlemen."

Donovan looked at his doodles. Crosses and small daggers. Yes, Holt had to be watched. He was a good man, but, by profession, he was on the hunt constantly for Communist conspirators in every possible and sometimes impossible corner. Like the Vatican. "Now let us have lunch."

He was finishing a piece of shad roe on toast when he heard some disturbance coming from the pantry. The Marine sergeant entered. His face flushed, he announced Phyllis.

She rushed in and kissed her father on the forehead.

"My, do we look smart," Donovan said.

"You like it?" Phyllis pirouetted like a trained mannequin.

"Come and have some shad roe."

"No, thanks. I'll settle for coffee. I had my lunch at the club."

Donovan poured some coffee in his own cup and handed it to her.

"What's new with you?"

"Nothing much. I just wanted to see if they feed you properly."

"They do. Very nicely. How was your tennis?"

Phyllis shrugged and took her glasses off. "My backhand is getting a little better." She cleaned her glasses with the napkin and put them back on. "What is the name of your sergeant?" she asked. "He is quite handsome."

Donovan looked at his daughter. He did not think her remark was funny. "Phyllis, what has become of you lately? I asked you before: Are you taking a graduate course in nymphomania? You, the most advertised virgin since Holy Mary in our hometown, are chasing all the macho physical specimens in your reach. I don't like it at all."

Phyllis laughed gaily. "Dad," she said, "you know it's only for fun. I promise I won't disgrace the name of Donovan. Satisfied?"

"Yes, if you give this Donovan a kiss."

Phyllis leaned forward and kissed her father's forehead. "Besides," she continued, "I've had my adventure with a handsome man today."

"What kind of adventure?"

"On my way back from the tennis club, I stopped at the A&P to get Mother's special cherry jam. There, a very handsome, elegant young man bumped into me. My glasses fell and the frame broke. He apologized, picked them up, and offered to take me to his oculist just a few blocks away to have them fixed. I accepted, and he drove me there in his Rolls. The frame couldn't be repaired, so he offered to buy me this new one in blue. Isn't it pretty? The man gave me his card. Wait a minute . . ."

She reached into the bottom of her purse and found the small printed card.

He read it out loud. "Dennis Crawford. The Stonehenge Arms, Fourteen Calorama." He looked at Phyllis. "Sounds British."

"Come to think of it, he did sound slightly Oxonian." Phyllis stretched her hand out for the card.

Slowly, deliberately, without looking at the card, the President tore it to pieces. "We don't like unknown gentlemen bumping into us. We shall dismiss Mr. Crawford to oblivion. I don't know how you managed to shake that poor man who's been detailed to guard you, but I wish you wouldn't."

Phyllis shrugged. "Okay, Daddy, if you say so. I sort of fancied presiding at tea in one of those stately mansions." She got up and added, "See you later. Be a good President."

"I promise." As she reached the door he called out to her, "Phyllis!"

She turned, "Yes, Dad?"

"The young sergeant's name is Fred Shaffer. And I remind you of your promise."

She blew him a kiss and left, leaving a scent of violets in the air.

XXI

Michael was working on his new spy book in his apartment on East Seventy-third Street. When the phone rang, he was happy for the interruption. He could not figure a clever way of getting his CIA agent out of a morgue in Tashkent, where he had been trapped by some Moslem fanatics.

The bachelor apartment was comfortable, and Michael made good use of the small kitchen and even more of his king-size bed. The apartment was indeed an asset in New York. His fertile imagination helped not only in shaping his intricate spy plots but also in his sex life. Nubile girls of some intelligence (and Michael had sexual appetites only for intelligent ladies) liked spinners of tales. There was no paucity of king-size-bed–sharers, although he sometimes wondered why he had not found a more reliably stable tenant.

The telephone call came from Max Brand, his friend, editor, and publisher. "How you doing, fellow?"

"I'm stuck in Tashkent," said Michael.

"Where the hell is Tashkent?" Michael was about to tell him but Max continued in a fast staccato. "Never mind Tashkent. Get your ass over to Washington."

Incredulous, Michael asked, "Washington, D.C.?"

"Yes. Washington, not Tashkent."

"May I ask why?"

"You may. This fellow called from Washington. He asked for Tom Coady."

"I hope you didn't reveal my right name."

"I didn't. I can read contracts."

"Okay. What did the man want?"

"He wants to see you. He says he has a very interesting offer for you. He wants you to be at the Jefferson tomorrow morning at ten o'clock and ask for Mr. Brown in Room Ten-twenty-four."

"That's crazy. What else did he say?"

"He said he likes your books. Especially the last one. And he wanted a short résumé—your age, whether you're married, et cetera, and, if not, are you gay?"

"Hope you told him I am—otherwise he can trace me too easily."

"Listen, Michael, the man's voice sounded important. It will do you good to get out of Tashkent and hop over to Washington. Call me when you get back. I want a full report. I'm bursting with curiosity."

Why not, Michael thought. He had not been in Washington for two years. He could call Art and Peter, both at the State Department. Maybe he'd stop in to see his father, a three star general. In fact, he did not need the excuse of seeing anybody. There was a mystery about the call, an intrigue, and Michael thrived on intrigue.

In the morning, he almost overslept. He gulped down a cup of coffee in record speed and caught the shuttle for Dulles Airport.

On time for his appointment at the Jefferson Hotel, he asked for Mr. Brown in Room 1024. When he heard the "Yes," he announced himself as Tom Coady. He was told to come up. He knocked on the door of

Room 1024 and heard a voice say, "Come in." He opened the door and stared at the man standing by the low coffee table. The man stared back at him. It was hard to say which of the two was more surprised.

The man in the room was his friend Peter Frank, the State Department career diplomat.

They broke out simultaneously, "What the hell?" and began laughing.

"How did you get in here?" Frank asked. "I expected to see somebody else—a writer."

"A writer by the name of Coady?"

"How do you know?" Peter's face turned serious and uneasy.

"Because I'm Tom Coady, or rather Michael Burren is. Coady is my pen name."

"For Chrissakes. Welcome to Washington." He stepped up to Michael and shook his hand. "Let me look at you. You haven't changed."

"Nor you. Perhaps a little more prosperous or pompous. Probably goes with your job. By the way, what is your job?"

"You'll find out. First, do you want coffee or tea? A little early for a drink."

"Just had coffee in the coffee shop."

"Let's sit down then."

They sat down and looked at each other. Or rather stared. Peter broke the silence. "I believe we have established the fact that you are Coady né Michael Burren."

"We have. Where do we go from here?"

Peter knotted his black knitted tie hanging loosely from the collar of his Brooks Brothers button-down shirt. He said, "Excuse the few well-chosen clichés, such as—since my cover is broken, I'll have to level with you, friend."

Michael's imagination was working faster than Peter's. "Don't tell me you're with the . . . the . . ." He couldn't get the initials *CIA* out. "I think I will take that coffee. I might just as well die of coffee poisoning. After I leave this room, my life won't be worth a peso in Patagonia."

Peter laughed. "You've got this all wrong, Mike. It is *my* cover that is broken, not yours."

"And what about my nom de plume? That's broken, too."

"I promise your secret will die in this room." He picked up the receiver, asked for room service, and ordered two coffees.

"Okay," Michael said, "tell me what you want from Coady."

"I want to recruit him into the agency."

"Why Coady?"

"The books. The boss thinks we can use a man like Coady for his lively imagination."

"To do what? Listen to tapes of senators talking to their secretarial concubines or plan assassinations of South American rebels?"

"Nothing as wild as all that. We are . . ." He stopped when the doorbell rang and the waiter brought in the coffee. Peter continued, "We are the section of anti-infiltration. The defense against KGB moles penetrating our government agencies. The Germans had the notorious name of Abwehr for this. Deflection. Protection."

"Aggressive protection, I guess."

"Good guess. You see, the Russians have recruited a force of the best young brains from the Lubianka University. They use new, highly original approaches and devices. The leaks we discover from top-secret files of the army, the navy, and the electronics industry are incredible. So the boss wonders whether we could pick Coady's brain. He said the experience with us might even improve Coady's future plots."

"I see that your boss reads spy books. As I presume he's an expert, he should know that previous attempts at enlisting writers as spies have not met with success. Somerset Maugham was a disaster, and Graham Greene hasn't been so great."

"True. But there was Ian Fleming. He was damn good."

"When did you switch from State to the agency?"

"Let me see. You went to Vietnam with the Marines in 'seventy-one?"

"In 1972, blast it."

"That was the year I moved over."

"You like your work?"

"Frankly, yes." He took his pipe out of his pocket and offered Michael some tobacco. "The peace pipe." Peter looked at Burren and said slowly, almost timidly, "So now that Coady is out of the closet, could I possibly interest Burren in the job? To continue, as it were, a family tradition?"

"I don't think so, Peter. One spy in the family is enough."

Peter shrugged but made one more attempt. "Forget about the past. The KGB is ruthless and needs to be counteracted. By the way, how is the general?"

"Still strong and stubborn. Maybe you could use *him*. He is not the retiring type."

"How do you know we are not using him? You know the saying, once the CIA, always the CIA."

Michael looked at his watch and got up. "Look, Peter, it was great seeing you again. Please call me when you get to New York. I am in the book. Under my real name."

Peter walked him to the door. "I will, but I don't want you to walk out on a completely negative note.

Think about it. Give yourself a few days. There is
truth in what the boss said, the experience might be
good for your next books."

In the plane Michael said to himself, Yes, I will
think about it. Alone and with nobody advising him.
But I hate the idea. He knew that he could not and
should not reveal this conversation to his father, nor
to his publisher, Max. Still, his father could be a great
help in making a decision. A decision about what?
This proposition was more, he felt, than a free training in cloak-and-dagger techniques. Perhaps it was a
trumpet call for action.

Michael recalled his father's reminiscences about his
activities in the Second World War—good, suspenseful
stories. Because he had been crippled in the First
World War, General Lawrence Burren had only a
desk job with the OSS. But he was of great help with
his suggestions. One of them was to pool the millions
of Americans of German descent and have them write
Red Cross cards to their relatives in Germany with
questions such as, "How is Uncle Herman?" The answers, "Uncle Herman is not at home . . . ," gave the
Pentagon a clue as to how many men the Wehrmacht
had under arms.

Another idea needed more direct action, involving
the British ambassador to Turkey. This titled gentleman—his ancestors occupied a full page in *Burke's
Peerage*—was a heavy drinker and generally inclined
to carelessness in his daily behavior. The OSS repeatedly warned the British MI6 of the security risk these
habits presented. General Burren conceived the idea of
putting the slovenly habits of the ambassador to the
advantage of the allies. False information marked TOP
SECRET was planted with him. The OSS knew that
sooner or later the papers would find their way into

the hands of the Abwehr or the Canaris organization. The plot paid off.

Even before the plane touched down at La Guardia, Michael had made his decision—to accept Peter's offer.

XXII

The club was not really a club, just a meeting place for the "foreign press." As the name, *Sunrise*, indicated, the premises were reserved officiously, if not officially, for the Eastern rather than the Western members of the noblest profession. The reporters for the East German, Polish, Hungarian, Bulgarian, and Rumanian papers congregated daily, mixing freely with journalists from the "uncommitted" nations. "Uncommitted" by local definition meant that they were not committed to the West. They were strictly "neutral" in favor of the East.

The long room with its imposing crystal chandelier, small marble-top round tables, barbarian baroque windows, and parquet floor had a pleasant, sloppy, half-elegant atmosphere. It crowded up every evening after seven, and the air densed with the fog of vodka vapors and cigarette fumes.

Cholmondley liked the place. Vodka was cheap and plentiful, and at least three times a week caviar was available if you arrived in time. He also liked to chat with the chaps from Africa—blacks from ex-British colonies who spoke what Houndsworth called "Jungle Oxonian." He knew that he had to be on guard. There was his drinking problem, which he thought of as a "sobriety problem." Drinking itself was no problem. He could consume immense quantities of vodka, not always available, and still keep a fairly level head, he hoped, but alcohol did loosen his tongue. There were no British or American reporters; even the Communist Western press preferred other bars, but Cholmondley knew that among the roughly one hundred men in the room—black, white, and yellow—there were at least ninety-eight spies like himself. Spying for whom? Or just *l'art—pour l'art?*

Relaxing in a comfortable Georgian leather chair, his tall drink of vodka with ice on the round marble table beside him, he stuffed his large-bowl Dunhill pipe. He was quite contented, and he chuckled when he thought of the latest information from Washington. How had it gone? How had the President worded it? Something like You wish to graduate as a nymphomaniac? You, who used to be the best-advertised virgin in our hometown. A good one. "The best-advertised virgin . . ."

Who in this crowd would appreciate the story? He was getting decidedly loose-lipped in his old age. But he couldn't resist this time. And what harm would it do? Everybody had their bugs, their scramblers, their ins to the White House—indeed every head of every major nation was constantly bugged and recorded. It was a game they all played. It didn't really hurt anyone. It was kind of a sophisticated game of chess.

"Hello, Kovacs," Cholmondley greeted him. "Do sit down. Have a vodka on me and listen to a story that will amuse you."

XXIII

The President had to squint as he looked at General Holt. If I can't adjust to this harsh light, I will have to wear dark glasses, he thought. Holt was carefully weighing every word as he finished his report on South Africa. He would like, he said, to send one of his best men to Cape Town on a fact-finding mission.

Donovan tried to restrain his impatience and his built-in bias against CIA secrecy and overcomplications. But, gradually, he became interested and involved. For the first time, he began to feel that they could help the situation, not exacerbate it, if they proceeded with caution. The weeks in the office were showing him that power could be used in lots of ways, important ways, and power didn't necessarily have to corrupt. If his heart and his mind were in the right place, perhaps it was wrong of him to turn his back on Kenyere in the name of discretion—of laissez-faire. Hell, he should be honest with himself—it was cowardly to walk around the situation. Rodney was making sense to him for the first time.

"Let me get this straight, Rodney," the President said. "You want to send a captain . . ."

"Captain Fred Blakely, Sir," Holt finished, grateful for being called by his first name.

"Blakely—is he aware of the dangers of this mission?"

"Yes, he has been on dangerous missions before. In Odessa, Thailand, even Amin's Uganda, and he speaks all the local dialects—Zulu, Kaffir, Bantu. Bishop Kwa knows him personally, and he agrees with me that he is the best man to penetrate the APC."

"Okay, Rodney, then go ahead. If I understand correctly, only the three of us—you, I, and Bishop Kwa—will know about this undertaking."

"Correct, Sir. I will personally cut his orders, issue the fake travel orders, and take care of money needs."

"Well . . . if you can avoid the media, and see there's no leaking. Anything else?"

"I'm afraid, yes—I need to trouble you for a few more minutes. Something strange has come up."

"I'm curious—what is it?"

"I want to quote this verbatim." He opened his briefcase and took out a folded sheet of paper. "Please excuse me, but I must ask a very personal question: Did you say something like this to your daughter? I quote, 'Are you taking a graduate course in nymphomania? You, the best-known virgin in our hometown?' "

The President looked startled. "I'm afraid I did. Who repeated this? Phyllis? Or was Sergeant Shaffer eavesdropping?"

Holt's trained poker face did not betray his shock and anxiety. "It came to me this morning by scrambled code—from Moscow."

Donovan thought he had misunderstood. He repeated, "Moscow?"

"Yes, Mr. President. It was told at the foreign-press club yesterday, and one of our men, a soi-disant Hungarian journalist, picked it up."

"I don't understand. They amuse themselves at the press club in Moscow with private conversations I have with my daughter?"

Holt looked straight into the President's eyes. He

said very slowly, "The anecdote itself is not important. How did they get it? That is, did your daughter repeat it to a friend? Did you tell it to your wife or anybody else?"

Donovan had to think. He put his hand to his forehead. "I don't think so . . . but let me ask to be sure. It's very odd."

"Even more odd, Sir, if Moscow thinks it important to let us know that they have heard of this conversation. Are they trying to tell us something? Or doesn't the KGB care whether we know that there is a leak?"

"Well, this is not a very serious leak, Rodney."

"Sorry, Sir, but to us all leaks are serious. And this leads me to point two: I want you to meet our new recruit, whom I would like to post in your own household here. He is waiting outside."

"A new recruit? Who is he?"

"He's your own suggestion, Mr. President. Your favorite writer of spy stories, Tom Coady."

Donovan remembered. As a matter of fact, he was deep in Coady's new book, *Trap for a Lonely Spy.*

"Coady. Of course. Bring him in."

"Before I do so, Mr. President, just a few words about him. He went through rigorous training in Virginia. He speaks good Italian and French with some German. He is very intelligent."

"Why did he agree to join the agency? Money? Ambition?"

"I guess kicks and adventure. He doesn't need money. He makes a fortune on his books."

"And his background?"

"Harvard. Stretch in Vietnam. Captain. Won lots of ribbons. But more important, Sir, Coady is a pen name. His real name is Burren. Michael Burren."

"Any relation to General Lawrence Burren?"

"His son, Mr. President. That's why he uses a pen name. As a writer of spy stories, he doesn't want to be known as General Burren's son. But on this mission in the White House, he wants to use his real name, not the nom de plume."

Donovan had a pleased expression. "Michael Burren. Show him in, please."

Curiously, Donovan looked at the tall lanky young man—upturned nose, reddish-blond hair, fair skin. Not bad, he thought. Too innocent looking and, therefore, too obvious for a spy.

"Michael Burren," he said. "I am one of your fans—and now they have assigned you to spy on me. Do you like the assignment?"

"It will be an honor and a pleasure, Mr. President."

"Actually, Sir," General Holt said, "his official assignment is secret-service protection for your daughter, Phyllis."

And, Donovan thought, my official assignment will be to see that Phyllis does not seduce her secret protection.

"Where will he be quartered, Rodney?" he asked and hoped that nobody had noticed his quick Rorschach reaction to the word *Phyllis*.

"I am afraid it will have to be in the servants' quarters," Holt answered. "The rooms are comfortable, but not fancy."

"And no room service, I am afraid," Donovan said. "You will have to forage for your own breakfast."

"No trouble, Mr. President. I'm not the breakfast-in-bed type."

"And you're not missing anything here. The coffee is awful."

"I always carry my own special mixture. I'm a nut about good coffee."

So he is not married, Donovan thought. "Well, Michael, welcome to the White House. Make yourself at home. Tonight, over drinks, I will introduce you to the family. Six thirty okay?"

"Thank you, Mr. President. Six thirty."

XXIV

Michael could not understand his dissatisfaction at being with the President's family. Did the Royal Family hamper his style? Or did he feel like a lackey on call to Their Majesties? The President sipped his Scotch-and-water and talked freely, very much at ease. An aura, a halo surrounded him, a halo of success, of leadership. With him alone, I could be at ease, Michael thought. Even with Mrs. President . . .

The trouble, he decided, was Phyllis. Surreptitiously, Michael watched her, observing her minutely. Not bad, not bad at all. There was something feline about her, a tangible mixture of the passive and the predatory. Thank God, he thought, she isn't wearing slacks. He could see her legs—long, strong, athletically curved. The blond hair was soft and wavy, the mouth wide and sensuous below the retroussé nose. The color of her eyes had to be guessed at through the horn-rimmed glasses. Blue or blue-gray or an opalescent green?

Michael quickly lowered his head when he noticed that Phyllis was returning his gaze. He had read somewhere that in the game of staring, the stronger character was the first to give up. He was surprised when he heard himself addressed.

"Do you play tennis?" she asked with directness.

Caught off guard, he answered idiotically, "Not at the moment."

Phyllis laughed, "I can see that. I mean, do you play the game?"

To repair his obtuseness, Michael said, most emphatically, "I do. I do."

"How good are you?"

"Middlingly superb. My backhand, trained in holding poker hands, is quite effective."

"Fine. You can come to the club with me," Phyllis said. "Pick me up here tomorrow at eleven. Okay?"

"It will be a pleasure."

Yessiree, it sure will be a pleasure. I am supposed to guard this gal against evil forces and sinister Bolshevik conspirators. What I am not supposed to do is to want to take her to bed. How am I going to navigate between duty and pleasure? Fight off the gnomes of temptation? The flesh is weak; the spirit is strong. Or vice versa. Be serious, he admonished himself. You are on a government job, and you are an intellectual and raconteur of stories. You're supposed to be sophisticated and experienced, so act your age.

He was relieved when the President stood up and said, "Well, it's time to dress for dinner. How will I ever survive the nonalcoholic session with that Moslem head of state?"

Back in his small, austere room, Michael dialed his friend at the State Department. He must know some available gals to take to dinner, with the accent on *available*.

XXV

She slid lithely and easily into Michael's red XJ Jaguar. He drove carefully, curbing his desire to push down the gas pedal. Phyllis was too precious a cargo, and he was responsible for her safety.

"Nice car. Obviously not one that belongs to the secret service. It's too show-offy."

"She's my very own."

"Do they pay you well in the service?"

"Add ten percent to the wages of a New York cop."

"That must be very high. I'm not very good at adding."

"Nor am I. My agent does the adding."

"Oh, yes. Your spy books. I haven't read any."

Is she being aggressive or only provocative? Let's test it. "If I send you the latest, will you read it?"

"Eagerly. If you autograph it."

"Gladly."

"What will it say?"

"I don't know yet. Depends."

"On what?"

"Your tennis game."

In fact, her game was excellent. Her movements, the swing of her hips, the way she ran for the ball, were all feminine, but her strokes, especially her forehand drive and her serve, were powerfully masculine.

Her partner with a Dutch name, "Van den some-

thing," was an older man, between fifty and sixty. He
was lean and looked harmlessly brittle. But he was a
shrewd, experienced player—almost a pro and good at
retrieving Michael's overhead smashes. His own partner was the club's trainer, a sturdy Serb peasant, Mila
Bulatovic. Michael vaguely remembered her as being a
member of the Yugoslav team in Wimbledon.

The game was quite even. After a score of six-all,
Michael and Mila won on the tie break.

"Good game," Phyllis said as she walked to the
locker rooms. "Will you play with me again?"

"Whenever you wish."

"What about the day after tomorrow? Same time?"

"Great. Pleasure before duty. You play a good
game."

Mila Bulatovic had enjoyed the game, too. Now, she
sat down on the long wooden bench in the ladies
locker room and stretched her sturdy legs. She watched
Phyllis undress and nonchalantly walk naked to the
shower. Mila envied all about Phyllis—mostly her figure. The blessings of capitalism, she thought—good
food, vitamins, and a lot of exercise. She slowly got up,
opened her own locker, and took out an air travel bag.
She zipped it open and took out a pair of horned-
rimmed glasses. She picked up Phyllis's glasses and replaced them, in the exact position in which she had
found them, with the glasses from her own travel bag,
into which she put Phyllis's glasses.

Phyllis reentered, wiping herself with a large Turk-
ish towel. "Good game, Mila," she said. "Day after tomorrow we should take on the two men."

"Yes. We will win. Nice man this new one. Handsome. Friend of yours?"

"Not yet. He is my guardian."

"Guardian? What does it mean?"

"He is secret service. He is supposed to keep me out of mischief."

Mila laughed. "Funny. With him, I would have to be careful not to get into mischief."

Phyllis shrugged. "The idea crossed my mind, too."

Mila took her travel bag, went to the parking lot, got into her Beatle, and started to drive into the city. She stopped the car near a phone booth and dialed a number. When she heard a male voice say, "Hello," she said, "Rally."

The voice answered. "Smash. All set?"

"All set. The mailbox in thirty minutes."

"Okay. Anything else?"

"Yes. She has a new partner. Secret service. Michael Burren. About twenty-eight, tall, red hair."

"Burren. Will check. Okay?"

"Yes. Just one question—any news of Fred?"

A pause. The voice asked, "Where are you calling from?"

"Phone booth."

"The committee collected Fred. All taken care of."

"Splendid. Call you the day after tomorrow."

XXVI

Monticelli was tired, very tired. These last days had been busy, too busy with the agenda for the impending trip and with lessons in economics. He had been especially impressed with the figures in the collection known as "Peter's Pence"—a personal contribution to the Pope that had to be distributed to the poor. The figures were imposing.

As a matter of fact, this job of being the Pope was frightening in its power. Monticelli had never realized that the office of the Pope carried so much power in a small state inside a state, without one single armored division. There were moments when he was afraid of that power and of the possibilities of his own use of it to benefit the enemies of the Church. It was an enormous task, perhaps surpassing his own physical strength. He remembered the words of the good Pope John XXIII when they told him that he was to be the Pope. Quoting the Book of Job, he had said: *Horrefactus sum*. "I am terrified." He sat at the large desk, lost in his thoughts, covering his face with his right hand and was startled when he heard the Maestro di Camera's voice: "Your Holiness . . ."

He looked up at the Maestro, who held a large leather folder in his hands. "What is it, Alessandro?" he asked.

"Tomorrow is the first of the month, Your Holiness.

I have prepared the checks for your signature. With your permission, Your Holiness . . ."

He put the folder in front of Monticelli and opened it. Attached to a white sheet of paper were four individual checks, all made out to a law firm, Sassoferrato e Consorti. *Sassoferrato*. The name meant something to him but he could not remember what.

The names listed on the white sheet next to each individual check meant a great deal to the "Pope." All of the names were Monticellis. Giorgio, Rafaelle, Alessandro, Paolo . . . The sums were the same—four hundred thousand lira each.

He stared at the checks without making a move. Again, he started when he heard Alessandro's gentle and polite voice, "The monthly checks, Your Holiness."

The monthly checks. His first shock turned to anger—his brother, the pious sonofabitch, supported his equally pious brothers by monthly checks. To ease his conscience.

He quickly signed the checks with his well-trained hand. He was about to close the folder when, again, he looked at the name *Sassoferrato*. Slowly, as the meaning of the name came back to him, Monticelli broke out in a cold sweat.

"Alessandro, when did this Sassoferrato file start. I mean how far back did we have that file?"

"Your Holiness, the file started before my time. I have the whole file. It started in the year when you became the bishop of Livorno."

"Alessandro, would it be too difficult to get me the file?"

"Now, Your Holiness?"

"Yes, Alessandro. Please."

While the Maestro di Camera was away, he had time to think. He was quite sure now that the lawyer

who had informed him in Bergamo in 1946 that an
"unknown benefactor" had left him some money that
would enable him to complete his studies at college
was Sassoferrato.

He was in a state of shock. The file was an anticli-
max. His suspicion had been right. His holy brother,
bishop, then cardinal, then Pope, had supported him
anonymously all his life. Monticelli had become a professor at the university and a leader of the Italian
Communist party at the expense of the Pope.

"Are you all right, Your Holiness?"

"Yes, thank you, Alessandro, though I do feel somewhat faint. Perhaps, I need a stimulant . . ."

"How about that old grappa from Parma?"

"That will do fine, Alessandro."

In his bedroom, he almost finished off the grappa.
His saintly brother must have been smugly amused at
the idea of supporting his worst enemy. Very biblical, he thought and laughed. And how immensely no-
ble. On top of the file, he had found a note that read,
"To be destroyed on the day of my death." Sonofabitch. The best student. The darling of all the teachers. A first-class finagler, paving his way to heaven
with blood money to his brothers. Where did it come
from? Peter's Pence? Stolen from the poor?

In spite of the liquor, the shock would not subside.
There was a bilious taste in his mouth. He took a double number of sleeping pills and threw himself on the
bed.

It was four o'clock in the morning when he woke
up. For hours, he had been only half asleep, half
awake. Now that he woke up completely, he felt very
fresh, very vigorous. And greatly relieved from his half
dreams, which he remembered with crystal clarity.

The dreams of heresy. Of all kinds of heretics. The
Albigenses, the Jansenists, Calvin, Huss. And the her-

etics of the Marxist-Leninist religion, like Toynbee or Koestler.

It was quite obvious to him why he had this fight with all the traitors to a higher cause. Because of his own unpredictable weakness sustaining such a shock just on account of his brother's charitable acts. A very personal, very skin-deep earthquake caused by a minor fraternal conflict.

He got up feeling an immense craving for a cup of coffee. But he knew that at four in the morning room service did not function in this archaic chateau. He had to content himself with eating the one half of the apple left over from his supper.

He searched inside himself for a clue to get a hold of his feelings. Know thyself. The incident with his pious brother's banking accounts was dismissible, unimportant. Many years ago, he had analyzed this situation, this antagonism with his brother. True, it had probably started with what the analysts like to call sibling rivalry, the hatred and envy against the eldest brother who received all the benefits to the detriment of the others. This hatred, which in his adolescent years was probably very virulent and all-consuming, ceased to exist with his Marxist education. The hatred against the brother became a Marxist, cold, rational contempt and enmity against the Church as representative of capitalist sanctuary. That his brother was the Pope became an accident, a historical joke.

He shrugged, shook himself out of this family quagmire, and said: "Let us go for deeper and more important scrutiny of assets and liabilities." What have I accomplished so far, he thought. The list was there in the computer of his good brains. Information about some anti-Communist activities in Poland and Hungary. One not-unimportant pastoral message to the world about the opening to the Left. Two incisive and perhaps very effective speeches aimed at the still-hesitating Roman Catholic voters in Italy and Spain. And the subtle preparation for his meeting with the American President about the noninterference in Africa and the abolition of all atomic arms. He had to smile when he thought of his forthcoming proposition for the destruction of all atomic weapons.

Yes, these were some accomplishments. Not too spectacular, but not so minimal either. And time was working for him, for the party. He started to feel a little better about his trip to America.

XXVII

Quite obviously both men were upset. The brutal light seemed to bother the President more than ever, and the room was overheated. He stood up, took his jacket off, and threw it on a chair.

General Holt did not dare to emulate him. I've got to sweat this out, he thought, literally and figuratively.

The President sat down and said, "To repeat, the body was found in a stolen car in front of our consulate in Johannesburg. Positive identification?"

"Positive. Also corroborated by the photos in the local press."

"And your report says he was picked up at the airport. How is this possible? Where were our own people?"

"Right there, Mr. President. The enemies created a distraction with the use of a plastic bomb. In the panic and commotion, they must have grabbed him and forced him into a waiting car."

The President shook his head in despair. "Rodney, this is really terrible. To send a good man, Captain Blakeley, to his death . . . I don't know how to face this."

Holt did not flinch. Cold and determined, he said, "Mr. President, at the risk of sounding cynical, I have to remind you that we have taken such calculated risks with our agents before, and we will do so again. In cold fact, this means no more and no less than the loss of one expendable agent. And I am sorry to have to state this is not my main worry. What frightens me is the leak."

Holt stepped closer to the desk.

"Sir, our electronics team will check every corner in the White House. Plus your personal effects, such as watches, cameras, fountain pens, coins, wallets, ear-rings, cuff links."

"You sound like you have a certain fixed goal. What is it?"

"Mr. President, the KGB has developed oversophis-ticated listening devices of such precision and sensitiv-ity that we do not trust ourselves in our own offices. As a matter of fact, outside of standing under Niagara Falls with a transistor radio playing a Sousa march at high volume, we don't dare to speak openly anywhere. There are things I would not say in this room."

Suddenly Donovan felt a chill. He stood up and put his coat on.

"You certainly have the gift of frightening people. What do you suggest?"

"Nothing for the moment. At the agency, we resort to the primitive device of talking in some kind of pig Latin. Mostly in nursery rhyme—words no foreigner would understand."

"Sounds a bit primitive, Rodney. I will report to you of my talk with Gladys."

"Thank you, Mr. President, and good day."

XXVIII

Michael drove the black Chevrolet to the Blakeley apartment. He tried some small talk with the two "plumbers" assigned for the job. They looked like two alert, skinny, schoolboys. I hope they are better technicians than the Watergate burglars, Michael thought.

The apartment house was located in a not-so-chic suburb and had no superintendent. One of the boys took out an assortment of keys from his pocket and opened the outside door in a split second.

Opening the door of Apartment 707 was less easy. On the way, so far, they had encountered no one. Michael knew that the CIA used the house for transient agents. Perhaps they were all out on important spying jobs. He watched the two men working on the lock. Still no success.

"Something wrong?" he asked.

The other man answered, "This door has been picked before. By pros."

So other uninvited visitors had visited Captain Blakeley. How will I find out what they took, Michael wondered. I don't have an inventory.

Suddenly, the door cooperated and the three men entered the dark room. With the aid of flashlights they found the wall switch. The small living room was in spotless order. As they searched, one of the agents spotted a drawer in the desk that had been opened forc-

ibly, probably with a knife. Michael pulled out the
drawer and found a travel folder of Oregon; an un-
used checkbook of the Morgan Guaranty Trust Company; paper clips; red, blue, and green pencils; a
three-week-old copy of *Time* magazine; dental floss.

In other words, nothing. In the bedroom closet,
there was one heavy Harris Tweed suit, a pair of English brogues, three shirts. In the bathroom, used Gil-
lette blades and a pair of ragged, worn bedroom slippers.

Nothing. Except something on top of the desk,
which Michael instantly put in his pocket. His move
was quick and furtive. He had a good reason for it. In
the open agenda, he had caught two items of interest:
a hastily penciled note, *SAA Flight 803*; underneath,
underscored were the words *Club. Phyllis. Eleven.*

The hour, the club, and Phyllis. The combination
could, of course, be an accident, a strange coincidence.
His CIA training and his own plot mind had taught
him not to believe in convenient coincidences.

While driving out to Langley Field to report to
General Holt, he had a tough fight with his conscience.
He knew he had to question Phyllis about the note.
Should he question her first before speaking to Holt?
If she did not know Blakeley, there was no reason to
involve her. He had no illusions about his Galahadian
feelings—it had nothing to do with his assignment as
her guardian. It had a great deal to do with her legs, her
scent, her provocative mouth.

He squeezed the steering wheel tightly. You fool, he
said to himself, don't go blowing this for a kid with
myopic blue eyes—for a biological urge.

Holt listened carefully to the report.

"Thanks for the debriefing," he said. "Clearly, if
the KGB got in there first, they saw the note. They

were probably not interested in Phyllis. They were very interested in Flight Eight-oh-three of South African Airlines. The question remains: How did they know that Blakeley was about to leave?"

"Do you mind, sir, if I question Phyllis Hayley about this myself?"

"Hayley? Oh, I forgot—that's her married name. I insist that you question her. The sooner the better. Don't forget—we are installing the whole electronic circus in the White House this afternoon. At five. You should see her before that."

"Yes, sir." He turned to go. Suddenly, he stopped and said, "Sir, may I make a suggestion for the electronic team?"

"Certainly. What is it?"

Michael approached Holt's desk, "General, if they have any bugging devices and we announce what kind of search we intend to do, they will learn about it immediately. I suggest that instructions be given in writing with the request to be completely silent during the operation."

Holt looked up at Michael's intelligent face and congratulated the President and himself for having picked him.

"A very good idea, Michael. It will be done."

"Thank you, sir."

XXIX

It was five in the morning when he finally sat down on the wooden chair and started to pound the old battered Olivetti. He had been up all night correcting the handwritten pages of a long letter—a letter to the President of the United States.

He had thought about the letter for months. He had procrastinated, undecided whether to write it or not. Now, the matter could not be delayed any longer. Election day was close, very close. Was it the deadline of the election which eventually triggered his decision or was it the brutal assassination of Captain Blakeley? Or both?

His steel-rimmed glasses were as badly in need of repair as the Olivetti. He had neither the time nor the money to repair either. He sighed deeply, drank the rest of his tea, and started to type. His fingers were a little stiff from the cold. Have the weather conditions changed too in this crazy, changing world? It seemed that the wind coming from the ocean was colder and more penetrating than it used to be.

Dear Mr. President,

I am writing to you in the hope that you will read my letter and read it carefully. I dare write you because the matters I wish to speak of are of vital interest not only to my country but to the United States and to the whole world.

We are in deep trouble here and we are faced with mighty and ruthless enemies. They don't hesitate in using methods of terror and infiltration as you saw by the merciless murder of your own envoy. I am sure that our good Bishop Kwa will give you my messages and his own report but this is not enough. You have to know the real situation as it presents itself here today.

Apartheid is finished and the Afrikaner Nationalists know it. I write not to tell you of my hatred and contempt for the policies of apartheid in the past but because of my fear for the future of my country, for the transition from apartheid government to a free South Africa. I am afraid that there is much blind hatred among my people, perhaps strongest among the young, even the very young, the schoolchildren, who for generations, but mostly for the last thirty years, have been treated as nonexistent persons with no voice in their own affairs, forbidden to own land or houses in the cities. Hatred is a bad advisor in times of crisis. We want a peaceful, rational transition and not irrational chaos fostered and enhanced by our enemies. We don't want our schoolchildren to burn down their classrooms and terrorize their own parents. We know who teaches them how to make Molotov cocktails; we know who is pulling the ropes. You will remember that the first eruption of this children's revolution came when the apartheid government wanted to impose Afrikaans as the obligatory language. The schools revolted not because they wanted to speak only their own native Zulu or Tswana or Basuto, but because they wanted English to be the official language. English—they still have faith in Anglo-Saxon decency.

We, the black leaders of the so-called moderate groups, believe that emancipation will not be accomplished (or will be of no practical value) unless we blacks unite. And there have been more deaths in tribal disputes this year than in the political upheaval against the government.

These bloody tribal fights are encouraged and sponsored by the local representatives or agents of the Soviet government. And this is what I am deadly afraid of unless we get immediate moral and practical support from you, there will be a holocaust on the day after the election. There will be mass killings of the whites, who, however, will have better means of defending themselves than the blacks. The operators of organized chaos will see to it that the antagonisms between migrant Zulus and city Zulus, Tswana against Swazis will be exploited fully and viciously. One of these agents preached the supremacy of the country Zulus in order to establish a Zulu dictatorship. All these agitators preach the might of the Soviets, the financial omnipotence of the Russians and the paradisical life in a Marxist economy.

My party believes in a multiracial government of all tribes with no special privileges for any individual one. We want the whites born in Africa to live peacefully with us, to have the same rights but no more than we hope to have.

And we don't believe in Marxism as the solution for South Africa. We don't think we should accept any Western or Eastern political and economic ideas and theories but conceive and develop our own.

Kenyere was getting tired. He had to warm his hands and drink more tea. The kettle served both purposes. He gulped down the scalding tea, cleaned his fogged glasses, and continued typing the letter.

Mr. President, I thank you for your patience in reading this letter so far. Now, I will dare to take the liberty of giving you advice.

My people are naïve and primitive, easy to impress. Your State Department has made vague references to financial aid if we get elected. I would like you to turn this promise into reality. A 500 million dollar loan if the election takes place without bloodshed and violence and if the new government will be a democracy and not some kind of dictatorship.

And, Mr. President, I respectfully ask that you send the Seventh Fleet on the morning of the election into the port of Cape Town. With all your aircraft carriers, cruisers, and destroyers flying the Stars and Stripes. I know that you think "showing the flag" is outdated, and I also know that you want to avoid any confrontation with the Russians, including a face-to-face with their Indian Ocean navy.

I am convinced, Mr. President, that there is no danger of any real confrontation—they will back down just as they did in Cuba. And the pictures of your 7th Fleet, carried by our television cameras, will have an immense effect on my primitive and naïve people. You will have earned friends for many, many decades. A positive answer will greatly oblige your very obedient servant,

Kenyere.

He chewed on his glasses again. He had a long wait for the private car of his friend, the editor of the *World*, to arrive to take him to the American embassy in Pretoria.

XXX

When Michael burst into the small blue "salon," Mrs. Donovan and Phyllis were just finishing drinking their tea out of the fine English Wedgwood service.

"Won't you join us?" asked the First Lady.

"I am afraid I can't. I'm sorry to disturb you but I must speak to your daughter alone for a moment."

"Shall I leave?" asked Mrs. Donovan.

"No, Mother. We'll go up to my room, Mr. Burren."

Mr. Burren. She knows this is official, Michael thought.

The bedroom was in disorder. Michael tried not to look at the black silk panties on the bed. Phyllis caught the nonlook and quickly put them in the drawer.

"Forgive me. I did not expect any visitors. Especially male ones. A drink? Cigarette?"

"Thank you, neither. May I smoke my pipe?"

"Certainly. I love the smell of your tobacco. English?"

"American. Made in San Francisco."

They sat down. Phyllis crossed her legs and pulled her skirt down when she again caught Michael's nonlook. The move proved to be more provocative than otherwise.

"Mrs. Hayley—" Michael began when she interrupted.

"The name is Phyllis, Michael."

"Thank you. Phyllis, did you know Fred Blakeley?"

"Yes. He is one of my best tennis partners. I do
know him. Why the 'did'?"

"He is dead. Killed in South Africa."

"Oh, my God. Who killed him and why?"

"I am afraid I am not in a position to give you the
details. He was on an official mission in Johannesburg. Did you know he was leaving?"

"Yes. He told me that our date for mixed doubles
the next day had to be canceled."

"Did you tell anybody about Blakeley's departure?"

"No. Wait a minute. I had to tell the pro to look for
another partner for me as Fred was leaving."

"Who is the pro?"

"Mila."

"Mila Bulatovic who was my partner in the game
yesterday?"

"Yes. Mila. Is this important?"

"We think it might be."

"Will you question her?"

"Maybe. But not today. Today is electronics day."

"What the hell is that?"

"A team of electronic wizards are going to invade
this house and find out if it's bugged."

"Sounds eerie. Are you helping them?"

"Not really. You will get your instructions in writing from my boss, General Holt. An unpleasant invasion of privacy."

She was momentarily frightened, feeling threatened,
and in her fear reached out to her guardian. Within
seconds she was folding herself in him, unaware of and
unconcerned with propriety. She needed to feel secure,
and he was there for her.

They kissed—once, twice, arms entwined around each other. Before things could go too far he stopped her.

"For God's sake, Phyllis, you're the President's daughter."

"I'm a woman who happens to live in the White House."

He looked at her and realized she was not only an attractive woman but a confident one. A woman aware and in control of herself and her desires.

"Let's wait until the smoke clears."

She nodded her assent—things were happening she couldn't quite explain. She too needed the time to think things through.

They walked arm in arm down the stairs to the family room, where the family waited to see Michael.

The electronics team performed with great skill and speed. The gadgets resembling small vacuum cleaners scanned the walls, the windows, the curtains. No sound could be heard but the buzzing of the electric snorkels.

Twenty-two men worked on the bug-detecting job, and ten more were employed for the scrutiny and analysis of the personal effects of the President, his family, and the household employees.

Phyllis sat with her mother in the small salon and read. They were virtually incommunicado, for the printed instructions given them warned them not to talk while the search was on. The "company" had collected in rubber-lined baskets all personal paraphernalia, earrings, watches, rings, fountain pens, lipstick, keys, even Phyllis's horn-rimmed glasses. The baskets were taken to the pantry, now converted into a laboratory, where electronic microscopes were set on two white tables with heavy wires connecting them to an outside generator. The men working in the room could have been professional anesthetists.

It was at 6:15 that Michael entered the Oval Office. The President had to check the time by the old grandfather clock—his own wristwatch was still in the hands of the company. He could see by the look on Michael's face that he had some important, perhaps serious, news for him.

"Mr. President," Michael said, "I need you for a moment."

"Okay, Michael, I am all yours. What is it?"

"Not here, Sir. May I ask you to step out with me to the front lawn?"

"And take my coat off and pull up my shirt sleeves?"

Michael smiled. It was good to have a President with a sense of humor.

Donovan stood up and looked at the contraption in Michael's hand. It looked like a heavy umbrella.

"Is it raining?" he asked.

"No, Mr. President. This is just in case."

On the lawn, Michael opened the "umbrella." It was heavy with a steel rod holding a tent of aluminum foil. When Michael pushed a button on the handle, a low buzz was heard.

"Sir, let me explain. We don't know to what degree and to what distance their new Enigma II listening device can pick up voices and conversations. This umbrella is our most sophisticated scrambler, and we have reason to believe that it is safe."

"Well, let us hope so. What is the result of the scrutiny?"

"We found no bugs and no mikes in the White House. But we found one in your daughter's horn-rimmed eyeglasses."

"In Phyllis's glasses?"

"Yes, Mr. President. A microscopic, very new, very advanced tube."

"So whatever Phyllis hears, they hear too?"

"Yes, Sir. Of course, we don't know where and how they planted it and how they collect it."

"Wait a minute. A week ago, Phyllis told me that a man had bumped into her at a supermarket and knocked her glasses off. He took her to his oculist who repaired the broken frame. I am sure that this is how it started."

Michael suddenly felt chilled. "Sir," he asked, "did your daughter describe the man?"

"Yes. She said he was handsome and tall and had a British accent. The man gave her his card with his address, which, I am afraid, I destroyed."

"Do you remember the name?"

"Wait a minute. It sounded like Warwick. No, Crawford. Yes, it was Crawford. The address was the Stonehenge Arms."

"We will try to find him, although it is most likely that both the name and address are fake. But, Mr. President, what is of the utmost importance is that Phyllis, I mean your daughter, should *not* know of our discovery."

"You mean she should go on wearing the bugged glasses?"

"Yes. We can use it to our advantage. For the time being, it is imperative that they should not know that we have found it."

"Is this not very unfair to Phyllis?"

"Not really. It will in no way inconvenience her. And for us it is vital that they do not know that we know."

"The next step is to find out how they collect the tube?"

"Yes . . . and I have a hunch."

"Well, good luck. Evidently, I'll have to watch myself in my conversations with Phyllis. No political talk—normal, fatherly stuff. In other words, I will have to put on a good act."

Oh, boy, Michael thought, so will I—but it sure will complicate my private life. Tomorrow the bells of the Kremlin will announce that I'm having an affair with the President's daughter. What the Kremlin doesn't know yet is that I'm afraid I'm in love with the President's daughter. Well, such is life. Blame or bless the CIA for it. And the KGB.

Castor was sitting in his small apartment on Cherry Hill Lane in Washington listening to the amplified sounds coming from the tube. "Cholmondley will like this," he thought as the sound finished. The President's daughter making passes at a spy.

He put the tube on the scrambled transmitter and pressed the green button. Then he grabbed the phone and dialed a number. When he heard the female voice, he said, "Smash." He barely waited for the answer—"Rally"—and said, "Scramble." He heard the click, "Red. Immediate. With the Polish passport straight to the airport in not more than ten minutes. First flight to Montreal. Fedja will be there. Confirm."

"Confirmed. Question, replacement?"

"Lili Fagyas as foreseen. Call the club. Repeat, utmost urgency."

"Confirmed."

Neither General Holt nor Michael were surprised to find that nobody had ever heard of the Stonehenge Arms in Washington and surroundings.

While Michael was driving to the tennis club, he had time to think of the surprising and fascinating events of the previous day. Or the previous night. Dinner at the Sans Souci with Phyllis was not only good, it was epicurean. She disliked champagne just as much as he did, but the Château Haut Brion tasted like nectar. They did not dare yet to exploit the possibilities of togetherness in the White House, either her room or his, so they made love in his car in a grove off the main road to Virginia. A little uncomfortable (and a little dangerous?), but who cared? And who cared for explanations? He had carefully removed her glasses and put them in her purse. When she said, "You know I never did this in a car before," he knew she spoke the truth, just as when she said later, "I knew this was it, the moment I met you." It was "it" for him, too. He smiled, happily, and took out her white handkerchief from his breast pocket and sniffed it.

At the club, again, he was not too surprised to learn that Miss Mila Bulatovic had left. She had received an urgent phone call from a very sick relative in Mexico. Her replacement, Miss Lili Fagyas, was expected in the afternoon.

XXXI

Washington was a peaceful haven after New York. Like a real bad dream, Monticelli thought as he relaxed in a deep leather chair at Bishop Glenville's home. No street noises, no fire engines. He stared at the television screen, trying to understand this country. Some naïve, some amusing, some exciting programs, always interrupted by what Monticelli found to be tasteless and coarse advertisements. Still, he could push a button and stop the show. In New York there had been no end of visitors, priests, senators, VIP's. And the mad ticker tape parade on Fifth Avenue, which he would never forget. What had impressed him the most in this strange country? The President had sent a special, immense plane to Rome for him, a Boeing 747. Before landing, they had circled over New York, and the first impact had been that of power—steel and electric power of unfathomable proportions. The well-named skyscrapers, the neon signs, the incredible efficiency, which he sadly compared to both Italy and Moscow. The Asiatic, monolithic inefficiency of the Russians; the lazy, Mediterranean laissez-faire inefficiency of his own Italians. What made these capitalist slaves so efficient? What made these zealots work so hard? Would they ever become Socialists?

He was tired and wondered why he was not enjoying himself more. To play a good part and to play it well, to impersonate so excellently the world's most important person should have been more than satisfactory.

He did not look forward with any enthusiasm to his meeting with the President the next day. Of course, he had to perform and try to make this pacifist President a little more pacifist. He almost used an American slogan he had heard on television, "I am paid for this." But he wished he weren't so weary.

His faithful Maestro di Camera brought his tea with apologies. The kitchen had only Chinese jasmine tea in stock. Monticelli resigned himself to his fate, or to his brother's fate, and turned on the television again. He leaned back in his armchair and watched the young black San Francisco cop on his motorcycle chasing a gangster in a black Porsche.

For a change the Donovans had their drinks in the yellow Louis XVII oval-shaped room. After all, the premises had to be made use of.

Phyllis was reading a brochure and laughed out loud.

"What's so funny?" Donovan asked.

"The protocol."

"Protocol is a serious matter."

Phyllis disagreed. "To me it's silly and ridiculous."

"But necessary," the President said. "The chief of protocol might take his job too seriously, but that's his duty."

Gladys intervened, "After all, when the President and the Pope meet, they can't just say, 'Hello, how are you?'"

Phyllis shook her head. "Why not? Both Dad and the Pope are sons of simple workingmen. Common people. They work, they sleep, they eat. Dad likes cheeseburgers, and I am sure the Pope likes spaghetti."

The subject interested Gladys. "I read somewhere," she said, "that Mrs. Roosevelt served hot dogs to the King and Queen of England."

"Phyllis, thank heavens your mother doesn't like hot dogs," Donovan said.

"Mrs. Roosevelt was a great woman," Gladys defended. "She was too busy to bother with menus."

"Anyway," Donovan said to Phyllis, "stop picking on the protocol. Just follow it."

Phyllis had another look at the sheet of protocol. "It says here that the Pope has diplomatic priority. He is the father of all kings and princes. Nevertheless, I am warned not to genuflect before him nor kiss his ring."

The voice became presidential, "Because I don't receive the Pope as a Catholic. One head of state receives another. He is not my spiritual leader. My allegiance is to the Constitution, not to my religion."

"Period," Phyllis said. "Sounds like one of your campaign speeches."

"Well, I did win, didn't I?" Donovan said. "With the solemn declaration, which, by the way, I intend to keep, that for me the Pope is just another foreign ruler. Our status is equal."

"Except that you are more equal," Phyllis said. "You can press a button and drop that thing. He hasn't got the thing."

"Don't mention the thing, Phyllis, you know I'll never drop it."

"Why not? Everybody is mentioning it."

"You are not everybody. You are the President's daughter. You have to watch your language."

Phyllis shrugged. "I have to watch everything."

"So have I," Gladys said. "Security goes wherever I go. And all my visitors must be screened. The price to pay for being First Lady."

"I can't even have a date," Phyllis said. "Except with my own guard, God bless him."

The furtive exchange of looks between her father and mother did not escape Phyllis. How much did they know or guess? At this moment it was not important. She would take greater risks than just parental disapproval of an "affair" that had become much more important than just an affair.

"Back to my solitary confinement and *The New York Times* crossword puzzle," she said. She put her cup down, stood up, and went to her room.

In the Oval Office, Monticelli felt elated, almost euphoric for the first time. He sat next to Bishop Glenville and the American secretary of state and faced the President. It was pleasantly warm in the room, and the stark light did not unduly disturb him. The importance of his mission gave him a spiritual boost, and he considered himself intellectually superior to these Americanos.

At the initial phase of the meeting, President Donovan warmly congratulated the Pope on his liberal stand on several important matters: he approved of his encouragement of the worker-priest movement and of his easing the Church's stand on birth control.

Monticelli sighed. "I wish, Mr. President, I had the same understanding by my cardinals in Rome. The patina-encrusted tradition of the Church is a difficult barricade to take. I must proceed slowly. There are many more important improvements I would like to announce but don't yet dare."

"Such as?" the secretary of state interjected somewhat dryly.

"I wish to propose that the Pope should be elected not by the College of Cardinals but by the bishops.

Even more important for me is the question of Catholic schools."

"What are your intentions with them?" Donovan
asked.

"Mr. President, at the time we're living in, I consider religious schools an anachronism. They divide
the children into two groups. I think this is unnecessary and outdated. Schools should be the state's responsibility with teachers of religion attached to
them."

"A revolutionary idea," the secretary of state said.

"Revolutions can be peaceful. When I declared that
there was no rank in the Church that I lead, the
crowds invaded St. Peter's. A tidal wave flooded the
Church—rich, poor, young, old, cardinal, bishop, friar,
priest. My secretary of state called it revolution. If it
was, it was very peaceful, very serene. Now all the
newspapers, the radio, television speak of a 'revolution' coming in South Africa. What kind of revolution? If the major powers like you, Russia, or China
will leave the South Africans to decide for themselves,
the announced 'revolution' will be quiet and peaceful."

The secretary of state shook his majestic head.
"Bishop Kwa would disagree with that, Your Holiness."

The "Pope" put on his most benign papal smile.
"Bishop Kwa," he said, "is entirely in the hands of a
Fascist group."

"Shall we say a moderate group?" the secretary said.
"Fascist is such an outdated adjective."

"Not where I come from." Monticelli regretted saying it immediately.

Donovan felt the mounting antagonism between the
two men. "Well, Your Holiness, I don't think the ma-

jor powers will intervene in the elections. I certainly have no such intentions."

"And your Seventh Fleet? Will it stay out of territorial waters?"

The President felt slightly shocked at the direct question. Slowly and very quietly, he said, "You are the head of state yourself, Your Holiness. You know that a head of state should not announce decisions ahead of time, especially where developments might remain beyond control. I can say this much and say it in strictest confidence: I hesitate to use the Seventh Fleet for what the Kaiser used to call a *Flottendemonstration*. I wish the Russians had sense enough not to parade their hammer and sickle at Cape Town either. Such confrontations are always dangerous, especially in Africa. I am sure, Your Holiness, that you remember your history and know that the simultaneous presence of the German and French fleets in Agadir almost brought about the outbreak of the First World War."

Monticelli got up, and Bishop Glenville and the secretary of state did likewise.

"I thank you for this interview and for your hospitality, Mr. President. I expect you for lunch tomorrow at Bishop Glenville's residence. I trust Mrs. Donovan will join us, too."

"Certainly. She is very much looking forward to meeting you."

"And your daughter? Please bring her along."

Bishop Kwa hoped that it was not blasphemous to compare this to heaven. The soft bed with the fine white linen sheets, the discreet lights, the nurses silently sliding by on rubber soles, bringing celestial dishes of beef broth, grilled fish, orange juice, and good hot coffee.

For two days, he had not moved nor spoken. On the flight from Cape Town north to Basutoland, then over the jungle to Mozambique, he had always been in danger of being discovered by hired assassins who followed him everywhere. He had reached Kenya with false papers fearing to be demasked. He was picked up in Nairobi by one of General Holt's men, and, as far as he could remember, from then on it had been simple. As far as he could remember. It is easier to forget the simple, the self-understood, the civilized manner than the mortal danger, starvation, and unquenchable thirst. He was amazed at his own strength, returning so quickly under the tender and thoughtful care of the doctors and nurses of the hospital in Washington.

General Holt had brought him a bottle of liquor with the label INVALID PORT. He sipped the sweet drink and savored it with pleasure.

With no urgency, gently, Holt asked him, "Do you think you are strong enough to move into the bishop's residence and to see His Holiness the Pope?"

"Most certainly," Kwa said in his melodious, primitive, lilting English. "I wish to see His Holiness with much urgency."

"Do you really think that there is imminent danger in your country?"

"I do not think. I know. They killed not only your captain, they killed three of my best men who got into their group. I still have two men who bring reports, and I am glad you do not ask for their names."

Holt had to smile. "Your Eminence," he said, "I know something about security. Keep your secrets to yourself."

"Does His Holiness know of my arrival?"

"Not yet. We kept it a secret. We told it to his Maestro di Camera, and he will learn about it when he returns from the White House. He is seeing the President now."

"Your President is a good man. I do hope that he will help us. The future of the world depends on it—not only South Africa."

"We have collected quite an impressive array of facts. And we would like to hear more from you after you have seen the Pope."

"How do I travel to Bishop's house?"

"In an ambulance, and you will be guarded like the crown jewels. You will be safe, and I hope, well. How do you feel now?"

Holt looked down at the ascetic face, the hollow cheeks, the eyes sunk deeply in their sockets. I hope he can make it, he thought.

"Fine," Kwa said. He added, as if reading Holt's thoughts, "Not to worry, please."

It was Wednesday the fifteenth, a date that Monticelli would never forget. The day had started in the euphoric mood of the previous day. He was looking forward to the visit of the President and his family, and he was quite unprepared for the fate in store for him.

He knew that the reception room was filled with visitors and that he could only devote five minutes to each. He sat behind a massive Louis XVth desk in a high-backed chair that looked more like a throne in the salon of the bishop's residence, when the Maestro di Camera announced Senator Duffy and his son. Something in his devoted servant's voice made Monticelli ask, "Do I know them?"

"They came to see you in Rome last year to ask for your blessings."

"Of course. Please show them in."

As he left the room, the Maestro di Camera tried

not to shake his head. Sometimes the Pope seemed strange and absentminded. Was he getting slightly senile? He opened the door wide and announced, "Senator George Duffy and his son."

"Please be seated," Monticelli said. "I am happy to see you again."

As if conveying some hidden message, the senator said to his son, "Tommy, you sit down too." The boy pulled the heavy chair a little closer to his father and sat down.

"It is a great honor to be received by you, Your Holiness. You must be terribly occupied. But I had a reason to seek this appointment. Or rather, my son had a very important reason."

Monticelli looked at the boy. About eleven years of age, neatly dressed, healthy looking. He was waiting for an explanation. As he said nothing, the senator continued, "Your Holiness, last year in Rome I asked you to be so charitable as to bless my son's eyes. As you remember, he was blind—the consequence of an accident. You very kindly blessed him, and he can see now. May he kiss your hand in gratitude just like he did when you blessed him?"

Deeply disturbed by this account of such voodoo nonsense, Monticelli could hardly bring out the words, "Of course."

The boy went up to him, looked into his eyes, bowed deeply, and kissed the hand with the papal ring.

"Is his eyesight completely restored?" Monticelli asked.

"Completely," the senator answered. "Three months after you blessed him he was able to see again."

Does he really believe in this hocus-pocus? My brother puts his hand on the boy's head and, presto, he can see. What makes this man, this senator who looks like a reasonable human being, believe in such "miracles"? The will to be healed? The Lourdes syndrome? Bleeding nonsense and superstition.

The shock would not wear off, not even after the senator and his son left. He forced himself to look at the remaining list of visitors. Time was getting short before the President's arrival.

His eyes scanned the names of those seeking an audience with him. When he ran across the underlined name of Francesco Bologna he stopped short. It was Castor's code name in case of an emergency. Why would Castor try to see him in person? When the Maestro di Camera entered, Monticelli said, "Alessandro, I have very little time left before the President's arrival. But I must see this man Francesco Bologna. Please show him in."

The chamberlain thought it his duty to remind the Pope, "Your Holiness, Sister Elisabeth, the Mother Superior, is still—"

Monticelli stopped him short. "Tomorrow morning. Apologize, please. And bring in Bologna."

Castor burst into the room like a rocket. He stopped in his tracks when he saw Monticelli's drawn and haggard face. "Are you all right?" he asked.

"I am tired playing a part that is not mine. Never mind. We only have five minutes before the President's arrival. I am sure you have something very urgent on your mind if you dare to show yourself here in broad daylight."

Castor shrugged. "Another anonymous face among the mass of supplicants. And I have something of top importance. Bishop Kwa is in town."

"The Bishop from Cape Town?"

"Yes. He is now in this building, and you will see him later."

"How did he escape?"

"No time to tell you. Please do listen to this very carefully. I must reveal to you one of our best-guarded top secrets. I had to get Maximus's permission for this."

"Yes?"

"Kwa had five men who infiltrated our South African organization. We eliminated three of them. We have to have the names of the other two."

"You mean that you want me to get these names from Kwa?"

"Yes, that's what I am telling you. And you will see from the reason how important it is. We have no intention of going through these ridiculous elections. We must play it safe. At noon of election day there will be a putsch. We take over the barracks, the radio, the television station. Only our three top leaders know this. We cannot make preparations or give our orders as long as Kwa's men are at large. We must eliminate them before."

"What do I do? Burn his fingernails?"

"Use your excellent brains, your diplomacy, your charm. Use threats, subterfuge, lies, but, for God's sake, get the names!"

A bitter smile crossed Monticelli's face. "The first time you have used the name of God, my son," he said. "In what you think is a good cause."

Again, why was he so shocked? Spying on the enemy, using dirty means to obtain information was part of this "job." He heard the door open and knew that Alessandro was there to announce the President's arrival. Castor stepped up to him, kissed his hand reverently and whispered, "I must listen to your conversation with Kwa," and put a small, round box on the table.

As Castor crossed the reception room, he saw the President, his wife, and a very smartly dressed young woman with them. When he realized that the young lady was Phyllis, he turned quickly away and left the room.

Phyllis recognized him instantly. The man with the eyeglasses. She touched her father's arm, but the double door was thrown open just as she said, "Daddy—"

Donovan whispered, "Not now."

Two conversations had bearing on Monticelli's future. One took place in the presidential limousine on the way back to the White House after the papal lunch.

"Are you absolutely sure?" Donovan asked when Phyllis told him that she had recognized the "Englishman" as he was leaving the Pope in the reception room.

"I'm positive."

The President, knowing that later the Russians would monitor every word, felt very uncomfortable about their talk. He tried to think of a reason for her to remove the glasses. Not able to think of one he hastened to end the conversation.

"A Roman Catholic Englishman. I didn't know they existed. Very odd."

Phyllis glanced at her father. Unable to read the expression in his face, she let the matter drop. Her thoughts flowed to Michael. The President's thoughts were also on Michael. But for very different reasons.

The second conversation had taken place in another automobile, Senator Duffy's Cadillac.

"The Pope looked a little tired," the senator said to his son.

The boy was looking at the heavy traffic on the road. "He is not the Pope," he said.

The senator turned and looked down at his son. "What did you say, Tommy?"

The boy stubbornly repeated, "He is not the Pope."

The senator was both irritated and puzzled. "Why do you say that?"

"Because when I was blind my hands and lips were real sensitive . . ."

"And?"

"The Pope who blessed me in Rome had rough hands, full of calluses. His ring was on his first finger. The man here has smooth hands like a woman, and the ring was on his second finger. So something's fishy. He's not the same guy as the one in Rome."

"This is utter nonsense, Tommy. The Pope might have been given some hand lotion while here. And he could have changed the ring from one finger to another. Nonsense. I don't want you to repeat this to anybody. Understand?"

The boy nodded. "He is not the Pope," he insisted and went back to watching the traffic.

The senator managed to shrug while holding the steering wheel. "Have it your own way. He is the devil, impersonating God's deputy."

With a voice reserved only for people he liked and respected, the chamberlain announced Bishop Kwa.

Monticelli felt weary and jaded. There had been no time for his siesta. He wondered how he could ever fulfill his task.

Bishop Kwa genuflected and kissed Monticelli's hand.

"Let us praise the Lord who brought you here in safety," Monticelli said, and added with deep compassion in his voice, "We know all about the abuse, oppression, and maltreatment that forced you into exile."

"Alas, I left behind so many who suffer persecution in my diocese."

Monticelli lowered his voice to a deep baritone and said, "Blessed are the persecuted, for theirs is the Kingdom of Heaven."

"They still need help here on earth."

Perhaps this is my cue, Monticelli thought. Let's try it. He said, "That's why I am here, to help. We are well aware of the fact that there are many faithful Christians in Africa, ready to fight foreign intervention. We were told that you have a few fearless informants in the enemy camp—God's first line of soldiers. I will make a note of their names so we can be grateful to them and give them better protection."

Bishop Kwa shook his head sadly. "I wish I could, Your Holiness."

Perplexed, Monticelli looked at the bishop's face. "You wish you could? Why can't you?"

"Because I don't know their names, Your Holiness."

"You mean the identity of your best soldiers is not known to you? Is it possible?"

"This is a territory that is out of the Church's knowledge and jurisdiction. I will use a technical term that has nothing to do with the Gospel—*security*. Yes, I am their bishop, but the names are withheld from me, so that I cannot name them, not even under torture."

"Your Eminence, I have learned about security. A strange word that sometimes means just the opposite, as in the case of one of our men, Captain Blakeley."

Kwa shrugged helplessly. "Yes, our security was at fault in this case. More reason for my men to be extremely cautious."

I've hit a cul-de-sac, Monticelli thought. I won't get anywhere with this dedicated lunatic today. Let's change the subject. "What do you think will happen at your elections?"

"It is very difficult to say, Your Holiness. There are

days when I see only deep apathy in my people. There is a slogan in South Africa—*Phuza anandia*—'Drink health.' The Afrikaners used it when unrest threatened—they reduced the price of *maiza* or *marela*, a sour drink that resembles beer, and increased the production of it. Now our adversaries produce even more, and the price is only about twenty American cents for a two-liter paper container. The Bantus and the Zulus start drinking it early in the morning, and by nightfall they don't care which party comes to power."

"Beer is the opiate . . ." Monticelli started to say but checked himself. "Do they sell this beer on election day?"

"Not officially. The country is rampant with illegal bars, where the more affluent prefer to drink the white man's whiskey. The city population looks down on the *Isicazas*, the peasants who intoxicate themselves with *dagga*, the local marijuana. It is these *Isicazas* who have been enlightened by us. I believe they will not get drunk on election day, especially if we get some help from the West."

"What kind of help do you expect?"

"Teachers, doctors, financial aid. And the American fleet in the harbor of Cape Town."

He is dedicated, Monticelli thought, but very naïve. It will do no harm to let him have some information. "I had a meeting with President Donovan yesterday. I would not count too much on the presence of the American fleet."

Doggedly, Kwa replied, "God will help us . . ."

Monticelli stood up to indicate the meeting was over. He suddenly had an idea. "Your Eminence, this meeting was too short, and I have so little time here. The day after tomorrow I will be back in Rome. Please be my guest in the Vatican. Come as soon as you are able to travel."

Kwa thanked him, genuflected, and kissed his hand.

"A stroke of genius," Castor remarked to Robles, as the two were listening to Monticelli's conversation.

"Why?" Robles wanted to know.

"Don't you see—Monticelli was getting nowhere with this black bastard here. In Rome, in the atmosphere of the Vatican and with more time, he might get some useful information."

"You really think Kwa doesn't know the name of his agents?"

"They've been trained by the CIA—they know all about that thing Kwa talks about. Security. Sure, it's possible. But when he's in the Vatican, Kwa is bound to receive messages and give orders. And we will bug his room. I think Monticelli is a shrewd old bird. All roads lead to Rome, especially ours."

XXXII

When he got up that morning, Donovan knew that it would be an irritating day. It started with his breaking the crystal on his watch, and sure enough, matters began to fall into the arbitrarily preordained pattern of annoyances.

Duncan Mulford read his memo to him about what he called "the Pope's strange behavior." Donovan suspected that one of the main reasons for Mulford's antagonism toward the Pope was due to Donovan's own admiration and respect for him. Mulford strongly opposed the mixing of politics with religion. Well, he might be biased, but I should not be, the President thought. I should listen carefully and patiently. He put his palms on the desk and looked at the fine patrician face of the secretary.

Mulford concluded, "Well, you've heard the summation. We have monitored all the speeches made by His Holiness, read all his statements. Taxes on the rich, give the Socialists more power, the Right way is just as bad as the Left. What emerges is a pure Marxist pattern. He is under a strong Socialist influence. We want to know whose influence and what we can do to counteract it."

To gain time, the President turned to General Holt, who sat, as always, stiffly erect, ready for action. Donovan could not guess that Holt's thoughts were elsewhere, on something disturbing. He was jolted back by the President's question, "What is your opinion, Rodney?"

"I have read the minutes, Sir," Holt said. "I fully agree with Mulford. I've ordered a minute check in Rome, but I think our ambassador could be of help, too."

"Let me think about this, Duncan," Donovan said. "We'll talk about it again tomorrow. And Rodney is right. Perhaps you should talk to the ambassador."

When the two men left, Donovan reached for his already-stuffed pipe. It had a bitter taste.

Holt had not wanted to mention the conversation at the Ambassador's Club with Senator George Duffy. He had been inclined to dismiss the episode Duffy had recounted. A young boy's sensitive lips were not important evidence. Still, maybe he had better talk with Michael.

"Sounds like a page out of my last spy book," was Michael's reaction. "I think I should talk to this boy alone. Do you agree?"

"That's what you're paid for; to use your plot mind against the boy's fantasy. I will call George Duffy and arrange for a meeting."

Michael got up and went to the door. He made a decision and turned back. "General," he said, "I think I should mention another incident at the bishop's residence when the Pope was here. It's only a maybe or perhaps event, but it might have some bearing on the case."

Curious, Holt said, "Well?"

"You see, sir, Phyllis, the President's daughter, thinks that she recognized the man who bumped into her at the supermarket and had her glasses fixed. Remember?"

180

THE JANUS POPE

"Very clearly. What about that man?"

"Well, Phyllis is not quite certain that the man who came out of the Pope's reception room was that person. She says that she thinks it was that man, but as I repeat, she is not one hundred percent sure."

Holt was furious. "Mike, what the hell took you this long to tell me. If it *was* the same man, what the hell is he doing with the Pope?"

Michael stepped closer to Holt's desk. "Look, sir, you hired me for my plot mind. Well, it's beginning to work. I'm trying to put the pieces together before I present you with the puzzle. Writers have to work in solitude. I can't think any other way. Perhaps I will have more to say after I see the boy."

"Okay, Mike, but don't keep things from me."

"I'll do my best, sir."

The boy was eager and cooperative, especially when he learned Michael was a writer of spy books.

They sat in the conservatory of Senator Duffy's large, old-fashioned house. The air was warm and humid and smelled of exotic plants and flowers. The boy played with the branch of a dwarfed fir tree, resisting the temptation to eat the needles.

"So this was last year in Rome. The Pope blessed you in Latin, I suppose?"

"Yes."

"And you kissed his hand with the papal ring?"

"Yes."

"Could you replay the scene for me with the exact movements?"

The boy stood up, went over to Michael, and genuflected. He grabbed Michael's right hand and asked, "Do I have to kiss your hand?"

Michael laughed. "No, Tommy. So you held his

right hand with yours, lifted it up a little, bent down and kissed it?"

"Right. His hand was rough and callused. The ring was on the front finger."

"You are sure of that?"

"Sure, I'm sure. I thought of that all the time, hoping his blessing would help me."

"And it did. Fine. Now tell me exactly what happened here in Washington at the bishop's residence."

"Same thing. I knelt, picked up his right hand, and kissed it, next to the ring. Only it was someone else's hand—like a woman's—smooth. And the ring was on the third finger."

"And again, you are absolutely positive?"

"Sure am. I got awful sensitive when I was blind. Only, thank God, I can see now."

"You can also thank the Pope."

"Yeah, the real one. What are you going to do now? Arrest the phony one?"

Michael sighed. "Whoa—not so fast. We haven't any proof. Even your father suggested that maybe the Pope used a hand lotion and that he might have changed the ring from his index to his second finger. Or the Vatican might use a replacement for receiving less-important visitors."

The boy was indignant. "I *know* that the man who blessed me was the Pope. You think a stand-in could have brought back my eyesight?"

"I don't know what to think, Tommy. Perhaps I had better take a trip to Rome." For a moment he wondered whether they ever fingerprinted Popes. Not bloody likely.

XXXIII

On his return to Rome, Monticelli had difficulties in adjusting himself to life there. The difference in time disturbed his sleeping and eating schedule. Was it time for breakfast, lunch, or dinner?

He woke up at three in the morning and wanted to retire at noon. He felt depressed, lethargic. It was not only the jet lag. Everything in America seemed new, functional, with no traditional ballast weighing it down. Here, everything was patina, pomp, and pedantry.

Even the weather irritated him. Spring just refused to come. The wind from the Alban hills was icy, the skies gray. What was the name of the place in the Abruzzi where Colonel Skorzeny had picked up that buffoon Mussolini, to deliver him into the hands of the Machiavellian Hitler? It must be even colder in the Abruzzi—a slight consolation.

He had to concentrate and prepare for the "big show"—his Easter message to the world. His thesis would be that socialism was not the enemy, that the foundation of Christian religion was socialistic. He read and reread his paper in philosophy, where he had so lucidly stated this some twenty years before. The thesis was too well known to be used verbatim. Some zealous student might point out the similarities between Professor Monticelli and "Pope Clemens." Yes, some changes had to be made.

He laughed when he thought of his brother listening to the speech. He did not know where Clemens was imprisoned, but he hoped he would be allowed to listen.

Oddly, when rereading his thesis for the tenth time, he felt that it was hollow, an empty conglomeration of words, an abstract dissertation. He knew the reason. Intellectuals all over the world spoke of "Marxist philosophy." Monticelli knew that there was no such thing. Marxist theory of national economy, of the political power of the masses, of a better and more equal society, yes, but not philosophy in the original Greek sense. Philosophy means the love of wisdom. Socrates was a philosopher and so was Kant. But Marx?

What the masses needed was not philosophy. Not even the highly overrated and misunderstood term of *freedom*. What they needed was food, the security of jobs, the certainty that they would not starve in their old age.

Through Castor, whom Monticelli disliked more and more, the Politburo repeatedly demanded to see the text of the Easter message. Monticelli procrastinated. The speech was not ready yet. At the last minute he would refuse to let the Politburo censor and advise him. Of course, he would also refuse to submit his message to the College of Cardinals for approval or the scrutiny of his secretary of state.

The night before his next meeting with Bishop Kwa, he received a radio message from Castor. "Make him talk," Castor had said when he was told that no headway had been made with Kwa. "If friendly persuasion does not work, bribe him."

"He's not interested in money," Monticelli answered.

"Then bribe him with power. I have been told that even bishops are venal. Promise him power."

"I will try," the false Pope said without conviction. Monticelli studied the face of Bishop Kwa. He seemed to have recovered somewhat. He carried himself well and sat erect in the high-backed chair, attentive and alert, a black Don Quixote.

He tried in his manner to be friendly, warm, and open with Kwa. "Of course, I understand your sorrow, my brother in Christ. Torn away from your flock, you must be living in a vacuum."

"The emptiness is filled by God." Kwa seemed reserved and evasive.

"Nevertheless, you are a bishop without a diocese." He sighed deeply and meaningfully. Like a trained snake charmer, he continued, "It's a great loss. But I might compensate you with *more* than a diocese."

Kwa did not understand. Uncertainly, he just said, "Your Holiness . . ."

Monticelli continued in the same breath, ". . . with a membership in the Sacred College."

"I am not a cardinal, Your Holiness," Kwa protested.

Monticelli was ready. "You are, in my heart." He saw the surprise on Kwa's face. Yes, Kwa was impressed. With more hope, Monticelli continued, "The cardinal of South Africa. With all its dioceses at your command."

Kwa's answer came fast. His tone of voice was gentle but firm. "No one should strive after command. It is better to wash the feet of one's brothers than to rule over them."

Monticelli looked up at the ceiling, trying to remember. "You are quoting St. Francis?"

"With your permission, Holy Father, I would like to retreat into a Franciscan monastery."

"Abandoning your suffering brothers in Africa?"

"Your Holiness, suffering, united with love, is the one thing we should desire in this valley of tears." He stopped as he detected the trace of a cynical smile on the "Pope's" face. "I am too weak and fragile to return to Africa."

I won't let you off that easily, Monticelli thought.

"As a cardinal," he said, "you do not need to go back to Africa. You could guide them from here. Send your messages through me. I could ease their trials."

His voice carried conviction. "Trials help us to detach ourselves from this earth," he said. "They make us look to God rather than to the world."

Monticelli shrugged. "The world has changed since St. Francis."

Undeterred, Kwa followed his own line of thinking. "The Savior's love for man never changes. He takes into account our weaknesses, and He knows all about the frailty of our natures."

Monticelli raised his voice. "We can ill afford weakness and frailty now. The time demands action."

"God knows no time. He is eternal."

They sat in silence for a moment. Monticelli realized with mounting impatience that he could not break through this man's armor of faith.

Kwa broke the silence. "With your permission, Holy Father, this is the time for my Rosary."

In a sudden impulse, Monticelli stood up and said, "Would you mind if I joined you?"

He took Kwa by the elbow and helped him to stand. "We could say it in my private chapel."

Monticelli opened the door for the bishop. He saw a Franciscan monk standing outside, waiting.

Kwa nodded to the monk. "Your Holiness, let me introduce Brother Anthony, my acolyte and retreat master. He prepares me for my entrance into the Franciscan order."

Brother Anthony, aristocratic looking, despite the simple Franciscan garb, said, "Holy Father," and genuflected to kiss the "Pope's" ring.

Monticelli led the way to the private chapel.

While the bishop and Anthony murmured the concluding prayers of the Rosary, Monticelli watched, feeling contempt for their empty and pointless prayers.

"Hail, Holy Queen," Kwa murmured, "Mother of Mercy. Our life, our sweetness, and our hope . . ." echoed by Anthony's, ". . . To thee do we cry, poor banished children of Eve . . ." Kwa concluded, ". . . pray for us, O Holy Mother of God, that we may be worthy of the promises of Christ . . ."

The promises of Christ. Promises, promises. Monticelli could stand this no longer and walked out of the chapel, back to his study.

Monticelli sent Castor a message that he had to see him, and received explicit instructions. He was to be driven in the Vatican car to a certain address—"The same where we made the switch. The driver knows how to get there."

In the shabby room badly illuminated by a naked electric bulb, Castor stood by the table.

"The room in which I became Pope." Monticelli looked around him.

Castor nodded.

"By the way, where is my brother now?"

"He is in a safe place in Switzerland and he is well. Did you ask to see me to talk about your brother?"

Monticelli flared up. "Sorry to take up your valuable time. How many CIA agents have you killed today?"

Nothing could change Castor's manners. With his

routine cynical smile, he said, "None, Your Holiness. What can we do for you?"

No use to try and teach this sonofabitch manners. He spoke quickly, "I don't feel well, and I cannot expose myself to the Vatican physician. You have to contact Professor Buonamano and prepare him for my visit."

"Holy Mother of Lenin, this means one more person will know this top secret."

"Buonamano is one of ours and a close friend of mine. I think you can trust him."

"I trust nobody, not even myself. Is this really absolutely necessary?"

"I am afraid it is. I fear that something is radically wrong with me."

"Well, if it has to be, it has to be. By the way, I also have a message for you. Maximus is not happy with the reforms you made in the Vatican."

Monticelli was proud of his loosening the rigid birth-control standard. He was beginning to think about easing up on the Church's rigid standards about divorce.

"Not happy?" Monticelli was puzzled. "They are all good, democratic reforms in the interest of the people."

Castor shrugged. "Maximus says you were put in this position not to reform the Church but to destroy it. With your reforms the Church is getting more popular every minute."

He could not discuss theological matters with this gorilla, so Monticelli just said, "You go to Buonamano and prepare him for my call. I need to see him soon."

He returned to the Vatican.

XXXIV

The faithful chamberlain helped Monticelli into his coat. His dark-brown Saint Bernard eyes were clouded with anxiety, fear, puzzlement. Why did His Holiness want to consult another doctor? He did not understand, and what he did not understand, he could not approve. He consoled himself with the thought that the Pontiff's actions were guided by God.

Followed by the car of the security guards, the black Alfa crossed the Tiber and arrived in the expensive, exclusive residential section. Not far from the Eden Hotel the driver opened the door, and Monticelli entered a modernized building of the late nineteenth century. He knew it well. In the brightly lit entrance hall Professor Buonamano's butler awaited him. He genuflected and kissed Monticelli's ring.

The slow hydraulic elevator took them to the third-floor apartment where a bronze plaque on the door read, PROFESSOR FELICE BUONAMANO—BY APPOINTMENT ONLY.

The two men embraced. The professor, a gnome with a totally bald head and an unruly black beard, said, "Giulio. It is so good to see you. It is almost a year since you came here. You looked somewhat different then—the plastic surgeon did a good job." He paused. "Now sit down and tell me what is wrong. You look a little pale. Anemic."

"There are no specific symptoms," Monticelli said. "I am just tired, abnormally tired. Not much appetite, either."

"It seems to me you lost weight. Did you?"

"Yes. A few kilos."

"How few?"

"Five or six."

Buonamano shook his head. "Not surprising with the job you took on. It must be a tremendous strain. Why did you do it? Did they force you to?"

"No. You cannot call it that. You can imagine how important this masquerade is for our party. But let us not talk about politics. What do we do about me? Pills, iron, vitamins?"

The little gnome laughed. "Maybe," he said. "Today everybody thinks that vitamins are the panacea for everything. Take your shirt off. I will take your blood pressure."

He examined Monticelli's chest, abdomen, even his prostate. He noted the rash on his friend's leg. "Have you had these sores long?"

"They're nothing—they don't even itch much—they appeared a few weeks ago."

"Now I will take some blood. I have my lab here. I want to do the test myself. You will be patient for half an hour. As you see, we have magazines, books, *L'Epoca*, the *Corriere*. I don't recommend *Playboy*. Your blood pressure is high as it is."

Monticelli had just finished *L'Epoca* when Buonamano came back. He did not look happy. "Not too good, my friend. I don't like the overall picture. Too many white corpuscles, not enough red."

Monticelli put the magazine down. "Don't tell the party," he smiled.

The gnome remained serious. "I am afraid I will

have to test your marrow. It will take only a minute.
Lie down on this table, please."

Monticelli did as he was told, and the doctor started
to shave the hair on his chest. Then he took a long,
pointed steel instrument from a case and said, "It
won't hurt. I use a local pain killer."

When the test was over the doctor said, "You have
to wait again, Giulio, but only for a few minutes."

He sat down at his desk and did not say anything.
Monticelli eyed him expectantly, and when Buonamano still kept his silence, he asked, "Well, what's the
verdict?"

The gnome looked at his upturned palms on the table. "Not good, Giulio. Not good at all."

"Can you be a little more explicit?"

The doctor stood up, took a chair, and sat down
next to Monticelli. "My friend. This is so difficult.
You're not well, Monticelli. I'm afraid you have acute
leukemia."

"Leukemia? My God, say it's not so."

"I am afraid that's what it is."

The shock did not take its full effect yet. His voice
even, Monticelli asked, "How much time have I got?"

The gnome looked at his hands again. "Six
months," he answered.

Monticelli did not remember how he got back to the
Vatican. In a total daze, his mood changed from the
anger of a wounded animal biting the lethal weapon,
to celestial serenity. The words of Cicero, of Socrates,
came back, encouraging the dying to die. He knew
that on this earth, only two things are certain—that
we are born and that we have to die. It was no consolation. He repeated constantly, "The end. Finis."

One moment he sat up, erect and alert, at his desk,
looking at his agenda and thinking of the task he had
to fulfill. The next moment he slouched down in infi-

nite despair, with the total abandon of a ' what's the use" attitude.

The Maestro di Camera felt that something was radically wrong. He did not dare to ask. Finally he said, "Your Holiness, can I get you some tea and biscuits? You ate nothing for lunch."

Monticelli grabbed the edge of the table until his knuckles went white. "Alessandro," he said, "do we have any champagne? French champagne?"

The chamberlain's face lit up. "Yes, Your Holiness. I shall bring it instantly. I trust you had good news from the doctor."

' Excellent news. I intend to get drunk a little Please cancel all appointments for this afternoon."

It took him several days and superhuman energy and concentration to stop thinking of nothing but "the end." The manifest destiny, th fulfillment of the all-important task was all that mattered; his own fate was secondary, trifling. He disciplined himself to the routine of his "job." The item he could not master was his mounting impatience; time was the enemy.

In his study he awaited Brother Anthony. He could not sit still. He got up from behind the desk, walked to the window, drew the curtains and looked at the gray sky, dotted with blue between the clouds. He knew the room was warm, but he was shivering. When he heard the opening of the door, he quickly returned to the desk and sat down in the armchair.

Brother Anthony entered, a tall and dignified figure of a man in the brown Franciscan garb. He genuflected and said, "Your Holiness."

"I called you Brother Anthony ' Monticelli said, "because you are in close spiritual relations with our beloved African Bishop." He stopped for a reaction

Very humbly, the monk said, "I am just guiding him toward the sacred solitude of a Franciscan monastary."

"I know that. And I also know that, as his retreat master, you have great influence on him. That's why I need your help."

Brother Anthony was startled. "You, Holy Father? The help of a simple monk?"

Curbing his impatience, Monticelli quickly recited the prepared text. "St. Francis was a simple monk, too. But a great help to the Pope. He rebuilt churches, organized missions. He was not only a saint, he was also a very practical man." He added, perhaps a trifle too pointedly, "A beggar who collected fortunes for his holy purposes."

Anthony looked at him with puzzled expectation. He could not even try to guess the purpose of this conversation. Monticelli was aware of Anthony's confusion and knew that he had to get to the point. He put on his most benign smile when he said, "You can have a fortune, too, for the greater glory of God."

"I am wedded to Lady Poverty," Anthony answered with his constant and firm humility.

"The fortune I wish to bestow on you," Monticelli said, "is destined to help your African missions. All you need do is to persuade Bishop Kwa to send it to his friends."

Anthony shook his head. "He does not believe in human intervention. For him there is only one helping hand. God's hand."

Monticelli nodded his pious consent. "As a priest, I agree with him." He straightened his back and used his voice of authority. "But as the head of state, I know that sometimes, in addition to prayers, deeds are necessary. And you have the power to act for the bishop."

Helplessly, Anthony said, "I am not at all versed in money matters."

"You don't have to be. Just send the funds I will put at your disposal to the bishop's friends. Prepare a list of their names and addresses."

Again, Brother Anthony shook his head. "The bishop did not give me any names."

"But he will if you ask him."

"I am afraid, Your Holiness, that he won't. He is a very sick old man. He is not interested in this world anymore. His only concern is the world to come."

"He is still in *this* world. And he can't forsake his friends who serve Christ in secret."

"He forsakes no friends. He prays for them, he asks for the help of the Mighty Protector."

No good, Monticelli thought. I cannot shake this bigoted ox. At least, not at this moment. And how many moments will I have left to try to shake him?

With a gesture of his hand he dismissed Brother Anthony.

In his room at the Apostolic Palace, Bishop Kwa was kneeling in front of a small statue of St. Joseph. The statue was the only decoration in the ascetic room. The red Carrara marble floor had been walked on for many centuries, and the careful waxing had not erased the imprints of shoes, sandals, naked feet, since the early days of the Renaissance. The simple cot had antiseptic cleanliness, the white walls looked freshly washed.

Kwa was completely absorbed in his prayer and did not hear the heavy oak door being opened.

Monticelli, escorted by Brother Anthony, entered and stopped when he saw Kwa, oblivious to the world and lost in his prayers. He did not move. He stood still, impressed by Kwa's devotion.

Reverently, Kwa whispered, "Blessed St. Joseph, guard our missionaries in heathen lands, just as you guarded and led into Egypt Mary and His divine Son. Help them to sustain with patience the trials of the soul and the weariness of the body. Grant them your grace and the material aid they may need to set up tabernacles for Jesus, among them who know Him not . . ."

Monticelli tried hard to keep the image of his inner struggle from his face. His cynical skepticism fought the impact of such unbounded faith.

He had an uncertain instinctive feeling about this prayer. It had the sound of a personal message, an answer to an unasked question. He was curious to know whether he was right. He turned to Brother Anthony.

"I'd like to have a private talk with him."

Anthony bowed silently and backed out of the room.

Monticelli stepped up to the bishop and knelt down next to him, joining him in his now-silent prayer.

Bishop Kwa looked at the statue of St. Joseph, his eyes filled to the brim with faith and adoration. Oblivious to the world, he did not even sense the "Pope's" presence. After a few minutes, Monticelli looked at the bishop and gently touched his shoulder. The touch broke the spell. Kwa turned his head to the right and stared at Monticelli. His eyes did not register any recognition, as if he had never seen this face before. After a few seconds Kwa closed his eyes and then opened them again. Now he seemed to focus properly. Surprised, he said, "Your Holiness?"

Monticelli nodded, fully understanding the bishop's surprise. "Forgive me for the interruption."

Kwa did not answer. His silence emphasized his puzzlement.

"You are in conversation with a saint," Monticelli

continued, "but there are certain matters down here on earth . . ."

With absolute conviction, as though just stating a fact, the bishop said, "I am going to leave it soon."

How soon? Monticelli thought. Sooner than I? As if talking to himself, he said, "You can't tell the day."

Kwa stood up and adjusted his cassock. "Every day can be the last," he said.

Monticelli stood up, too, and looked at Kwa's face. "But as long as you're still here, you have certain duties to perform." He continued with blunt frankness. "Protect your friends in Africa. Help me so I can help them. But, strangely, you refuse to tell their names."

"I have already disclosed these names."

Monticelli was startled. Had he? Perhaps a little too eagerly, he asked, "To whom?"

Kwa answered simply, "To God. And I will tell him again when we meet."

Irritated by Kwa's dogmatic idiocy, Monticelli asked, "How do you know you'll see God?"

Kwa answered humbly, "Penitent sinners go to heaven. Even the thief who died on Calvary joined the Lord in His paradise."

With a touch of self-irony and sarcasm, Monticelli said, "Then even a poor Pope has a chance."

The bishop seemed unaware of the sarcasm. "I'll put in a good word for you," he said.

Kwa felt weak. His legs seemed to cave in under him. Seeking support, he put his hands on the prayer stool. Almost silently he whispered, "He is already calling me."

Monticelli felt very uncomfortable. Do I really need all this? he thought. The bishop seemed to be looking at some invisible presence, whose arrival he had sensed.

Monticelli touched the bishop's hand tenderly.

"Please, Your Holiness, leave me with my God."

Monticelli, moved to tears, both for himself and for Kwa, made the sign of the Cross over the bishop's head. Unaware of the irony of his blessing, he left the bishop to his prayers.

XXXV

Monticelli hated the smell of a sickroom. He was allergic to hospital odors, but this place reeked of something else—it smelled of death. And the room had been readied for it. A small table covered with white linen stood near the bishop's bed, with a bronze crucifix, flanked by two burning candles. A bowl held the holy water; a small towel lay next to it. These were the routine preparations for the Extreme Unction.

He looked at Kwa's drawn face, the dry parchment skin, the eyes tightly closed.

Will I look like this and smell like this? Monticelli thought. And when? He had accepted the inevitable; he wished now only for a date—a deadline.

He had been sitting next to Kwa's bed for some time now. Suddenly he perceived a movement on the bishop's face. Kwa slowly opened his eyes. Wetting his lips with his tongue, Kwa started to speak.

He said, "How gracious of you, Holy Father, to come and bid farewell to me."

With reassuring comfort in his voice, Monticelli said, "You are not leaving yet."

"I am ready for my journey."

Monticelli looked at the peaceful smiling face. Almost incredulously, he said, "Ready. With a smile on your face and without the trace of fear."

"Christ is my Savior. His words give me comfort. 'I am the resurrection and the life, and whoever lives and believes in Me shall never die.'"

"The Gospel. And you believe every word of it."

"Don't you, Father?"

Monticelli shrugged. "Books are open to interpretation."

With strength and conviction, raising his voice a little, Kwa said, "And yours is the false book."

The words hit Monticelli with a shock. Did this black bishop know? "Why do you say that?" he asked.

"Since the moment we first met, I had a peculiar feeling . . ."

"About what?"

"The questions you asked me. Very worldly, very practical questions. Never a word about Christ, never a hint about heaven."

"We are on earth, and I am an earthly ruler."

"You are still God's servant." He stopped and tried to raise his voice higher. "Nobody should serve two masters."

Monticelli was alarmed. What was hidden in the sick man's brain? "And I serve two masters?"

The bishop answered with another quotation, which carried the sound and meaning of a judgment. "Jesus knew from the beginning who they were, who did not believe, and who it was who would betray him."

This was so obvious that Monticelli could not pretend to misunderstand. He had to meet the challenge with a challenge.

"Why are you telling me all this?" he asked.

"I am a dying man," the bishop said. "But you still have time to repent." With no transition he glided into a prayer again. "O Holy Lord, Father Almighty, with all love You watch over Your creatures. Deliver Your servant, Pope Clemens . . ."

In uncontrollable anger, Monticelli spat out the words, "I am not Pope Clemens."

Totally undisturbed, the bishop whispered, "God knows who you are."

The shadow of death had not blunted this man's thinking. Incredulous, Monticelli asked, "You believe I am a traitor and you are still praying for me?"

Too weak to form his own sentences, the bishop quoted the Bible again. " 'There is greater joy in heaven for a repentant sinner than . . .' " He was too weak to continue, and his head fell back on the pillow.

Monticelli bent down to look closer at the dying man's face. To his own surprise, he said, with infinite tenderness, "God be with you, God look out for you . . ."

He stood up and went to the window. The rain had stopped. From this room, higher than his study, he had a good view of Rome, the piazza in front of the Vatican, the residential houses across the river, the outline of the Monte Pincio. He stiffened when the concerto started—the bells of all the churches and the distant sound of the whistle of factory chimneys. My two worlds, he thought. Technocracy and progress on one side, and faith with a capital *F* on the other. The other that still fought progress and would crucify Galileo and Darwin even today. He knew that he did not have the strength anymore to be his own arbiter in the conflict between the two worlds. He stood by the window and stared at the panoramic view, stopping the thought of how long he would be able to see what he saw.

He did not hear Brother Anthony enter, carrying more of the paraphernalia for the sacrament of the Extreme Unction.

Anthony stopped at the table and placed on it a dish with six small cotton balls for the anointing and a second dish with a piece of crustless bread. Lastly, he put down a small pitcher with the holy oils.

When Anthony started, "Peace to this house and all who live here," Monticelli whirled back. He wanted to ask, What makes you think that this is the right moment? Radar? But he said nothing.

"We are ready, Your Holiness," Anthony said. "Would you kindly assist me?"

Reluctantly and with an inner shrug, Monticelli nodded his consent.

Brother Anthony started. "Let us pray. Look upon Your servant, for he is growing weak and his body is sinking. Strengthen his soul whom You have created, that his suffering should purify it and deliver him from the power of the devil."

He blessed the bishop with the sign of the Cross. Then, pouring some oil in his palm, he started the anointing. With his anointing finger, he touched the eyes of the bishop. "May the Lord forgive you for whatever wrong you have done through the use of your eyesight." Then he touched the ears of the bishop. ". . . whatever wrong you have done through the use of your hearing." Anthony continued, touching the bishop's lips, hands, and finished with his feet. ". . . whatever wrong you have done through the power to walk."

When Anthony started the anointing, Monticelli wondered how long this absurd act of witchcraft would last. The ceremony was almost heathen in its primitive symbolism. As Anthony proceeded, Monticelli's strong self-defense of cynicism started to fade. Suddenly it was *he* who lay on the bed; it was he who was being anointed; it was he who was receiving the Extreme Unction. Don't feel so sorry for yourself, Comrade, he said to himself. You still have a long way to go.

Brother Anthony finished the anointing and wiped

his fingers on the towel. He stepped back and started another prayer.

"Lord, have mercy. Grant salvation to Your servant. Send him aid from Your Holy Place. Be a tower of strength to him . . ."

Without knowing it, Monticelli repeated, "A tower of strength . . ."

Anthony continued, ". . . against the attack of the enemy . . ." and Monticelli said the words in unison with Anthony: ". . . and let not the son of evil come near to him."

Anthony looked at the ceiling and put more force in the words. "O Lord, hear my prayer . . ."

Monticelli followed with, ". . . and let my plea be heard . . ."

"The Lord be with you," Anthony said, and Monticelli concluded: "And with Your spirit. Amen."

He rushed out of the sickroom.

XXXVI

It was cold in the church and almost dark. Monticelli sat apart from the others, and he did not enjoy himself. He had to attend this last rite of Bishop Kwa's burial, and he heard, not too distinctly and not devoutly, the words, ". . . *De profundis* . . ."

He had suddenly become deeply aware of Michelangelo's mural "The Last Judgment," the painting in the Sistine Chapel, of which Michelangelo had said, "This will drive men mad." Monticelli stared at the painting and focused in on certain groups—the doomed being dragged down to hell by demons, the tortured faces of the damned. It could have been painted today by the hands of a genius, fresh, emotionally vivid, with the impact of the immediate. Every hand, every foot and leg were masterpieces of precision and imagination. For the false Pope, the mural carried a very personal message, an important communication.

The burial mass continued, the words and gestures completely lost on Monticelli. He started when the bishop of Bologna gently touched his elbows and said, "It's finished. Let's walk back to the Apostolic Palace."

He could not fall asleep for hours. And then he slept fitfully, sweating and tossing his body around. The dream he had was incoherent, vivid, vulgar. Christ, with the scorn and wrath of a judge, raised his arm in damnation, while twisting bodies of the doomed sinners were sucked into the dark chasm of annihilation. The boat of Charon carried the emaciated bodies across the River Styx around a big rock. After the turn, the gaping mouth of hell was waiting for it. Charon returned to the landing and Monticelli was thrown into the boat by some ugly demons. He said to Charon, "I don't belong here. I have the key of the Kingdom!" And Charon answered, "It is a stolen key! Inside with you!"

He was tossed into the flaming entrance and woke up screaming. Dazed, he jumped out of bed, and it took him a few seconds to realize that he had been dreaming.

Helplessly, he looked around for some solace, some assistance, and unwittingly, his hand touched the rosary, and he started playing with the beads. With a sudden impulse he put his robe over his nightgown and walked through his study and the corridor, straight to his private chapel.

What was he looking for? Consolation? A private conversation with his "Boss"? He stopped abruptly when he realized that he was not alone. A man was kneeling before the altar, engrossed in fervent prayer. The "Pope" crept closer and recognized the man.

"Brother Anthony," he said.

Not at all surprised, Anthony just said, "Your Holiness."

"It's after midnight. Rather late for a visit."

"I hoped to meet you here, Father."

"Is it so urgent?"

"I've met the devil."

Shocked, Monticelli drew back and looked at Anthony's face.

"There is a devil in the church," the priest continued.

Monticelli nodded automatically. *"Diabolus in Ecclesia."*

"Ironically, he attacked me just as I exorcised the dying bishop," said Anthony. "The devil switched from the dying body to the living one."

"He didn't attack me through my senses, but through my reason."

"You're a Franciscan. Your faith should defeat your reason."

"I am a belated Franciscan. And obviously my original name isn't Anthony."

To answer the unspoken question of Monticelli's raised eyebrows, Anthony said, "My original name is Vittorio. Vittorio Monticelli."

Startled, the "Pope" repeated "A Monticelli?"

"We are the poor cousins of your successful Monticelli family. Very minor Monticellis, Your Holiness. My concern is not with you, but another Monticelli. Giulio, the professor, who died in a plane crash in Russia. I feel guilty about his death."

"Guilty?"

"Yes. We, the servants of the Church, drove him into the arms of the Communists. It was our scorn that made him an atheist. We gave him contempt instead of love."

"And now you are praying for atonement for him?"

"I ask you to pray with me, Holy Father."

"You believe my prayer will help?"

"You are the Vicar of Christ. Giulio died without receiving the sacraments. You have the power to relieve him from his suffering in hell."

"Have I?"

"Well, haven't you?"

"Do you have any doubts about it?"

"The devil gave them to me. And that's why I am here. You alone can dispel my doubts. Confirm my faith. Prevent me from asking dangerous questions . . ."

"Whether God really exists? Is the Gospel true or nothing but fiction, myth and superstition? Born in credulity and ignorance in a time when people believe in a three-story universe—heaven, earth, and hell."

"The devil's words."

"Is the Pope infallible? Or just a simple man, full of faults. A pretender. A charlatan."

Horrified, Anthony exclaimed, "Holy Father!" Brother Anthony looked at the "Pope" with such anguish, such pain, that Monticelli felt that the wrong answer might destroy the man. To his own surprise, he suddenly felt an upsurge of pity and charity for this simple priest.

Very gently Monticelli said, "I agree with the devil in one point only. All men are sinners. Including myself. I see no fault committed I could not have committed myself."

Even more tenderly he added, "Don't worry about Giulio Monticelli. He might be dead, but his soul is alive. And alterable. His opinion about right or wrong could have changed."

"You sound so certain. Like Giulio himself."

"I've met many men with the same problem. I am sure that Giulio went through life without suspecting the existence of a subconscious faith . . ."

His face lit up with hope.

Anthony said, "And do you think it surfaced before he died?"

His voice, firm and clear, the "Pope" said, "I feel in my heart he did not die an atheist." He returned to the same God he ran away from."

His voice carried the conviction of the final judgment. The statement was so clear and so definite that

Anthony could not help but ask in devout amazement, "How do you know that?"

"As you said, I am the Vicar of Christ."

"Holy Father, will you forgive me for my doubts?"

With full papal authority Monticelli said, "I absolve you in the name of the Father and the Son and the Holy Spirit."

He blessed Anthony with the sign of the Cross. Kneeling down, the monk kissed the papal ring, and Monticelli returned to his bedroom. He fell asleep immediately and peacefully.

XXXVII

The President of the United States, still in pajamas, cleaned his teeth very thoroughly in the bathroom and gargled a long time with Listerine. His throat felt dry, probably from too much talking and too many pipes. I must cut something down, he said to himself. He switched the light off and went into the bedroom. He looked forward to his routine before-going-to-bed conversation with his wife. This habit was as old as their marriage. Before turning the lights off they always discussed the events of the day, although Gladys secretly resented that the President's day was so much more interesting than her own. Donovan felt the resentment, but what could he do about it? A President has perforce a more exciting daily agenda than a President's wife.

Gladys was propped up on the double pillows on her side of the double bed; the Donovans had insisted on the double bed. She wore a transparent cotton voile nightgown, and she looked pretty. Donovan told her so, and she thanked him with a smile.

"How busy was the President's day?" she asked.

"Not more than usual," Donovan answered. "Except that I have some added work with the plans for our European trip."

"You know I am really looking forward to it. Is a President's wife allowed to shop? I want to walk down

the Fauborg St. Honoré and Bond Street and the Via
Veneto and visit my favorite museums again. Do you
know how many years it's been since we were in Europe?"

"Let me see. Ten?"

"Twelve. I wonder whether that little dressmaker
wizard who copied all the Dior and Courrèges models
still exists?"

Donovan laughed. "Now look, cookie, a President's
wife can afford the originals."

"I know. I just hate to spend so much money on
rags. That's all they are today, rags."

"Well, get yourself some nice, silk-lined velvet rags.
I can't afford to buy any clothing in London. I would
be criticized for patronizing foreign tailors."

With no palpable transition Gladys said, "Michael's
sport jackets come from London."

Donovan realized that this was clearly an introduc-
tion to a major topic. Suddenly, Gladys had that unde-
finable matchmaker's look on her face. She patted her
hair and said, "Pat, this thing between Phyllis and Michael. I have the feeling it's becoming serious."

"You really think so?"

"Definitely."

"Well, what can we do about it?"

"Nothing. They must decide for themselves. I like
the boy very much. Talented and attractive. Good
family, too. But I don't think he's ever mentioned
marriage to her."

"We don't know that. He might have. Both of them
know that, in any event, personal plans have to wait."

"Wait? For what?"

"Sweet, you are not supposed to know. Secret and
sensitive. We are sending Michael to Rome on a top-
priority mission. Until that's completed, his private
life will have to wait."

"How long will the 'mission' take? I mean, how long will he stay in Rome?"

"We don't know. Perhaps a couple of weeks. Perhaps a couple of months."

"Does Phyllis know?"

Donovan thought of the bugging device in Phyllis's glasses. How can Michael handle the situation?

"I don't think so. Not yet."

Again, with that happy matchmaker expression on her face, Gladys said, "I bet you the crown jewels I don't own that Phyllis manages to get to Rome while Michael is there."

"I don't know if that will be wise. His mission is not without a certain danger."

"That would not stop her. As it did not stop me. Did I object when you accepted the dangerous job of the Presidency?"

"Not for a moment. Actually, you pushed me into it."

"Okay. Come to bed, Mr. President."

Michael had needed a certain amount of daring and bravado when he asked General Holt for a room in a safe house for his meetings with a "lady of high society." Holt had showed a surprising understanding. He had not asked any questions and Michael could not determine by his boss's poker face whether he had heard any gossip about Phyllis and himself.

The room was on the outskirts of Washington in a complex of poorly built modern buildings. All that mattered was that it had a comfortable bed, a telephone, and a bathroom. Of course, Michael could have afforded a suite at one of the best hotels, but the risk of their being recognized was too great.

Since his trip to Rome had been decided, Michael was "on call" by the CIA. His suitcase was packed and

ready. The time of the flight was up to Holt, who had
to prepare the Rome CIA, and assign a "director" to
assist Michael there. The director was to operate under direct orders from Holt. Michael had been offered
the choice of three men to work with, and he had selected Jim Sullivan, who knew Rome well. He was
about a year older than Michael, a stocky, muscled,
intelligent, and experienced agent who had earned his
medals in Beirut and in Kosovo, Yugoslavia.

Being on call, Michael had to report all his movements through the Indicator 3 machine, a gadget small
enough to fit into his pocket. The code was simple
enough: when driving his car, he pushed the button
that said MOVE; back at the White House, he pushed
HOUSE; and now, in the rented room with Phyllis, he
pressed the button SAFE.

Phyllis lay happily exhausted in his arms. They had
made savage and hungry love and all was peace now,
nothing wrong with the world. Except that Michael
had to announce that he was flying to Rome any minute and tell it in a way that would give as little information as possible to the Kremlin. Her eyeglasses were
on the small table next to the bed, and Michael as-
sumed that the apparatus functioned at a distance of
four feet.

Half asleep Phyllis said, "This was very, very nice,
love. It gets better every time."

Michael pretended to be hurt. "It was no good yesterday?"

"Excellent. And today it was even better."

"I am afraid we will have to suspend our activities
for a while."

Phyllis sat straight up in bed and touched Michael's
penis with her left hand. "Why? Is he too tired?"

Michael laughed. "No, he is not. I have to fly to
Rome."

"To Rome, for God's sakes! Why?"

"General Holt's orders. Some reorganization in our local group. And preparations for the President's arrival."

"When are you leaving?"

"Any minute. Perhaps tomorrow."

"And how long will you stay?"

"A week. Ten days."

"Oh, Michael, how dreadful. How will I survive?"

Michael patted her buttocks affectionately. "You are," he said, "a very well-built, strong kid. You will survive."

"You have that happy look on your face. I'm sure you enjoy the thought of leaving me for the sexy hookers on the Via Veneto."

"I don't think I'll have time enough."

"And if you had the time?"

"There is only one woman I want to make love to, and she is right here in bed with me."

She looked at him with that very special, very provocative feline smile of hers and said, "So why don't you?"

Michael was happy to oblige. Later, lying in his arms, she suddenly said, "Is it beneath your social status to marry the President's daughter?"

Michael's face was flushed. "Is this a firm marriage proposal?"

"It is. Firm."

He sat up in bed and said, very seriously and ceremoniously, "Madame, will you take me to be your wedded husband, for better or for worse?"

"I will."

"Okay. Now we are married."

She laughed and pushed the pillow down on his face. "Not that easy, you bastard. I want the biggest, fattest, shiniest wedding ever. With all of the CIA lined up in gala uniforms."

Michael shook with laughter. "The KGB would like that. All the boys of the agency in uniform. Dozvidanya!" He suddenly stopped, remembering Moscow was listening.

"So we line up the Marines. All right?"

"Fine with me. But it will have to wait until I'm back from Rome."

She wrinkled her forehead. "Or perhaps we can get married in Rome. Because, whether you like it or not, you sonofabitch, I will be in Rome, too."

"Great. But how will you manage to convince your family that the trip is necessary?"

"They know I love to visit my friend there—the Principessa Buchhari. She and her husband, the prince, have a charming little palace."

"I didn't know you move in such aristocratic circles. How can you stand a plebeian like me?"

"I'll take a plebeian like you anytime. I've read your résumé—summa cum laude at Harvard. Officer's rank yourself."

"Where did you meet this princess?"

"In summer school in Lausanne."

"I didn't know you went to school in Switzerland."

"Well, what do you really know about me, lover?"

"Only the essentials. You play a good game of tennis, you like hamburgers but hate hot dogs. And," he cupped her right breast, "you have the prettiest breasts this side of the Swiss Alps."

"All this is enough to ask me to be your wife?"

"You did the asking. And it *is* enough. And I forgot to mention—we both like Tolstoi and Bellow and are not fond of Kerouac and Stendhal. A solid foundation for a marriage that will last eighty-nine years."

XXXVIII

In the decoding room of the embassy, Castor, in his role of a "voyeur," listened to the conversation between Phyllis and Michael. He understood Michael's interest in her. He would not have minded getting laid by her, either.

The important point was Michael's trip to Rome. Some reunion, he thought, with the "Pope," Phyllis, Michael, and the President. He wasn't impressed with Michael's mission—he considered him a rank amateur, not at all a professional.

But Castor did not cherish his own role in this charade. He knew too much, and it was not healthy for an operative to be so knowledgeable. Previously, in Athens and Caracas, his instructions had been simple and precise. Find the subject and "waste" him. In the present situation he feared that he would be the one to be wasted. He was exposed, through the Boss's whim, to too much knowledge, to too much contact with the intended victim. He had no doubt of the future fate of Monticelli. Sooner or later he would have to go. And it was he, Castor, who would have to carry out the "going." He did not like to know his future victims. There was always the danger with human contact that he would develop human sympathy. Of course, Castor denied the possibility of this. A contract was a contract. It consisted of a man with his hand on the trigger aiming at a faceless target.

The disturbing factor was that the target had suddenly developed a face. He did not admit it, but Monticelli had made an impression on him. He hoped all this would be over soon and he could return to Venezuela.

Even if he wanted to, he could not discuss his problems with anyone. The mere mention of a "problem," the hint that he had some thoughts of his own, would be fatal with Houndsworth. He would not last forty-eight hours. And his underling, Robles—an empty-headed, thoughtless gorilla. He could never talk to that ape.

Lately, the ape had dared to make some remarks about Castor getting a little sloppy and neglectful of security. He had told Robles of his encounter with the President's daughter at the bishop's palace in Washington. "Why had he not used a disguise?" Robles had asked. His answer, not illogical, was that Phyllis had seen him only for a fleeting second and her description of him would lead nowhere. The KGB, with all its experience, knew that such a nondescript description was worthless. And, there was no immediate danger of breaking his cover in Washington. He did not need a cover. He could not be caught in gathering classified material because this was not his job. Enigma II was enough and not traceable to him. Furthermore, in twenty-four hours, he would be out and on his way to Rome.

XXXIX

Kenyere sat in front of his "residence," the mud hut, and held the newspaper in his hand. His steel-rimmed glasses, sliding over his perspiring face, had the tendency to fall down on the paper. It was hot and humid, not as dry as it had been years before civilization had brought about changes in the atmosphere.

Kenyere adjusted his glasses and read out loud the news that interested him so much—the news of the American President's trip to Europe.

"President Donovan will be in Rome tomorrow," he told the two very tall, very black bodyguards. They sat on the ground, leaning against the mud-brick wall, their Second World War Sten guns on their laps.

The bodyguards nodded. It was difficult to say whether they understood the meaning to Kenyere of the American President's voyage. Of course, they could not know of Kenyere's feelings about the President, about the strange affinity the black man felt for the new head of the United States. Kenyere liked his face, his gestures, his openness, his straightforward way of grappling with problems. He was convinced of President Donovan's help, if he had received his letter. Perhaps, due to the President's voyage, the letter had been delayed.

He thought of his friend and secretary, Bwato,

whom he often called "my vice-president." He had taken the letter to Pretoria. He trusted Bwato implicitly. "He will do all right," he said to himself, thinking of his own succession if anything happened to him.

Many things could happen. Kenyere was not in the best of health. His kidneys gave him trouble, and his heart was getting weak. And there were other dangers: mysterious, unknown "tourists" were circling his house like black vultures.

"I am sure that in Rome the President will see the Pope," Kenyere said. He heard the noise of an approaching car. The Land-Rover threw up a cloud of dust, driving too fast on the dry dirt road. With screeching brakes it came to a stop in front of the house, and four men holding automatic guns jumped out of it.

The two bodyguards sprang to their feet, their guns on the ready. Too late.

All was over in less than a minute. After gunning down Kenyere and the guards, the assassins, for good measure, riddled the house with bullets. They seemed to take great delight and pleasure in their actions. While pulling the triggers they gave out little animal cries of joy.

After a last blast they jumped into the Land-Rover and drove off. All that remained was the heat, the three bleeding bodies, the excited cackle of the chickens, and the distant bark of mongrel dogs.

XL

Patrick Donovan took off his green-tinted eyeglasses, especially designed to soften the glare in the Oval Office. He wanted to see the faces of the three men as clearly as possible.

Duncan Mulford, secretary of state, impeccable as ever in his freshly pressed suit; Oliver Hampton, the secretary of defense, the overworked, steel-nerved executive with his bushy gray-brown hair (the secretaries were amused at his obvious toupee); General Rodney Holt of the CIA, fit, athletic, ready for action. They looked expectantly at the President's face.

"Look, boys," Donovan said. "I know that you expect a decision from me, and you are entitled to it. I must confess that I have not, repeat *not*, made a decision. I have here, right in front of me on this desk, all the data and information. I still need time, and frankly, I would like to have at least some conversation, if not consultation, with our allies."

He is procrastinating again, Hampton thought. He needs more time while Admiral Rokosowski is moving the Soviet fleet into Cape Town.

"As I told you," the President continued, "all the information has been meticulously presented by our secret service. My important, perhaps fatal decision, is based on this. However, as you know, the data is not entirely homogeneous. We've had alarms and panics in previous years about the missile gaps, the superiority of their fleet, et cetera. We made corrections, perhaps even overcorrections. Our fleet today is at least equal to theirs. The missiles? A decade ago, that often-misunderstood genius Kissinger said then that both parties have the capacity of mutually extinguishing each other. He said that a few hundred or even thousand missiles more for them or for us could make no difference. I think this is true today. The still-strong progeny of the Cold War speaks frequently of the 'gaps,' the submarine gap, the dollar gap, the missile gap. I don't believe in the gap theory. The most serious threat, according to you, Mr. Secretary"—he looked at Hampton—"is their program of civilian defense."

"It certainly is, Mr. President," Hampton said.

"Well, on this point, the information furnished by General Holt differs from yours. The CIA does not believe that such a gigantic operation could be undertaken without our satellites noticing it."

"Mr. President, you saw the items we referred to that took place in Kiev, Odessa, Leningrad, and even in Moscow."

"I saw those, Mr. Secretary. Let me digress for a moment."

He reached across his desk, picked up his pipe, and lit it. "Civilian defense, or the building of immense underground shelters, is not a defensive but an offensive move. No radar system gives enough time for any city to evacuate the population into the shelters. The power that will decide on a first strike will, at least theoretically, have the possibility of moving millions of people into the shelters before they press the button. However, as I repeat, the building of such shelters cannot be kept a secret, just as moving the population underground in Kiev or Odessa cannot be done without our immediate knowledge. As part of the scaffolding of useful knowledge, I studied the briefings by the CIA very carefully. Preventing the gestation of global conflict is my main goal. And, weighing the data of the Pentagon against that of the CIA, I had to make an appraisal. The three of you know that the correct appraisal of information is the most decisive factor. My carefully studied conclusion is that the Russians are bluffing."

Even General Holt was surprised. He repeated, "Bluffing?"

"Yes," Donovan answered. "There seems to be a new trend, created by a new breed of adventurers in the Politburo. Being an optimist, I don't believe that they are in the majority. We have encountered lately, signs of bizarre activities—indiscriminate killings of agents and missionaries, fleet movements, threats to Berlin and to Labanon. And now comes this digging of shelters."

"These are very serious ploys, Mr. President," the secretary of state said.

"I am not treating them lightly, Duncan. But I repeat that I need more time and a few words with our allies." He paused. "I won't let you down. I will make my decision, and with God's help, I hope it is going to be the right one."

The three men stood up. Donovan said, "Duncan and Rodney, I will see both of you over there. Oliver, please stay a moment. I must talk to you about the emergency plan we've worked out with Duncan. You have been briefed by him?"

"Yes, Mr. President."

XLI

The whole operational facility of the agency had been put at Michael's disposal. He, who had often described in his books the functioning of the company, was staggered to see how reality surpassed his own fantasies.

He employed the same method as the one he used in constructing the plots of his books—a blackboard, chalk, paper, pads, a red pencil. On the blackboard he wrote the basic known elements—the Pope's speeches, his statements to the press, the incident with the boy kissing his hand, the unknown man who had been in to see the Pope and who, according to Phyllis, might have been the man who broke her glasses.

Now for the suppositions. If the Pope had been replaced, it would have had to be by somebody who knew his habits well and who would be well versed in the workings of the Vatican. His mind constantly reverted to the mystery of the plane crash of Pope Clemens's brother, Professor Monticelli.

"If I were writing this absurd story, it would have to be his brother who replaced the Pope." He quoted to himself the Latin proverb, "*Creo quia absurdum.*" "I believe it because it's absurd."

Well, he thought, let's work on the absurdity theory that Monticelli replaced the Pope. He knew he could tell this to no one—not to Holt and certainly not to

Phyllis. The bug must not be informed of his suspicions.

He jotted down his agenda for Rome. He must be as inconspicuous as possible; he had to tread very cautiously and proceed carefully. If the KGB should get wind of his suspicions, they might go to extremes. The false Pope could "disappear" to Siberia or even to hell or heaven. What had they done with the real Pope? Michael figured that it would be pointless from their position to have him killed; alive, Clemens could always be used for blackmail. Unless by some mishap during the kidnapping, he had been eliminated.

The CIA files gave him all the information he needed on Monticelli. As one of the heads of the Italian Communist party, they had all the data on him—his childhood, studies, speeches. He wondered whether fingerprints could be obtained.

When Holt's call came announcing that he was to fly to Rome the following morning, he took his large briefcase and stuffed the material on Monticelli in it. His packed suitcase was already in the safe house where he would spend the night with Phyllis.

XLII

The flight was smooth and pleasant. Indefatigably, the stewardess poured vodka martinis into Michael's glass, and Scotch-and-soda into that of his neighbor's. A very British businessman, Michael decided, judging by his pinstriped, double-breasted suit, no doubt custom-made by a Saville Row tailor, and a cream-colored silk shirt with an ill-fitting collar. Perfect fitting shirts were a sign of the nouveau riche.

Michael liked to fly. The euphoria of almost weightless levitation above the earth, above the clouds, the exclusion of communication with the busy humans thirty thousand feet below, was complete.

He thought of Phyllis and he happily anticipated their being together in Rome. He hoped to find time enough for her once this crazy mystery was solved, a mystery he could never use for one of his books. The plot could only fit into science fiction, which was not his forte. However, it gave him a plot idea for another book. He took a pad out of his briefcase and started to make some notes. Did he imagine that his neighbor was secretly trying to read his scribbling? No. The man was engrossed in a touring guide of Venezuela.

He exchanged a few polite words with him and determined by his accent that he was indeed an Englishman. Only Professor Higgins could have discerned his social and geographical background from the alternating speech between Cockney and Oxonian English.

On arrival at Leonardo da Vinci Airport he said good-bye to the English gentleman. He could not have guessed that the man was Castor, nor did Castor have an idea of Michael's identity. They would meet again under much less civilized circumstances.

After some haggling about the price ("When in Rome, do as the Romans do"), the taxicab driver deposited him safely, after slalomlike contortions and constant honking, in front of the Hotel Hassler. While signing the registration card, he heard the shrill outcry of the hall porter.

"Mr. Burren, Mr. Burren," the man was yelling, "please take the telephone. Washington has kept this line open now for forty-five minutes. Madonna mia!"

Michael yelled back, "I'll take it in my room." He rushed to his room on the third floor and picked up the receiver.

"Mr. Burren?" the voice asked.

"Yes. Who is calling?"

He recognized General Holt's voice. "Michael?"

"Yes, sir. Is something wrong?"

Holt said, "Scramble."

"One minute, sir. I must unpack it." He opened his travel case and attached the scrambler to the phone. He quickly scanned the room, but if it was bugged there was no time to neutralize it. The scrambler started to cackle. The unscrambling decoder translated by earphone.

"He escaped. The real one escaped."

Michael tried to understand but couldn't. Holt seemed incoherent. The incurable disease of all secret services: they use code words even on the scrambler.

"I don't quite . . ." he said when Holt continued, his voice a little calmer now.

"The 'Pope' in the Vatican is an impostor. The real one escaped from an asylum in Switzerland."

Staggered, Michael asked, "Where is he? The real one?"

"You get your ass this minute over to our embassy. Ask for the ambassador. He is the only one who knows. Total secrecy and silence. Call me back in an hour."

Michael picked up the phone and yelled into it, "Taxi!" When the hall porter replied that it would take ten minutes, he said, "Forget it."

The elevator was too slow so he ran down the staircase. Out on the street he realized that he had not taken his overcoat. He ran in the chill fog to the embassy, fighting his way through the usual barrage of the photographers, the *paparazzi*. In the entrance he was stopped by the Marine guard.

"State the purpose of your visit."

Breathlessly, Michael said, "The ambassador."

An elegant civilian standing next to the guard asked, "Mr. Burren? Please follow me."

The ambassador was standing behind his fine mahogany desk. He shook Michael's hand. "I am fully informed about you by General Holt. Please sit down. A glass of sherry or coffee? Both are right here." Michael thanked him and asked for the coffee, which the ambassador poured from a Thermos on his desk.

Michael looked up at the ceiling and noticed the glowing purple tube. He was relieved to see that they had installed the newest antilistening device.

"The Pope is here, in a room at the embassy. He is not well. Pneumonia. But he is on the way to recovery. He is fully informed of your arrival. It is only yesterday that he gave me permission to inform the President and our security services. General Holt holds you in high esteem."

"Thank you, Your Excellency. May I see the Pope?"

"In an instant. First, I must brief you. He escaped from a lunatic asylum in Switzerland, put there by his abductors. He managed to get to Rome, clad only in pajamas and slippers, and he caught a cold. He is frail and vulnerable."

"I will try not to disturb him," Michael said, a little impatient with the ambassador's slow manner.

"I know you won't. But it is essential that you know that he does not want the false Pope demasked, nor does he want to return to the Vatican at this time. That is why he refused to allow us to inform your office of his plight."

Amazed, Michael asked, "Why not?"

"I think he should tell you himself." He stood up. "Please follow me."

They walked down a hall covered with plush carpets and lined with fine baroque angels and crystal chandeliers. On the next floor the ambassador took a key from his pocket and opened a door.

Pope Clemens was resting, seemingly at ease, in a large double bed. He put the cup of tea he was holding down on the night table and said, "Good morning, Mr. Ambassador. I trust this is Mr. Burren?"

"Yes, Your Holiness. I will leave you alone with him and will see you after lunch." He opened the door and turned to Michael. "Mr. Burren, please come to my study after you finish your conversation with His Holiness."

"Come closer, Mr. Burren. I met your father when the Yankees entered Rome. At that time, alas, I was only a cardinal."

Michael sat down and looked at the gentle face of the old man. A wise, tired, all-knowing face. "The ambassador told me, Your Holiness, that you don't wish to expose the impostor who usurps your place in the Vatican. Is this true?"

"Yes, Mr. Burren. Please try to understand me. The ambassador told me that you work for the CIA—I believe these to be the initials of your organization."

"Yes, Your Holiness."

"The ambassador also told me that your real profession, a successful one, is that of an author of spy books. Is this correct?"

"It is, Your Holiness."

"Now, my son, I most certainly do not wish to offend you. But this episode of my life is *not* the subject for a spy story. Not at all. It might have started as one, misleading a few people, perhaps even you. I repeat, it is not a detective story or a spy yarn."

"I understand, Your Reverence. But you must admit that your kidnapping and replacement by a man whom we suspect of being a Communist has the makings of an espionage plot. By the way, is the false Pope your brother?"

"Yes, he is Giulio Monticelli, whom God has chosen for this test."

"God? Not the KGB?"

"Even the KGB—you mean the Russian counterpart of your organization—is subject to God's decisions."

"And Your Holiness is ready to accept the KGB's decisions, inspired as you say, by a Higher Power?"

Pope Clemens nodded. "I am. But not forever. I want to see the deeds and actions of my brother in the next days. God will lead him in the right direction."

"And—this is a hypothesis—if not, what are your intentions?"

"I will make my decisions in time. If I recover and gain back my strength, I wish to return to my office. The Vatican."

"Your Holiness, do you realize that you are in mortal danger?"

Pope Clemens smiled. "Aren't we all? Our entire life holds that menace of mortal danger. *Menatio mortis.* My life is in God's hands. He will do with it what he thinks is best. Your duty, my son, is to assist the Heavenly Father in keeping me alive. You will be, as I hear, in charge of my security?"

"Yes, Your Holiness, my office has so informed me. And I assure you that I will do all that's possible to ensure your safety."

"I am convinced that you will. Please keep in touch with me. Come and see me every day while I am here at the embassy."

Michael stood up. Pope Clemens said, "God be with you, my son."

"Thank you, Reverence. I might need Him."

The ambassador dismissed his secretary and asked Michael to sit facing him. "Well, what is your impression?"

"The same as yours, Mr. Ambassador. He won't give in. His faith is stronger than my sense of reality and yours combined. If we would try to act against his wishes, he could make our lives very unpleasant with unforeseen catastrophic consequences for the Church. We must play the game according to his rules for the time being."

"What do you intend to do?"

"First of all, I must contact our liaison with the Italian state security, Colonel Romanelli. I don't like to involve them and there is a potential danger, but it is unavoidable. I need their assistance."

"In what respect?"

"Sir, I am certain it is the Box at the Kremlin who thought up this scheme for the KGB. They know that the real Pope has escaped. By now, I am sure that they have staked out the residences of all of Pope Clemens's friends. Perhaps even our own safe houses, insofar as they know them. If possible, I would like to try to bring them out in the open, which I won't be able to do without the help of the Italians. By the way, Mr. Ambassador, how did the Pope get into the embassy? Was he brought by a car, by a cab?"

"No, he walked. I don't think anybody saw him enter. We know about Russian surveillance of this building. Last year, knowing that they were photographing our visitors, we had to rent three floors in an apartment house across the street. There are, as you saw, always dozens of *paparazzi* out front. Lord knows how many of them are in Soviet pay. But frankly, I don't think they would pay much attention to an old shabby-looking man. What excites them is the Libyan ambassador's Mercedes limousine. And another thing: I don't think that the underlings of the KGB knew that he had escaped at the time Pope Clemens entered here."

"I think that you are right, sir. In any case, I urgently need more men for the Pope's surveillance, both inside and outside the embassy. And they will have to be placed without arousing suspicion. The number of *paparazzi* will increase somewhat by tomorrow."

XLIII

Michael checked the address. The street was correct, so was the fading number on the house. Still, the old dirty facade, the boarded-up windows, the half-broken rain pipes did not seem to fit the address given him by Colonel Romanelli's secretary. On this narrow side street, close to the Piazza del Popolo, all houses looked badly in need of repair. Shaking his head in disbelief, Michael entered the once-elegant porte cochère. Once inside the picture changed completely. An arched Renaissance inner court with evergreen plants on marble pedestals advertised the affluence of the owner.

A regular storybook witch, seemingly left over by King Vittorio Emenuele, materialized from a niche in the wall. With a toothless grin, she said, "La Contessa," and pointed with the skeleton of an arm to the right corner of the courtyard.

"*Grazie,*" Michael said, and went through the small *piazzetta* to a staircase covered with a faded red carpet. He walked up a few steps and faced a fine walnut double door. Before he could touch the bell the door was opened, and a melodious voice asked, "Signor Burren?"

The maid, straight out of a Goldoni comedy, was young and pretty. She wore a very short black silk skirt, a white blouse partly covered by a starched lace pinafore. She took Michael's coat and led him to the

salon. Michael inhaled a strong fragrance that seemed
like a mélange of incense and essence of roses. A low
table with an antiqued mirror top sat between a low
couch and two rosewood armchairs upholstered in a
light-green velvet. On brocaded yellow silk walls hung
two large Canaletto oils of the Arsenal of Venice and
the Rialto Bridge over the Canale Grande. The gilded
frames surrounded a green passe-partout—a Venetian
green made of aquamarine and blue tints, which reminded Michael of the Adriatic.

A melodious voice called out his name in English.
He turned and saw the Contessa. She looked fragile,
like a Tanagra figurine—small, elegant, and so very
attractive in black pajamas and a long string of white
pearls.

"Please sit down. I apologize for the colonel. He is a
little late. May I serve you a drink?"

From a crystal decanter she poured the ruby wine in
tall, slender glasses for Michael and herself. As though
making polite conversation, she said, "I am Colonel
Romanelli's official mistress."

Michael reacted to this by choking on his drink. Un-
perturbed, the Contessa continued, "In Rome, as you
know, all important men must have an official and
well-advertised mistress."

"I congratulate Colonel Romanelli on his official
choice."

A voice in the background answered, "I thank you,
Mr. Burren."

Michael stood up and shook hands with Colonel
Romanelli, the legendary head of the Italian counter-
espionage department. Romanelli was reputed to be
one of the most astute professionals and highly appreciated by the CIA and the British M16. He was small
and wiry, and every movement he made seemed to be
activated by fine inner springs.

"A drink?" the Contessa asked, and Romanelli said, "Sorry, no time. Please follow me, Mr. Burren."

The study was small and lined with bookcases. They sat down in two black leather armchairs. In excellent English, the colonel said, "I want to apologize for being late. An urgent call."

Michael noticed a low buzzing sound. The colonel explained, "It is an old-fashioned antibugging device. We don't yet have your Meddler X2, nor, of course, the Russian Pleskow. I understand from General Holt that you have very important information for me."

Michael gave him a full report. Romanelli listened, alert and concentrated. His well-educated face showed no reaction, not even to the incredible news of the false Pope in the Vatican.

When Michael finished, Romanelli said, "Fantastic. We had no inkling. The only item I can trace back was some info coming from the Chiasso border about the escape of an Italian banker or manager from a Swiss lunatic asylum." He leaned back in his chair and repeated, "Fantastic. Still, I am not too surprised. I've expected those boy scouts in the Kremlin Box to be coming up with some hairbrained scheme."

"You seem to agree with General Holt that this was planned and invented by Houndsworth?

"I'm sure they meant to use Clemens to negotiate with us when Monticelli had outlived his usefulness. Perhaps they thought they could have the Vatican and also ransom Clemens back to the true, die-hard believers. Neat trick. Thank God for His Holiness's electrician's license!"

"Now, what is our course of action?"

"First and paramount, the security of Pope Clemens."

"Naturally," Romanelli nodded. He thought for a moment and suddenly said very rapidly, "I know how to proceed as a professional. But I learned from my friend, General Holt, that you were engaged by him mostly because of your imagination as a writer. Putting your fantasy to work, what would you do if you were the KGB?"

"I would try to find and kill the real Pope. And I would have the Vatican surveyed around the clock, because sooner or later Pope Clemens would try to get back to the papal apartments."

"Why?"

"Because an exposure of such a fiendish operation would cause immense harm to world communism."

"In the first place, I am sure that they have covered themselves well in every contingency. Secondly, they don't care about world opinion. And lastly, has it occurred to you that we, ourselves, might not want to disclose this escamotage? Have you thought of what harm it might cause if the Christian world learned of the replacement of the real Pope by a false Pontiff without causing a ripple in the Vatican?"

"Yes, the thought crossed my mind."

"Still, knowing their stubbornness in persevering on a project, it stands to reason that they will try to get at Pope Clemens. The surveillance of the Vatican, no matter how close, will not help them. Thousands of diplomats, cardinals, priests, come and go daily, not to mention myriads of monks—the Franciscans, those of Eastern sects, Capuchins covering their faces. We can get the Pope into the Vatican with little trouble. What I would want to do is to bring the KGB out into the open. Set them a trap, cause them to believe that Pope Clemens is at a certain place, for instance the bishop's residence. Or . . . wait a minute . . . perhaps Castelgandolfo, the Pope's summer residence, which is closed at this moment. We will create a sudden activity in Castelgandolfo, with all the lights on, with personnel

rehired, with guards. The KGB will have to investi-
gate. We will be ready for them. Holt told me that
you asked for reinforcements from the States. When
do you expect them?"

"Tomorrow."

"Fine. In the meantime I will see to it that your
embassy is well guarded. I will leak it to the press that,
in view of the impending arrival of your President, we
are tripling our guards around the embassy, your information center, and the airport. But first, immediately and personally, I must contact the Pope's majordomo and the Vatican secretary of state. Unpleasant as
hell. But unavoidable. And check with the man we
have at the Italian Communist party. Just ask him
some innocuous questions."

"How do we keep in contact?"

"Remember this number. It is easy. 333222. Day and
night. And let us meet here again tomorrow at four
thirty."

"And disturb the privacy of the Contessa?"

"Nothing disturbs the Contessa. She is the biggest
intriguer in Rome. And a blabbermouth, full of the
wrong information."

"And charming."

"That she is. Why do you think I selected her as my
official mistress?"

XLIV

Patrick Donovan disliked secrecy and intrigue. His highly intelligent brain was not programmed for it. An extrovert, he liked to bring matters out in the open, to discuss problems freely, and not in dark rooms full of antibugging contraptions. Secrecy made a special mental filing case necessary: with whom he could share the secret and with whom he could not. Why should the British know about the newest Python rocket and French not? He knew that this trend to cloak-and-dagger mystification was not his own doing, nor was it Duncan Mulford's. The secretary of state had no stomach for it: he always looked nauseated when he mentioned a subject marked TOP SECRET, FOR EYES AND EARS ONLY.

They planned to leave the next morning for their voyage to London, Bonn, Paris, and Rome. Donovan was not looking forward to this trip at all. The news Duncan had brought him about Clemens had shocked him more than he could say. It hit at his vulnerable point—his devotion to his religion. If the Vatican was vulnerable, what was solid and unshakable in this world?

And then there was the letter from Kenyere. Donovan could not explain why the letter of that primitive Kenyere had touched him so much.

In Donovan's mind the two seemingly unconnected

items—the planting of a false Pope and the Kenyere letter—were related. They were integral parts of the puzzle: Why have the Russians become suddenly so aggressive and so scheming? Were the reports in *Jane's Fighting Ships* and of the CIA correct, and are the Soviets now so much better armed than we? What are their immediate intentions? Are they still testing me and my reactions, Donovan wondered? Perhaps his devotion to pacifism had rocked the Church forever.

And he thought of Duncan Mulford's project or plan. "Top secret" sounded like a cheap euphemism for something that had to be really much more than just top secret. He had to make a decision on the project, and he felt, he knew, that he was drifting closer to the solution advocated by his secretary of state, of defense, and of General Holt. But he had to remind himself that he had not yet made a final decision on this scheme, named by Holt, "Operation Villa d'Este."

With all this, he had to laugh when he heard Gladys say, like a good housewife, "Don't worry so much, darling." The Russian fleet will sail into Cape Town to decide the elections there, and the Pope will announce on Easter Sunday that communism and Christianity are synonymous, and the wife of the President of the United States tells darling not to worry.

They sat in the den next to the bedroom, a room that he liked to relax in. He liked the chintz curtains, the working fireplace, the TV set, the comfortable couch. Gladys was arranging her address book for their voyage. He could not resist breaking his promise of secrecy and told Gladys about the Pope. To hell with keeping secrets from my own wife. There were security precautions even he must have.

Gladys was as deeply shocked as he had been. "Why?" she asked in disbelief. Donovan explained the practical reasons for this infantile caper. "Very practical ones."

He felt much better for having told her. At least there was now one secret that he shared with the woman he loved. He did not mind her advice when he sat and brooded, not to worry about these problems too much. She was right—worrying did not help.

"What makes it worse," he said, "is that we must go on this useless courtesy trip to see our allies and won't be able to breathe a word to anybody. We will sit, you and I, at dinner tables and think of the Pope and not utter a word. Like two cats who have swallowed two canaries."

"Will this thing with the Pope be resolved by the time we get to Rome?"

"I do hope so."

"Of course, Phyllis knows nothing about this?"

"Not if Michael can keep his mouth shut better than I can."

Of course, Michael had it easier. He can't tell Phyllis in view of the bug. To keep one's mouth shut, he thought. How long will I be able to keep this Villa d'Este project from Gladys? This time I really have to. She has to be kept out of it. Just like Phyllis.

"Are you all packed, love?" he asked.

"Of course. With all the help from the Marines and the secret service, packing was easy. Now, stop fretting, and let's go to bed."

XLV

Using the small table next to the bed to make notes, partly for himself and partly for his Easter message, Monticelli sat late into the night. His battle with himself was not finished. Was he trying to convince others or only himself? He, who had once believed, but was not satisfied now in his disbelief? Or the others who are not willing to approach the question of human condition with mere feelings, prejudices, and workable explanations? Why then remain a Christian? Was it not enough to have faith, to believe in guidance from a higher power? He felt no affinity with the pomp, the theatricals, the dogma of the Church. But he came to the conclusion that this major stage show might be a necessity for the masses. Behind the glittering facade of the Circus Maximus was the foundation of faith and charity. Perhaps it was his dying that had changed him. Finally, he wrote down the words, "Atheism cannot offer conclusive proof against the existence of God. If the atheist has a basic trust in reality, he cannot explain it. If he does not have the trust, the result is pure nihilism, the possible futility, worthlessness, emptiness of reality as a whole. Facing the radical uncertainty of the human condition, therefore, requires a belief in God. Without such a belief, reality itself seems unsubstantial."

He paused for a moment. It was pointless to list his

doubts in certain elements of the Old and New Testaments—he did not believe in miracles nor in the Immaculate Conception. The greatest importance, he thought, was Easter and Christ's appearance in the Holy Land.

He looked with hatred and even fear at the small alarm clock chiming midnight. The midnight instructions from the party. With a sigh, he picked up his small radio, opened his breviary at the page of the code, and waited for the signal.

Castor seemed very angry and very excited. "No code," he said. "No time for games."

Okay, no games, Monticelli thought. I want to plot no plot, he quoted Swift to himself.

"We cannot find your brother. He vanished."

"To bad," Monticelli said, not very sincerely.

"We need your help. You might hear something from your bishops and cardinals. And sooner or later he will try to sneak back into the Vatican. Keep me informed."

"I am not a spy or a policeman. I am the Pope."

"Are you kidding? Some Pope. Your Holiness," with heavy sarcasm, "we expect your report."

"Don't expect it. You promised me that you would not hurt my brother. You will excuse me, but I don't trust your promises or the KGB's."

"You know that I am reporting this conversation to the Boss."

"Of course. You do what you have to do, and so will I."

"Well, just as long as we understand each other. How far are you with the Easter message? Is it ready?"

"Not yet. But soon. Good night."

So they cannot find Clemens. He was very pleased that the mighty KGB could not find him.

Come back, brother, and take over, he thought. I wish I could get out of here, but when? He was not really ready to give up. Before he vanished from this agora, before he became something else (but what? He could never become again what he had been), before his illness reached the terminal phase, he wanted to deliver to the world his testament, his last will, his Easter sermon. He started silently to pray for the fulfillment of his wish.

XLVI

Among the "reinforcements," traveling under the cover of a group of agronomic experts, Vasily Glazunov was the dominating personality. Decades of experience in China, Cuba, Chile, and Japan had not blunted his alertness. His mind worked as sharply as it had twenty years before, at the time of the Cold War.

Portly of build, a Slavic countenance, and wearing steel-rimmed glasses, Glazunov listened intently to Castor's debriefing. He spoke of mysterious movements at Castelgandolfo, which his men had reported. "This has to be looked into," Castor concluded.

They sat on the second-floor reception room of the Soviet Information Center in their heavy overcoats. The Italians did not believe the early Roman spring was only a continuation of winter, and the heating was minimal.

"Perhaps," Glazunov said.

"Why are you uncertain?" Castor asked.

"Because it might be just a CIA trap."

"I doubt that the CIA is involved. They cannot risk a serious conflict with the Italians, and risk has to be taken. Agreed?"

"It is your show, Castor. My job is the surveillance of the Vatican. In the next few days they will have to get their man in, as you so emphatically stated. And

you want him killed, even before he gets in there. My
duty is to inspect, as far as possible, ambassadors' cars,
private vehicles, ambulances, the fire brigade, monks
and friars—everyone and everything that enters. A
damned big job. In addition to my men, I've hired
thirty thugs and cutthroats. All they know is that this
man has to be killed. They have his photograph."

"All right. You are in charge of the Vatican. Who is
your choice for Castelgandolfo?"

Glazunov shrugged with his whole stout body.
"There is not much of a choice," he said. "Yevgeny
will do, if you can keep him from using his automatic
on whatever moves. We don't want a dozen little
Popes killed. Only the one real one." He banged his
fists on his knees, enjoying his joke.

The Castelgandolfo ambush did not go well for either party. At 2:00 A.M., three of the KGB delegates
reached the inside of the huge building and headed for
the room on the second floor, where light filtered out
through the window. Two men kept guard outside.
The only casualty, a middle-aged night guard, was hit
on the head by Yevgeny, a blow that rendered him incommunicado for several weeks.

Yevgeny and his comrade, Yuri, kicked the door in,
posting the third man outside in the unlit corridor. In
the room two Dominican padres sat at a small table
reading. When the Russians entered, the muzzles of
their guns pointing at them, the padres jumped to
their feet. Yevgeny yelled in English and in Russian,
"Hands up!"

The padres understood and obeyed. Almost simultaneously Yevgeny lowered his gun: these men were not
what they were looking for. He was just about to utter
an effective and vulgar Russian curse when he heard,
in perfect Russian, "Drop your guns and turn

around." The voice used the professional imperative.

Yevgeny managed to say "Damn!" before dropping his gun. He saw six pairs of eyes, six guns of different calibers, and six neat green Italian uniforms.

"Welcome to Italy, Comrades," the man with the captain's insignia said. "Colonel Romanelli would like to have a word with you."

Yevgeny, his helper, and the two men standing guard outside were all put into an olive-green mini-bus. The third man, who stood in the corridor outside the room where the padres read, managed to escape through the roof.

"Not a smashing success," Romanelli reported to Michael. "Old-fashioned primitive operatives. I had hoped for a better catch. These boys arrived with the transport from Kiev, a decrepit Tupulov one-oh-two. Agronomes, they call themselves. They want to learn how to make more zakuski with less barley. However, it is clear that the operation is directed by the KGB, not the local party. And they know by now that our side is purely Italian."

"Who knows that?"

"The third man who escaped and who saw our uniforms."

"And the big brass of the KGB will conclude now that the CIA has nothing to do with the maneuver?"

"The big brass will know that we, the Italians, are in it, too."

XLVII

Problems, problems, mostly logistics. Michael consulted the small pad in front of him. He neatly numbered the problems to be solved. Number one was, without doubt, the smuggling of Pope Clemens into the Vatican. He had agreed to Colonel Romanelli's scheme because it appeared to be the simplest. Whenever the Pope would be able to move— (and he seemed to be recovering rapidly) —he was to be flanked by four Franciscan priests in their brown "uniforms," with the hoods over their heads, and the Pope dressed as they, would walk among them into the Vatican. Once inside, it became Romanelli's problem, which he hoped to solve with the help of the secretary of state and the majordomo.

Problem number two caused Michael real headaches. The crux of the operation rested with Phyllis's eyeglasses. They had no evidence of the usual escamotage and therefore had to play it by ear. Her daily tennis games were properly advertised, as demonstrated by the presence of a dozen *paparazzi* with telephoto lenses at the Lawn Tennis Club. Yet there was no trace of an eyeglass picker-upper. Damn the KGB, he thought, they are getting sloppy. And we have no time to lose.

Problem number three was his own "baby," the "secret" trip of President Donovan, with his family, to

the Villa d'Este on Lake Como. He had to figure out
how to leak this information to the press and what the
right moment would be.

He did manage to free himself in the afternoons for
his meetings with Phyllis. The pure Renaissance castle
of the Principessa Buchhari on the outskirts of Rome
was lovely, and the drive on the Via Appia Antica in
the *primavera* sunshine was especially so. Yes, spring
was in the air, and Michael felt it in his veins, in his
bones, and mostly in Phyllis's reckless passion.

The Principessa always served English tea in the
conservatory with finger sandwiches covered with
dainty, midget watercress. The attractive Principessa
made mondaine chitchat about the young film director who was following in the footsteps of Fellini, of
the new musical that had opened in Rome ("better
than your American musicals"), and about intrigue—
mostly political but frequently erotic—in the highest
circles of the Roman aristocracy.

After half an hour she looked at the tiny watch
embedded in diamonds on her blouse, and said, "Time
for my Russian lesson." She promptly took leave, and
the lovers were left free to be lovers. The Principessa
obviously took for granted that the betrothed couple,
the *promessi sposi*, were as good as married.

It was on the third tea party that Phyllis announced
to Michael, when he inquired about her game, that
the club had engaged a new pro, an Egyptian.

"He looks divine," Phyllis said. "Tall, slender, sat-
urnine . . . could be Omar Shariff's brother."

Michael excused himself and went to the telephone
to call Colonel Romanelli. Before he could speak Romanelli said, "Where are you? I've been looking for
you everywhere. The tennis club has hired a new pro.
Abou Hassid, he's called."

"Fine," said Michael. "Things are beginning to move."

"I'm told your President is due here on Friday. Do you think he will visit the 'Pope' in the Vatican?"

"I doubt it. But I can't explain now why not."

"Don't worry. My information says that the 'Pope' will excuse himself with some malaise or illness."

"That is the best solution. Any other news from the Holy See?"

"Nothing unusual. We, the watchers, are watching the watchers. In addition to their own trained agronomes, they have called in a large number of well-selected cutthroats. The tramps who sleep under the bridges of the Tiber now have washed faces."

"Are you sure you can handle all this?"

"I hope so. The Contessa sends her regards and suggests that you have tea at her apartment. Just the two of you."

"Flattering, but impossible. My teatime is otherwise engaged."

Very dryly, Romanelli said, "So it seems. See you later."

XLVIII

Castor sat brooding in his hotel room and waited for Robles. This one Pope, two Pope game was exasperating. Castor reminded himself that concentration on the main problem was highly essential.

The main problem—and no secondary operation could detract from it—was the preparation and execution if necessary of the Pope on Easter Sunday. The penthouse apartment on Monte Pincio had been rented and was ready. From the terrace of the apartment the view to the Piazza del Vaticano was unobstructed. The marine field glasses with a magnifying power of sixteen times, from the famous Zeiss optical factory in Jena, East Germany, had been placed in the luggage compartment of the Fiat 228, along with the newest Shebekov 300 long-range, long-barrel, laser rifle. Although the owner of the apartment had sworn that no one else had a key, Castor did not dare to leave the equipment there—with the Italians, you never knew. The Fiat was locked in the hotel garage.

The eyeglasses belonging to Phyllis had been picked up by the "Egyptian"—who was not an Egyptian but a Palestinian—and were promptly monitored. Nothing but society prattle and lovemaking with that amateur spy Michael. Castor was in no hurry to get them. He knew that before the arrival of Donovan he would not hear anything worth listening to.

Robles arrived and volunteered the information that he hated Italian food and wanted to return either to borsch or to paella territory.

"Soon," Castor reassured him.

They took the Fiat out of the garage and drove up to the apartment house on Monte Pincio. The concierge received a good tip for helping to load the two suitcases into the small elevator. Castor opened the door, and they entered an apartment that had been decorated as a love nest—shiny marble floors, a baby grand piano, silky Persian rugs, a whatnot full of useless bric-a-brac. On the walls, postcard imitations of Sorrento and the Bay of Naples.

Out on the terrace they fixed the position of the spyglasses and the laser rifle with the heavy telescope on it. They left the chairs, the cushions, and the metal table in the selected position, and packed the equipment into the two suitcases again.

The packing was done with the utmost care. They had been entrusted with this priceless equipment by the general of the KGB. This was to be the first time the electronic telescope was to be used. The laser rifle had been mounted with the same electronic telescope lens that could show the wrinkles on a face at a distance of five miles.

"It will work," Castor said.

"Unless we get fogged in," Robles answered.

"There is never fog—certainly not in the spring. Whatever fog there might be is at the airport. They look for the most likely places for fog and build airports there."

"But in the Vatican, no fog?"

"Never. God would not tolerate that. Let's go back to the hotel."

XLIX

Pope Clemens had a late breakfast in his secluded bedroom at the American embassy. "I am going to miss these fresh croissants," he told the ambassador.

"We have a French pastry cook here. I will be happy to lend him to you."

"Thank you, Mr. Ambassador. I must not pamper myself too much. You have done so much for me, keeping me, keeping silent when it must have been so difficult."

"Your Holiness, I would do it all again. Are you well enough to make it?"

"The doctor said yes, and I say most emphatically, yes, I will make it."

"Once inside the papal apartments, you will be taking over. You know that Colonel Romanelli has prepared everything for the transition. With the assistance of your secretary of state and Maestro di Camera, all will go smoothly."

The Pope shook his head. "No, my son, I will not take over. Not yet. Not before the Easter sermon."

"Your Holiness, I do not understand. Forgive me, but what are your reasons?"

Pope Clemens sighed and took a deep breath. He looked at the ceiling, and Michael thought that the Pope's face had suddenly become illuminated by some inner light.

"Reason," the Pope said. "In your profession and with your upbringing, you are bound to assume that everything can be explained by that magic word *reason*. My intentions connected with my brother cannot be explained by reason."

"We must accept that," the ambassador said. "But Your Holiness has made a decision that defies the definition of reason. Can you, without revealing something, give us an idea of the motivation for your decision?"

As though conversing with himself, the Pope said very quietly, "Auto-da-fé. An act of faith." He stopped suddenly. He felt he had said enough.

Stubbornly, Michael wanted to know more. He repeated in the same quiet tone, "Act of faith?"

Clemens covered his face with the palms of his hands. He thought of these two men, these two friends responsible for his safety. He concluded that they deserved an "explanation." An explanation that they would probably not understand, but it was the only one he could give them.

"This is a matter between the three of us—God, my brother, and myself. I am convinced that God is guiding my brother's actions and that his mission will culminate in his Easter sermon. I want him to make the sermon from the balcony of the papal residence, with all the papal regalia. It is imperative for me and my eternal faith in God that he act as Peter's messenger and delivers his own sermon on Easter Sunday. This, then, is my act of faith."

Michael and the ambassador sat in silence. They were impressed by the Pope's unshakable conviction. Michael said to himself, It is not without reason that this man was appointed to be God's general. He quickly supplanted the word *reason* with *merit*. Fur-

ther discussion and argumentation would lead nowhere.

"Thank you for telling us, Your Holiness. Our plan
is the following: I will be here at four o'clock this afternoon and take you to a waiting car. Colonel Romanelli will drive it himself. He will be wearing the
frocks of the Franciscan monks and so will the three
men with him. I took the liberty of bringing the same
Franciscan outfit for you. It is in this box." He
pointed to a cardboard box he had placed on a table
next to the door.

All smiles, the Pope said, "The Franciscan monk
will be ready for you, my son."

The nondescript black Lancia waited in the space
reserved for members of the embassy staff for the appearance of the four friars. The driver himself, dressed
as a Franciscan, kept his alert eyes on the wrought-iron
entrance to the embassy. The Marine guard signaled
the driver of the approach of his passengers, and when
the Lancia arrived in front of the entrance, he opened
the back door for the three padres. The eldest one
placed himself in the middle. The fourth Franciscan
took his place next to the driver. With a casual hand
salute to the Marine and to Michael standing inside
the door, Colonel Romanelli started his drive to the
Piazza del Vaticano.

Through the half-opened window of the car, the
Pope pleasurably inhaled the bracing spring air. He
filled his lungs and his veins with the prime of the
year. When they reached the Vatican Square, the Pope
saw with pleasure and perhaps a touch of pride the
large crowds of pilgrims pretending to be tourists and
tourists pretending not to be interested in the Church.
And, as always, there were the good people of Rome—
his flock.

The Lancia stopped at the main entrance. Flanked by both the Swiss guards and the Roman police, the heirarchy of the Church moved in and out of the buildings. Their various robes—the purple and vermilion of the cardinals, the black of the priests, the black and white of the nuns—made a kaleidoscope of color. To add to the motley crowd, a group of some forty Franciscan monks stood in front of the entrance, waiting.

Colonel Romanelli stepped out of the car and opened the back door. He helped the Pope out of his seat, and the five of them joined the waiting Franciscans. Immediately, the large group started to move with persevering steadiness toward the door. Pope Clemens was now in the first row, the two monks who had shared their ride in the car were in back of him, and then came a big man, with Romanelli behind him. They entered the giant door and continued their walk down the long corridor.

A tall monk, constantly squinting and scanning the faces of his colleagues, worked his way up from the last row. Now, only a few steps behind the Pope, his deep-lined aquiline face showed decision. He reached into the folds of his robe, and well concealed in the deep cuff, he opened the blade of his switch knife.

A few seconds later, Father Anselmus of the Bergamo Franciscan Order, heard a strange, hissing sound. He tried to locate its origin but all he could see was that the tall Franciscan seemed to falter and lean over. Two monks helped him by grabbing his elbows and leading him on with the group.

Before they reached the end of the corridor, Romanelli saw the door open on their right. He took the Pope by his arm and led him inside a small room under a spiral staircase.

Two sobbing and kneeling men kissed the Pope's

ring—the Maestro di Camera and the secretary of state. Still unable to believe that the Pope, the real Pope, was back with them, they stammered unintelligible words of blessings and welcome.

With Romanelli's help, the Pope walked up to the second floor. His room in the south wing was ready. So were the two Swiss guards and two of Romanelli's best men, stationed in front of the door.

Pope Clemens was back in the Vatican.

In the corridor leading to the entrance, Sister Angelique of the Sacré Coeur let out one half of a blood-curdling shriek. A hand over her mouth stopped her from finishing it.

The cause of Sister Angelique's terror was the sight of a bleeding, severed hand holding a knife, and lying in the center of the marble corridor with blood still oozing out of it.

Angelique turned her head to explain why she was so frightened to the Dominican monk who had stopped her outcry. She turned back again to show him the object of her horror and pointed to the spot where she had seen the hand. It was gone. So was the blood. The corridor was almost empty at this moment, except for three friars walking to the entrance. One was carrying a pail.

L

The crackling, shrill note of the scrambled telephone was a further irritant to Houndsworth's already frazzled nerves. He was with his two friends in the Communications Room at the Box and listened to Castor's debriefing.

"A total failure," he said into the receiver. "First, this blunder at Castelgandolfo, and now the real Pope is back, safe, in the Vatican. How could this have happened?"

"We all are bound to make mistakes, Boss."

"We cannot afford such mistakes. Dzerzhinsky Square sent me the best team they had, all graduates of the Verhovnoye School. We even took the risk of letting them take the newest Stechkin gun to Rome. And the result? Complete victory for the CIA."

"Comrade Boss, it is not a coup for the CIA. It was Colonel Romanelli who masterminded the Vatican entry."

"Well, did your men not recognize Romanelli?"

"Nobody knows what Romanelli looks like. He never participates in official meetings, and not a soul has ever seen a picture of him."

"So what do you propose to do, Castor?"

"Up to you, Boss. The real Pope is in the Vatican, but not safe as you think. We have ways and means of getting in there."

"And be butchered by Romanelli or the CIA?"

"We can defend ourselves."

"Under no conditions. We cannot risk a battle inside the Vatican. This is completely outlawed. Repeat: don't try to get inside the Vatican. This Pope-against-Pope business has to resolve itself. We don't know what they intend to do with Pope Clemens and they don't know what we will do with Monticelli. This case is closed as far as we are concerned. The minute it became known, even to a very small circle, that the 'Pope' was an impostor, Monticelli ceased to be an asset to us. On the contrary, he is a liability. I still expect some profit to us from his forthcoming Easter sermon, but have no idea as yet what we will do with him after that. It will depend on what they will do with Pope Clemens."

"So, for the time being, we leave Pope Clemens alone and concentrate on the sermon. I assume that your instructions have not changed?"

"No, they haven't. If, as you suspect, Monticelli has 'turned' and will say something against us in his sermon, you proceed as planned."

"We have the apartment and the equipment is in place."

"I hope you will use that expensive laser properly. Don't advertise the place on Monte Pincio to the CIA. Have you heard the expression—keeping a low profile?"

"Yes, Boss. A capitalist overreaction to publicity."

"You are getting too intellectual for your own good, Castor. Call me again at ten P.M. your time."

He put the receiver down and turned to his two friends. "Let us go back to the office and have some tea."

They sipped their dark Darjeeling tea out of Royal Doulton cups. The warm scones were delicious with the Crosse & Blackwell red currant jam and the Dundee marmalade.

How long? Houndsworth asked himself. Maximus cannot be pleased with the situation as it presents itself at this moment. They won't be enjoying good Darjeeling tea in Siberia, but some light Chinese tea from across the Chinese border. Perhaps a little excursion to Peking could be arranged.

He broke the silent tribal ritual of the adoration of tea.

"The joke has turned sour, gentlemen."

"As the CIA would put it, you can say that again," Cholmondley added.

"When did it start to misfire? What mistakes did we make?" Colvin wanted to know.

"We forgot about the damned 'human element,'" Houndsworth said. "We overlooked two factors."

"Which two?"

"First, we should have known of Pope Clemens's background and ability to handle electrical appliances. As I said before, we relied too much on the detailed Korean report. But the report was of the previous Pope."

"And number two?"

"This is really the worst psychological mistake we have ever made. We know how every man changes when he is thrown into a higher position. The higher the position, the more he changes, or more of his hidden qualities come to the foreground. Remember Truman the haberdasher who became a forceful decision-making President?"

"And you think that playing 'Pope' turned Monticelli into the real thing?"

"I am not saying that, but it's possible that the power and pomp of office turned his head. From an apparatchik, a Numero Due of the Italian Communist

party, he became the Numero Uno of the Christian
world. No wonder he lost his head and had the ver-
tigo. I think he still is trying to steady himself and
may get back into shape."

"What shape?" Cholmondley asked.

"Well, shall we say, our shape?"

"I'm not so optimistic. The signs point to his having
turned, and if so, he won't turn back. He will go down
in our books as the Koestler of the Popes."

"Koestler, the writer . . ." Houndsworth said.
"Haven't heard that name for years. I vaguely remember one of his books about the Jews not being Jews,
but Kazaks. Quite interesting. Shall we call it a day,
gentlemen?"

LI

Gladys anxiously looked at the face she knew so well and loved so much. The President looked tired this morning. The lines on his pale face seemed deeper. He did not speak during breakfast—he only stared at the memo pad in front of him.

They breakfasted in an adjoining room to the bedroom in the embassy in Rome—an unusually early breakfast, at least for Gladys. They had arrived the night before, very weary after the blitz visit of London, Bonn, and Paris. They had dined with the ambassador and his wife, and afterward the President disappeared to a conference room with the secretary of state for a "debriefing." The debriefing had not been brief. It was two o'clock in the morning when Donovan sneaked into the bedroom.

"These croissants are delicious," Gladys prattled. "I wonder whether Antoine could learn how to make them." As Donovan did not respond, Gladys repeated, "The croissants, they're delicious." Absentmindedly, Donovan said, "Wish I were back with my corn muffins."

She looked at her husband and asked very quietly, "Is it very bad, darling?"

"Yes, it is. This morning I must make a decision. Sorry, wrong. I did make a decision. Duncan is joining us"—he looked at his watch—"in ten minutes. And after I tell him, I will tell you, too. At least, as much as I can."

"Darling, look, we have gone through so many crises in our lives and came out of them all right. This will pass, too."

"Yes, Gladys, it will pass. But this is a different kind. It is not our own entirely. It involves a few hundred million people."

There was a knock on the door. The clerk of the embassy announced the secretary of state. Gladys took a last sip of her coffee. "I will take my bath now," she said, and went into the bedroom.

Donovan looked at the pad in front of him with the notes he had made during his sleepless night. In the conference room the secretary of state had handed him the news—the preelection predictions in Lisbon, the latest move of the Soviet fleet under Admiral Roko-sowski in the direction of Cape Town, the return of Pope Clemens to the Vatican after the abortive assassination attempt. A pattern seemed to connect all this news, and it was not a pleasant one.

Stuck into the memo pad was Kenyere's letter. Donovan started to reread it, although by now he knew every word by heart. And *heart* was the operative word: the letter had to be read with one's heart, not one's head. The letter was even more touching with a jolting impact now that he knew from the CIA that Kenyere had been assassinated.

Duncan Mulford entered. He was freshly shaved and impeccable in his striped double-breasted suit. How does he manage to be so freshly laundered, brisk, and elegant at this early hour, Donovan wondered.

"Good morning, Mr. President. Did you sleep well?"

"I did not sleep at all. Cup of coffee?"

"Gladly, Sir."

While pouring the coffee, Donovan said in his most

presidental voice, "Duncan, I've made my decision. It is the one you expected. I have had all this testing, and now I will do some of my own. I am sending the Seventh Fleet into the harbor of Cape Town."

The secretary of state took the cup from the President and said, "Thank you." It was not clear whether he was thanking him for the coffee or the announcement. After taking a sip he put the cup down. "I did hope, Sir, that you would make this decision. I take it that we start our moves on Operation Villa d'Este?"

"Operation Villa d'Este—a silly code on a very major operation. I think it came from Michael Burren. He has objections against telltale code words. He thinks it hurt our chances in the Second World War to call the Normandy invasion 'Operation Overlord.' Well, General Holt likes the name, and from now on he will be in charge. With you and with the secretary of defense."

"Yes, Sir. Let us synchronize our timetable." He opened his briefcase and took out a yellow legal pad filled with notes, written in a language that only he understood.

"Today, reception at the Quirinal. In the afternoon, excursion to Salerno and the American war graves. Tonight, dinner at the prime minister's house. Tomorrow, a short visit to the senate. Cultural exchange lunch at the Villa Medici as guests of the French ambassador. In the afternoon you may wish to visit some not-so-recent Roman ruins. In the evening, dinner at the embassy here with all the Italian big brass. The next day is Easter Sunday. You will be listening to the 'Pope's' Easter sermon here on television with the ambassador. After the sermon two Cadillac limousines will drive you, your wife, and your daughter to Lake Como."

"Did you find someone who resembles me?"

"Not necessary. The limousines have the un–see-through windows."

"Fine. Michael will escort me and my family to the Villa d'Este. And I will fly with you directly to Washington."

"Well, not directly. Holt suggested that we use a low-profile, battered Seven-twenty-seven to fly us from here to our own airbase in Verona, and we board the new supersonic to the States."

"And all is prepared for the Security Council meeting and the yellow alert?"

"Yes, Patrick." He looked at his watch. "Matter of fact, it is time for us to call Washington. Let's go downstairs to the Communications Room."

On their way down, the secretary of state said, "I hope that our security is watertight. In this operation secrecy and surprise are the decisive factors. Did you tell Gladys of our scheme?"

"Not yet. I intend to, but only the nonclassified part of it."

"And Phyllis?"

"Of course not. She gets the 'official' news tomorrow morning in time for her tennis game."

"How do we know that the bug has been picked up?"

"Colonel Romanelli is taking care of it. He's very reliable."

"Yes, it seems he is. If he weren't, we would be minus Pope Clemens today."

The Marine guard opened the heavy steel door of the Communications Room for them, and they went inside.

Gladys and Phyllis descended the Spanish steps and turned into the Via Condotti. They disliked being the center of attention, but there was no avoiding the secret service, the *carabinieri*, and the photographers surrounding them. Quiet window-shopping was out of the question. They entered Bulgari to admire the fabulous jewelry and the equally extravagant prices, and here Gladys managed to confide her worries to Phyllis.

"Your father hasn't slept at all, and he looks so drawn."

"What worries him so?" Phyllis wanted to know (and so did Castor and the Kremlin, listening later to the bug).

"I think pressure is being brought on him to make a decision."

"What kind of a decision?"

"I don't really know."

"Have you any suspicions?"

Gladys shook her head. "All I know is that he wants to be back with his corn muffins."

"Corn muffins . . . You know, in his heart he's still a country yokel."

Two KGB agents shook their heads and tried to decode *corn muffins* just in case they were missing something important.

LII

This was a moment of lovely relaxation. They had made love at the hospitable palazzo of the princess in the afternoon, and now they could quietly converse. Michael leaned back in the soft armchair and stuffed his pipe. He looked up surprised as he heard Phyllis say, "Mingle. I want to mingle."

"Mingle? Is this something new I should know about? Mingle with what?"

"People. Real people."

"Oh, come on. You want to leave your ivory tower, put on your Harun-al-Rashid dress, and walk in the suqs."

"Love, you are ingenuous. You are paid for using your imagination. I am tired of princesses, secretaries of state, and Popes. I want to sit next to you in a dirty little café and hold hands and see some real people. Invent something."

Michael thought for a moment. "Did you bring that gray loden coat with you?"

"I wouldn't travel without it."

"Put it on and meet me in ten minutes at the garden entrance."

After Phyllis left, Michael picked up the house telephone and called Mario, the head butler of the embassy. "Please move the black Fiat to the garden entrance and leave the keys in it," he said.

He opened the door for Phyllis, started the car, turned to his right, and drove the car at sixty miles an hour out through the garden into the Via Appia Antica. They reached the maelstrom of oil-burning ecology destroyers on the Via Veneto in minutes. Michael turned right in front of the Hotel Excelsior, heading for the service entrance. He jumped out of the car and helped Phyllis out. Waving a ten-dollar bill in the face of one of the doormen (nobody knew the exact value of the new Communist-Christian Democrat devalued lira), he asked him to park the car. The ten-dollar bill did the trick.

Through the service entrance they walked through the labyrinth of dirty corridors to the main hall. Michael noted that not much had changed in the last ten years: the crystal chandeliers were lit, with every second bulb missing, the deep imitation Tebris rugs were not too well vacuumed. The low tables were the same, only the chairs and sofas were now in the style of the new Finnish-Japanese chic. Among the guests there were less Arabs and Japanese and slightly more Spanish and Scandinavians. The number of German-speaking tourists seemed the same as in the seventies.

They were lucky. None of the *paparazzi* had caught up with them, and on the terrace of the café a stout Austrian couple had just paid for their iced coffee and whipped cream and had vacated the table in the second row.

And they were even luckier. A high-bosomed young blond attracted all the flashing bulbs. She was the new sex symbol, a Swedish star, the heir to the throne of another Scandinavian boob-owner of the sixties and seventies.

Michael, careful of their low profile, ordered two Americanos, as Italians from the provinces would. They held hands under the table while observing the show of pre-spring movement and excitement on the street. The café was as crowded as the sidewalks. The road was filled to overflowing with the new stream-lined and middle-sized cars. The minuscule Minis of the seventies were gone. Honking was against the law, but when had the Roman "plebs" ever observed the law? The *paparazzi*, a flock of birds of prey, fluc-tuated up and down the street, across the Via Veneto and back, without apparent reason. The smell of *pri-mavera* was in the air, a smell difficult to break down into its chemical components—gasoline, newsprint, heady female perfume, the Aqua di Selva eau de co-logne used extravagantly by most Italian males, even the odor of spring flowers from the baskets of the ven-dors of Parma violets and large pink carnations. Phyl-lis looked at the trees lining the street and noted with joy the appearance of small buds—the end of winter, the end of early darkness.

He was startled when Phyllis sat up and got out of her chair. She was staring at something across the street. She took her glasses off and said in an alarmed voice, "No. Not again . . ."

Michael asked, "What is it, darling?"

Phyllis pointed with an outstretched arm to a tall man across the street. In a shaky voice she said, "There. He just crossed the street. The Englishman who broke my glasses . . . the same one I saw at the bishop's residence in Washington."

Michael never heard the end of the sentence. When she said "Englishman," he jumped up and threw him-self into the whirlpool of traffic. The God of drunk-ards and idiots watched over him as he twisted his body in a slalom and gymkhana and reached the side-walk on the other side. He was now about fifty feet behind the "Englishman" who had been stopped for a moment by one of the street photographers. He had taken a candid shot of him and was handing him a yellow card, which the man promptly threw down on the sidewalk.

Shoving and elbowing his way, Michael was getting closer when he saw the man turn right at the intersection. He was about to catch up with him but he did not count on the ubiquitous *paparazzi* who forcibly stopped him for a picture. He shoved the men aside brutally and started running, but he could not penetrate the crowd.

As fast as he could, he reached the next intersection. The man had vanished. He rounded the corner and alternately cursed his bad luck and prayed to find the photographer who had taken the "Englishman's" picture. He had a good memory for faces, and this time luck was with him: the man with the camera was still there.

Michael grabbed his arm. "You just took the picture of a man. I want to buy the negative."

"I don't know which man, sir," the man said. "I have taken six shots."

"I'll buy all six. The whole roll. How much?"

The photographer made a quick calculation. This man was an Americano who wanted the film badly. "Twenty-five dollars," he said, overcharging 200 percent.

Michael reached for his money clip. "Here." He counted out three ten-dollar bills.

Helplessly, the Italian said, "Sorry, sir, not have change."

"Never mind," Michael said. "The roll, please."

Clutching the roll in his hand he snaked back through the flood of cars to Phyllis.

"Did you get him?" she asked with understandable excitement.

"Lost him. But I have his photograph on this roll. Please wait here. I have to make a phone call."

He rushed into the hall to the pay phone booth. Another prayer to the God of Italian telephones. This one cooperated. He dialed 333222 and asked for Colonel Romanelli. He gave his name as "Michael."

The female voice said, "Colonel Romanelli is not present. Is it urgent?"

"Very, very urgent."

"I'll call you back in a minute. Where are you calling from?"

"A phone booth at the Donnay."

"Please read the number. It is on the receiver."

"784477. I won't leave the booth until you call back."

He fumbled with his pipe. A pipe would soothe his nerves. Even before he could light it, the phone rang. It was Romanelli.

"Michael?"

"Yes. Where are you?"

"At the Contessa's. If it's urgent, come right over. Do you have transportation?"

"I have my car. Phyllis is with me, and we will need her, too."

"Bring her along."

The Contessa was very pleased to meet the American President's daughter. She offered refreshments but was turned down by Romanelli, who sensed the urgency in Michael's comportment.

They went into the library, where Michael explained to Romanelli the reason of his emergency visit.

"We'll develop the film right away and show the picture to Phyllis. If it is the man, the picture must be distributed instantly by your men to all the hotels, restaurants, bars, the airport, and the station. Immediately."

Romanelli's smile was understandably indulgent. "Michael, my friend, the word *immediate* in Italian does not have exactly the same meaning as in English. But I will prove to you that sometimes we can be fast. After all, the speediest race drivers and skiers are Italian." He stopped and picked up the film.

"I have to make a few calls. If Mrs. . . ." He groped for the name, but Michael had no time for civilities.

"Phyllis," he said.

"Yes. If Madame Phyllis identifies the man, we will put all in motion. I will need the help not only of our police but of some student organizations. By tomorrow morning we can distribute five thousand copies in Rome. Don't count on results before the afternoon, though. I'll have the film picked up here. Can you and Madame Phyllis have drinks now while we are waiting?"

They went back to the salon. The film was picked up by a uniformed motorcycle cop and the copy brought back in less than an hour. Phyllis made a positive identification.

Romanelli got up. "Sorry, but I have to leave you. The mechanism has to be put into operation right away."

Michael drove Phyllis back to the Palazzo Buchhi, where she had exactly ten minutes to dress for the State dinner. "See you later, my spy hero," she said, and went inside.

LIII

"I came to seek parental guidance," Phyllis said while munching on a croissant.

She paid a surprise visit to her parents in the embassy while they breakfasted. She was on her way to the club and looked radiant and happy.

"Parental guidance," Donovan repeated. "Sounds ominous."

"No, not yet. It is more a question of etiquette. The Baraggis and the Ghibertis are giving a joint party, a big, masked-ball thing. They say that it will be an updated *Dolce Vita* kind of shindig."

"Sounds like an orgy," Gladys said.

"That's what Michael says. He does not want me to go. Now, I am, of course, very curious and I say to myself, When will I have the occasion to see something like this? So I would like to go, but Michael is dead against it. He constantly harps on that 'President's daughter' bit."

Donovan put his cup down and looked at her. "Daughter," he said, "you bring up Michael's name constantly and speak of his advice. In what capacity does he advise you? As your security guardian?"

Phyllis laughed, her musical, staccato, irrestistible laugh. "Well, not exactly. As you must know by now, he is much more than my guardian."

"Well, does he intend to make an honest woman out of you?" Gladys asked.

"The question is whether I want to make an honest man out of him. With his present dishonest spy occupation."

"Has he asked you to marry him?"

"Daily. And the answer is yes. We would like to get married as soon as we get back to the States."

Gladys opened her arms, and Phyllis embraced her. Donovan saw with some surprise that the two ladies were on the verge of tears. Tears of happiness, no doubt.

Phyllis took her glasses off when she kissed him, and Donovan suddenly said to himself, This is just as good a moment as any.

"Phyllis." He started the game of deception and disinformation. "We have a surprise for you. A pleasant surprise."

"What is it, Daddy?"

"First, swear that you will keep this a secret. A complete secret."

"I swear. Cross my heart."

"Okay. In the afternoon of this coming Sunday we will all travel in private cars to the Villa d'Este."

"On Lake Como?"

"Yes. The ambassador has made the necessary arrangements. Now nobody but the ambassador and the secretary of state will know of this. We will stay in the Villa d'Este for four days, as incognito as possible."

"That's marvelous, Daddy. What about Michael?"

"I want you to invite him. You will go up in the same car with him. I'm going to enjoy the spring sun and smell the azaleas or rhododendron or whatever you smell at Easter on Lake Como. So, my little girl, come have a drink with us around six before we go to that State dinner."

"Will do."

She turned to go, when Donovan said, "Wait a minute. Parental guidance, remember?"

"Oh yes. What's the verdict?"

"Please don't go to that party. Promise?"

"I promise."

"He is late," Colvin said. "He told us it was urgent—to be here not later than eight thirty."

"What can the crisis be? Castor?" Cholmondley asked.

Colvin shrugged, "Who knows?"

The door opened and a very busy, very energetic Houndsworth entered carrying a thickly stuffed attaché case. He went to the desk with quick steps.

"A good morning to you, boys. I asked you to come in early as I am leaving immediately."

Four eyebrows went up simultaneously. Cholmondley had to ask the obvious. "Leaving? Where to?"

"Maximus wants me in Rome. This business with the Pope is of top priority and must be finished. And President Donovan's presence might open certain possibilities. So, I am under orders and my flight leaves"—he looked at his watch—"in one hour and twenty-five minutes."

Cholmondley said, "This is for the first time in twenty-odd years that one of us will be back in the Occidental fleshpots. How do you feel about it?"

"Elated. Not more. My immediate reaction was that getting out of this freezing weather will do me no harm."

"Where will you stay?" Colvin asked.

"The embassy, a diplomatic passport, a Polish one, an official car right at the exit of the plane. No danger of any contact with my old friend, Romanelli."

"And we?" Cholmondley asked. "We just sit tight and wait?"

"Yes. I will be in touch every four hours. Information from the South African desk and the South and Central American ones will come in to you and you will relay them to me. What can I bring you from Rome?"

"I could use some grappa," Colvin said. Cholmondley was undecided.

"Well—some of that thick Italian tomato paste. It's the best for spaghetti." He hesitated for a moment. "Alan, do me a favor. Have your liver checked there. I know we have wonderful doctors here, but I read about new medicines in the West that we might not have. Please do it."

Houndsworth looked at his friend. How much does he know? Nice of him, anyway. "I will have a checkup there. Promise."

LIV

It was past eleven at night when Castor finished listening to the latest tape coming from the bug in Phyllis's glasses.

'A sweet family scene,' he thought. 'Most touching.'

Houndsworth will be pleased with the big news. Things were going well. While he called he took out his address book to look for the telephone number of that sanitarium, Galenium, in Switzerland.

As he anticipated, Houndsworth was happy with the news—a big load off everybody's shoulders. And as Castor also anticipated, Houndsworth asked, "Did you check this out with the Villa d'Este?"

"I am doing it now. Calling Lebedev at Galenium. It's a half-hour drive from the Villa d'Este. If he can't do it tonight, we will get the info not later than nine tomorrow morning. I will call you back on this first thing."

"Nothing new on Monticelli?"

"No. He said that he is preparing his speech. His sermon, he calls it. I think we should leave him alone for the moment."

"All right. Call me tomorrow."

Lebedev was not too pleased with the call. "I have an important operation tomorrow morning at six. That's why I was asleep when you woke me up.

Schweiker will take care of this. When do you want his report?"

"Tell him to get his ass over to Como at six in the morning and call me at seven."

Schweiker arrived just before seven at the Villa d'Este. The hotel was to reopen for Easter, and the preparations were in full swing. The cars of the employees stood in the round courtyard, witnesses of the difficulties of recruiting personnel nowadays. License plates from Sicily, Switzerland, Novara—even from Spain and Reggio di Calabria.

Schweiker got out of his car and walked into the still half-boarded-up entrance. He crossed the hall and left the building through gigantic French doors.

So far, no trouble: nobody stopped him; everybody was absorbed in his own problems. When he reached the elegant baroque annex he was stopped by two energetic *carabinieri*. "Go back," they shouted.

Schweiker retraced his steps and realized that he would not be able to hear anything by the grapevine before the breakfast breaks. Across the street from the main entrance Schweiker saw a simple cantina and hoped that some thirsty members of the staff would go there for some local *vino*. He was right.

He selected two burly Sicilians and offered them a glass. Very cautiously, off-handedly, he asked why the *carabinieri* had stopped him from going into the annex.

"Wouldn't you like to know?" said the stocky Sicilian. "I would."

"Well, how about another pint of Valpolicella?"

The Sicilian took a good swig of the "red," wiped his mouth with the back of his hand, and looked around with a conspiratorial grin on his face.

"Il Presidente," he whispered. "They say that Il Presidente is coming. With his family."

274 THE JANUS POPE

"What president?" Schweiker inquired.

"I dunno. Some very big presidente. They hired special personnel for him. Mostly Swiss. Food, too. English bacon. Scotch whisky. All very *misterioso. Capisce?*"

"Not quite. Why the big secret?"

"How should I know? They don't tell us. All I know is nobody is supposed to go into that annex. They say they expect Il Presidente and his family Sunday evening."

Schweiker called Castor from the Galenium and gave him his report. Castor got on the scrambler to Houndsworth. "Looks real. My American friends would call it kosher."

Very dryly, Houndsworth said, "I did not know you had any American friends."

"Do we survey the Villa d'Este operation?"

"Only locally. Tell Schweiker that I want to know whether Donovan receives any visitors. Car registration numbers, et cetera."

"Will be done."

LV

The room was small and ascetic. The bed was rather a cot; there was a small washbasin, a wooden table that had seen better days under the Borgias, two high-backed chairs probably used by servants in the days of the Renaissance.

The inconveniences did not bother Clemens. Like a prisoner, he could not leave the room and had to use the chamber pot. This disturbed him less than the inaccessibility to his chapel. Even with the aid of the Franciscan hood to cover his face, he could not risk attending morning prayers.

He rose early, as always, and said his matins in front of the crucifix on the wall. Still weak, he laid down on his bed again. He smiled indulgently when he caught himself thinking of the comfort of the American embassy. What was the semantic difference between antiseptic and clean? This room was antiseptic; the room at the embassy was clean.

His faithful Maestro di Camera served him breakfast in bed. The Pontiff inquired about his back and was glad to hear that the spring weather favored the rheumatism. They heard three knocks on the door and the turning of the key. The Vatican secretary of state, Giovanni Petrarca, entered. He kissed the hand of the Pontiff.

"Did you sleep well, Your Holiness?" he asked.

"I certainly did. The room is very quiet. I even like this hard bed. What are the latest rumors? Do sit down, please, and you, too, Alessandro."

"Well," Petrarca said, "your brother certainly prays very frequently. He spent two hours in the chapel last night, and over an hour this morning. Of course, we do not know what he is praying for. The resurrection of Marx and Lenin?"

The Pontiff looked at the face of the secretary of state. His nose is getting longer, he thought. And the avuncular features show an inclination to intrigue.

"I don't think that his prayers have anything to do with politics."

With a sigh of impatience, Petrarca said, "I know how you feel about this impostor, Your Holiness, and I greatly admire your charity and trust. But, alas, don't you think this experiment is too dangerous to continue with it?"

"I don't think so, Giovanni. Look at the record. He has accomplished in a short time much more than I could have done. The reforms he has made serve the Church well. And, let us face it—he is a much better orator than I am."

The Maestro di Camera tried to interject. "Your Holiness . . ."

Undeterred, the Pontiff continued, "There are moments when I have a tendency to become fustian and bombastic. In the old tradition of papism. He has none of that. His training as a professor at the university serves him well. He is used to teaching; he has the habit of talking to the young. No, I don't see the danger in what you call the experiment and I call my act of faith."

"How and when will all this end?" Petrarca asked.

"It will end tomorrow. I want him to make the Easter sermon, and I will listen to it with you. Romanelli has made all the necessary arrangements. When he appears on the balcony, I will be in the room behind, wearing my papal clothes. If he makes any statement against the Church or against our faith—which I do not think he will—Romanelli will see to it that he has a fainting spell. I hope I will be strong enough then to replace him and continue the sermon."

Almost silently, the secretary of state said, "May God bless you and guide you, Your Holiness."

"Yes, we all need the help of the Almighty. I hope He will not deny me that help."

"Your Holiness," the Maestro di Camera asked, "may I ask—if the impostor's sermon is acceptable and if he does not hurt our Church, what are your intentions with him after that?"

Pope Clemens had a pleasant smile on his face and in his eyes. "I have only one definite plan. And much or all will depend on it. I want a face-to-face conversation with him. I need to find out what *his* intentions are. I am very much looking forward to this talk with my brother."

The secretary of state sighed deeply. "Tomorrow will be a big day. Perhaps a decisive day in the history of the Church."

"Giovanni and Alessandro," the Pope said, "let us pray together for a good day tomorrow."

And the three men started to pray silently.

LVI

Romanelli's task was an easier one than the others. He had set up headquarters in the Vatican on the third floor of the papal residence. He had not removed any furniture of this secretariat, but had installed several telephones, television and radio sets. Through the tall windows he could see the large piazza, as well as the terrace, and the balcony from which the "Pope" was to speak to his flock. He also had a direct line to the American embassy, where Michael had set up his own command post.

The chore of the Maestro di Camera was much more strenuous. He had to prepare the appearance of not one Pope, but two. He began early with the real one. At seven in the morning Clemens was ready. He wore the white and gold over the miter, the white dress with the lace ruffles, the ring and scepter. These had been quickly copied and were false ones.

Monticelli was ready. He felt strangely elated, free from fear, free from the burden of his own illness. This was the big day, the decisive day, and he admitted to himself without the slightest fear, perhaps it was his last day. He did not care. His own person did not matter anymore; what mattered was the fulfillment of the task he had set for himself—his sermon, which would be heard all over the world.

If Monticelli was in a euphoric mood, Pope Clemens was not. And he was frightened. The responsibility was his, no one else's. He did not stop believing for a moment that his act of faith would succeed, but he trembled when he thought of what could happen to his brother. It was too late now to change anything in the plan. But Clemens admitted only to himself that his trust in the Savior for Giulio's protection was strengthened by his full confidence in Colonel Romanelli.

Castor and his henchman, Robles, had none of these problems. They had a contract to fulfill, and they were well prepared. Since eight in the morning, they had sat on the terrace of the rented apartment on Monte Pincio. The large Thermos bottle was filled with strong hot coffee. The telescope was in place and so was the long laser rifle. They had two portable transmitters and a small Japanese television set. Visibility was good, with a clear sky occasionally dotted with fluffy white clouds.

Castor was relieved that this strange adventure was coming to an end. This Vatican business gave him the creeps. He had no feeling or understanding for the blind devotion of the crowd on the square. The business with priests, nuns, churches, holy water, and incense was nauseating—unfathomable, inunderstandable, in these last years of the twentieth century. He wanted to get back to good, solid, realistic acts of terror, blackmail, and political assassination of simple people, not Popes.

Of all the actors in the unfolding drama, Michael was the one with the uneasiest feelings. Romanelli did not want him in the Vatican, and he probably had good reasons. Conscious of the jealousy between secret services, Michael did not dismiss altogether the theory that jealousy was one of Romanelli's motives in keeping him off the premises of the Vatican.

He sat in a room in the embassy, listening to the crackling of the Italian radio and watching the TV set. He had plenty of time to think, and he tried to make sense out of the coming events of this day. History, world history, caught up with him forcefully. History. How did you define it? A panorama of human crimes? Tissues of disconnected accidents? Manifest destiny and predetermination? Was it morally right what they intended to do? Especially what the President was about to do? He quoted Benjamin Franklin to himself, a quotation that must have been older than Franklin; namely, that a bad peace was better than a good war. How true was it?

Dismiss this from your mind. Don't think of history. Not even of history repeating itself. Only historians did so. Think of Phyllis and your own future. Get out of politics and get back to your desk and your best-selling spy books.

At eleven thirty the Maestro di Camera knocked on the door of the papal bedroom. "It is time," he said to Monticelli. He was unable to add the title *Your Holiness*.

Monticelli slowly followed the majordomo to the balcony. They were joined by the secretary of state.

The "Pope" stepped out on the narrow terrace and looked down at the vast mass of people packed tightly on the square. The stage was set for the last act.

LVII

The crowd had come from all corners of the world; tall Scandinavians, swarthy Croats, neat, stolid Germans, and of course, the gay and warm-blooded Mediterranean Italians—all celebrating the resurrection of the Savior and the resurrection of the trees, the flowers, the dormant soil.

He could not and would not try to see any individual faces. Monticelli just stood there in the posture of blessing the masses on this square, blessing all the faithful of the world.

The small microphone was in front of him. He heard some distant church bells in the silence that had befallen the crowd on his appearance.

He did not have to clear his throat. He was ready. Slowly, with the power and authority of his lofty position as the servant and representative of God and His Son, he started his sermon.

God Almighty, send us the gift of spring on this day of the Savior's resurrection. A gift to enjoy and to cherish and not to despoil by strife and aggression. The race to which we all belong, the human race, often tends to destroy not only other humans, but nature itself. We waste land, we kill the forests, we make the air impure. We must remind ourselves in the strongest terms that unless we will do everything to preserve our heritage of nature, its flowers, its animals, its green trees, we will have no place in which to live, no place to savor. We pay lip service to the safeguarding of our ecology, but do little about it. Perhaps because our house is divided into two parts—one for the poor and one for the rich. It has been like that since time immemorial, but these are new, exciting, and promising times, and it is the moment for change.

When I studied American history, I found that one of their great Presidents, Thomas Jefferson, informed his parliament of conditions he had found in Europe in the eighteenth century. This is what Thomas Jefferson said: 'Under pretense of governing, they have divided their nations in two classes, wolves and sheep.' We haven't changed. We have to change. The world cannot go on being divided into classes of wolves and sheep. It is the duty of the Church . . ."

In the big reception room behind the balcony Pope Clemens listened with his friends, the majordomo and the secretary of state. So did Colonel Romanelli.

The three men watched Pope Clemens anxiously for a trace of reaction. To their surprise, what they saw was unexpected. The Pontiff, a warm smile on his face, was nodding his consent. He said, "Good. He puts it succinctly. He is right."

Romanelli did not understand. If the impostor continues in this leftist vein, will he be asked to intervene or just sit back and listen to the propaganda? Has Pope Clemens lost the sense of reality? Did the Communists get to him, and has he "turned"? At this moment he could not do anything but listen and wait.

If Romanelli and the two Vatican friends of the

Pope were surprised, so was Robles. He looked at Castor, who had his spyglasses focused on the terrace, and said, "Well, he still seems to be on our side. Shall we wrap up the laser?"

"He is not finished yet," Castor said. "Give me a cigarette."

Robles handed him a pack and a box of matches. They listened again to Monticelli's accurate inventory of the state of the world, the unrest and injustices in Brazil, in Poland, and in South Africa. Interesting, but predictable. The crowd was clearly interested but perhaps somewhat puzzled at the unorthodox, unconventional sermon.

When the sudden turn came, neither Pope Clemens nor Castor were prepared for it. Surprised, the mass tried to focus their eyes more clearly on the "Pope." They craned their necks, they turned, cupped their ears to hear better.

The voice that came out of the loudspeaker was different, sharper, with a steely edge to it. Despite the filtering effect of the microphones and loudspeakers, the penetrating, clarion call of the voice came through. This is what the "Pope" said:

> How can we unify the world in the struggle for peace and equality when there is the devil, represented by a group of evil men who sit in their tower in the Kremlin over a witches' brew of intrigue and terror? A group that governs over two hundred and fifty million souls who are taught to deny the existence of God? A group that does not shy from oppression and political assassination whenever it suits its goals? They are reaching out far, through the whole world, like a giant octopus with endless tentacles, even to the Holy Fortress of the Vatican. My children, they have to be

brought back into the world of peace and faith
and . . .

Pope Clemens looked at Romanelli and his two
friends, and with all humility, he could not wipe off
his "I was right" smile.

Robles's reaction was different. Through his radio
earphones, he was listening to the English translation
of the sermon. He took them off and said to Castor,
who seemed puzzled and engrossed, "What are we
waiting for?"

Castor shook off his thoughts. In a crisp commander's voice, he said, "Nothing. Pull the trigger."

Robles looked at the balcony and the hair-thin cross
in the laser telescope. When the center of the cross
rested on the "Pope's" chest, he very gently pulled the
trigger.

Castor had his spyglasses focused on Monticelli and
saw him fall backward. In his fall, he was caught by
the secretary of state. A loud cry came from the masses
on the square, while the secretary of state, aided by
two bishops, carried the "Pope" inside.

Monticelli's body was laid down on the carpet.
Blood started oozing on the white cassock on Monticelli's chest. Romanelli snapped his fingers and said to
his aide, "A doctor, quick." Shaken and trembling,
Pope Clemens knelt down and touched Monticelli's
face.

"My brother . . ." Romanelli grabbed him up by
his right arm and said, "Sorry, Holy Father, but you
must go to the balcony and finish the sermon."

The secretary of state did not believe his ears. "Impossible. I won't let him. They will shoot him, too."

Romanelli shook his head. "They won't. They
wanted Monticelli and they got him."

The secretary of state objected. "You cannot know whether they want to assassinate the Pope, too."

Pope Clemens stood up and turned toward the balcony. Very firmly, he said, "I am going to finish my brother's sermon. Pray for me."

The bishop of Parma had just entered the room from the balcony where he had announced that the Pope was recovering from a light fainting spell.

Pope Clemens stepped out and waited until the mass quieted down from a frantic ovation. He held the microphone and said, "My children, we shall continue our fight for a better, more just, and more peaceful world. God bless you . . ."

When Clemens entered the room he saw Romanelli and another man kneeling next to Monticelli. The man held a stethoscope in his hand. Romanelli stood up and said to the Pope, "He is dying. A shot to the heart."

Clemens knelt down and took Monticelli's body in his arms. He repeated the words, "My brother . . ."

Slowly, Monticelli opened his eyes. His trembling lips tried to say something. No sound came from his mouth. Clemens put his ears close to his brother's lips and heard or thought he heard the word "*Absolution* . . ." Clemens made the sign of the Cross over his brother's chest. "*Ego ti absolvo . . .*" He tried with all his might not to cry, but could not stop the flow of tears.

Romanelli rushed back to his command post. His orders were crisp and clear. Major Pedrazzi, in charge of the commandos, was to search every building from where the shot might have been fired. With strong binoculars he scanned the rooftops, starting close to the Castel San Angelo and up toward Monte Pincio. He was suddenly interrupted by an urgent call. He picked up the receiver. It was the prefect of police. He said, "We located the man on the photo. His name is James Bradford, and he is staying at the Hotel Eden. He is out now. He left the hotel at seven thirty A.M., but his luggage and belongings are still there. What are your instructions? Do we send our men in?"

"Under no conditions. This will be a CIA operation. Keep the hotel under surveillance, under complete secrecy. Your men must be invisible." He dialed the number of the American embassy.

Michael had been watching the events on his television set. He could not make out what had happened. He was as puzzled by the sermon of the false Pope as Romanelli was. When he saw him fall, he thought that the emotion was too strong for Monticelli and that he had fainted. He was relieved when, after a few minutes, the sermon continued.

The red light flickered on the telephone. It was Romanelli. "The man on the *paparazzi* photo is at the Hotel Eden. He is out now. His name is James Bradford. Over to you. Your baby. Just get the bastard."

"Thanks. I will. What goes on in the Vatican?"

"They shot Monticelli. He is dying or dead. I am chasing the killer. Call me later."

So they got Monticelli. But how? No time to think about it now.

He said to Sullivan, his assistant, "Jim, get your peashooter. Pronto. We're on our way to the Hotel Eden. I need five more men."

With efficient haste, Robles started to disassemble the laser rifle and put it in its case. Castor leaned back in his chair and lighted a Havana cigar. "What's the hurry?" he asked.

"Well, I just thought that the sooner we get the hell out of here and out of Rome, the better."

As Castor was not in a hurry, Robles picked up the

telescope and focused it on the Vatican. Suddenly he exclaimed, "Goddamn it! He is back." He grabbed the case and started to assemble the laser rifle again.

"Who is back? What the hell are you talking about?"

Robles handed him the telescope. "The Pope. He is back on the balcony. I missed him."

Castor did not bother to look. "Relax," he said. "That's the real Pope. He's replacing Monticelli. You hit him, all right."

"The real Pope? Clemens?"

"Yes. So put the cannon back in its case. Him, we don't want. Okay, let's get back to the hotel. I have to report to the boss."

A few minutes later they drove back to the hotel. Being pros, they could not resist the routine of cleaning up, wiping off fingerprint marks, washing glasses. The streets seemed empty, with most of the population on the square of the Vatican. They heard police sirens and saw an Alfa racing at a dangerous speed and whining noise up the Monte Pincio. Both Castor and Robles had their eyes glued to their rear mirror. Nobody shadowed them.

Robles locked the car in the garage and they walked up the stairs into the lobby, which was as empty as the streets. Only in the far corner a pair of long legs appeared from an armchair under the umbrella of the *Corriere della Sera*, held correctly, not upside down.

Up in Room 323 Castor pointed. "There is vodka in the icebox." He dialed a number and said, "All done."

"Fine," Houndsworth said. "Let's not waste time. The boys I sent you are already at the airport in a special room. You will be picked up in a diplomatic car and board the Tupulov to Moscow. I will be on it, too. How long till you pack and get out?"

"Ten, fifteen minutes. All right?"

"Yes. See you at the airport."

Michael saw the two men come in to the entrance hall of the hotel and recognized Castor from the photograph. He vaguely remembered having seen the face before, but his computer was not yet functioning.

Sullivan, who was standing behind a column, joined him. He signaled the two men at the revolving door to follow them. The garage exit and the delivery door were covered by Romanelli's men.

They avoided the noisy elevator and walked up on the soft carpet to the third floor. They listened to possible noises coming from Room 323, but all was silence. Slowly, Sullivan tried to turn the doorknob. It yielded. The door was open. Michael exploded into the room, followed by Sullivan. What they saw were two men drinking vodka out of mouthwash glasses.

Both Michael and Sullivan had their handguns ready. Michael's Smith & Wesson .38 was cocked, the safe on Sullivan's old reliable Colt .45 automatic was off. When he saw Robles reach for his breast pocket, he fired.

Sullivan was fast, but not fast enough. He never heard the hissing noise coming from the strange weapon held by Robles. Nor did Robles possibly hear the ear-splitting report of the Colt as the heavy copper-head bullet pierced his heart.

Both Sullivan and Robles fell to the floor. Why don't I shoot that reptile? Michael thought, as he saw Castor slowly raise his hands above his head.

"I am unarmed," he said, and incredibly and unpredictably, he smiled.

To the two men who burst into the room, Michael said, "Handcuff this man. And tell John to call an ambulance."

He knelt down to Sullivan's body and said, "Jim!"

Sullivan did not answer, but Castor did. He said casually, "Cyanide."

In the car that took them to Romanelli's headquarters, Castor made polite and urbane conversaticn. "We met before," he said. "On the airplane coming here from Washington. I did not know you then."

"Nor did I know you, unfortunately," Michael said.

"But I do know a lot about your habits. I found your conversation with Phyllis in bed quite amusing."

This was the moment when a lack of training showed in Michael's behavior. He hit a helpless, handcuffed man straight in the face and added, "You bastard!"

Castor made a feeble attempt to wipe the blood off his mouth with his handcuffed hands. He did not seem to be hurt or offended.

"By Jove," he said. "You are an amateur. No professional CIA man would have the nerve to hit a handcuffed man. Where did they dig you up?"

"Never mind. Let's talk about you. You seem very pleased with yourself and with what you have accomplished in the past. Would you like to know what's in your future?"

A handcuffed shrug and Castor said, "You take me to Colonel Romanelli. In ten days I will be flown out, by courtesy of your air force, to Langley Field via Washington, nonstop."

"Yes, the boys in Langley are eager to have a talk, a two-way talk, with you."

"I know. But their methods, both physical and chemical, are still infantile. And they know more or less all. From me they won't learn anything new. They will treat me fairly until my departure."

"Your what?"

"My departure. You know, back to Russia."

"How? You intend to escape?"

"No. That's not realistic. It's romantic. No. I will be flown to West Berlin and exchanged against a distinguished American or British spy on that famous bridge linking East and West Berlin."

"Anybody in mind?"

"No. Not yet. But in time there will be."

After delivering Castor to Romanelli, Michael's first thought was of a hot shower. He wanted to rid himself of all traces of contact with a venomous snake.

LVIII

Donovan did not feel at ease with himself about his part in the planned cloak-and-dagger operation. He considered it a childish masquerade and resented the playacting, not because it was below his dignity, but he disliked dressing up like a character actor and pretending to be someone else.

He left the embassy in the company of Holt. Both men were dressed in workmen's white overalls, and Donovan wore a visored cap pulled down low on his forehead. They left by the servants' entrance in a small Fiat van with the sign of the PASTICCERIA ROSA-TELLI, which furnished the embassy five times a week with the popular croissants and creampuffs. The windowless inside of the van smelled appetizingly of bakery goods.

They drove straight to the airport and on to the apron where the U.S. Air Force DC-474 awaited them—a troop transit of vintage make, which flew them swiftly to the Verona-Vicenza base.

The Bl jet, a once-controversial object of many congressional debates and now obsolescent, was ready with its four jet engines warming up.

Donovan put on his seat belt and leaned back in the comfortable chair. As always, when taking off, he automatically extended his right hand to hold Gladys's left. But there was no Gladys. She was on her way, with Phyllis and Michael, to the Villa d'Este. God, am I going to miss her in Washington tomorrow, Donovan thought. It could not be helped. Michael's idea of sub-terfuge and misinformation was a good one. Total sur-prise was the crux of total success.

After the shrimp cocktail and a split bottle of Moet & Chandon, Donovan felt better. When General Holt asked him, "Are you all right, sir?" he could truthfully answer, "Yes. I feel well and fit."

"I am very happy with your decision, Sir, and I'm relieved that we will be on terra firma, as it were, back home."

"So am I, so am I, Rodney. I trust that all is set for the meeting? All the generals, the secretary of defense, Admiral Fletcher?"

"All, Sir. And all meticulously briefed. And all on your side, one hundred percent."

"Your own CIA Gallup poll?"

"Yes, Mr. President. That's what I am paid for."

"Let's have another split of that French cham-pagne," Donovan said.

Holt guessed that the President was in a talkative mood. "May I ask you something personal, Mr. Presi-dent?" he asked.

"Go ahead, Rodney."

"What, ultimately, was the most important factor in your decision, Mr. President?"

"A good question. Let me think for a moment." He sat in silence.

"The assassination of the false Pope?" Holt asked, trying to help.

"No, Rodney. I try to keep personal emotions out of my decisions. Still, the killing of Monticelli had some-thing to do with it. Not the killing itself . . ." He stopped when he saw Holt's puzzled face.

"Let me explain. Political assassination, a contemptible extension of politics, is not restricted to one side. You, as the head of the CIA, don't need to be reminded of our own impure past. Remember Allende and Lumumba and the attempt on Castro?"

"Sir, that was two decades ago."

"Yes, but we have long memories. Both parties seem more civilized now, until these recent killings came up. And I confess that the slaughter of Kenyere shook me. Still, as I repeat, it was not the series of assassinations. I looked at the global picture, the unsettled situation in Spain, in the Middle East, the new nuclear-control agreement that we do not reach. I added it all up, and now I come to my main motive for my decision."

Eagerly, Holt asked, "Yes, Mr. President?"

"Well, damn it, it was this business with the Vatican. If the Kremlin could be so undisciplined, so irresponsible as to tolerate a scheme devised by some hotheads of the KGB to actually kidnap the Pope and replace him with a Communist, they must be told, they must be taught that such reckless, gangster adventures cannot be tolerated today. It was reckless and naïve of Khrushchev to assume that we would quietly allow Soviet atom bases in Cuba, and Kennedy taught him a valid lesson. I intend to teach them the same lesson in South Africa." He stopped for a moment and added, "Yes, that dirty Vatican caper played a large part in my decision."

"Thank you for telling me, Mr. President."

The head steward had approached and was waiting to get their attention.

"Excuse me, Mr. President. Would you prefer steaks or lobster for your dinner?"

"Decisions, decisions," Donovan said. "How about you, Rodney? We are both invited by the American taxpayer. You make the decision."

Holt nodded. "Steaks for both of us," he said to the steward.

"How would you like yours, Mr. President?"

"Rare. I made a decision. Okay, Rodney?"

"Fine, Mr. President."

When the steward did not move, Donovan asked, "Anything else?"

"Yes, Sir. About the movie."

"Oh, we have films, too?"

"Yes, Mr. President. With the compliments of Mr. Michael Burren, a film was delivered to us with a note from him."

Donovan read out loud from a folded piece of paper that was handed to him. It said, "Mr. President, this might distract you. It is a spy film based on my last book, *Levantine Roulette*. Respectfully, Michael Burren."

"Oh, I know the book," Donovan said. "By all means, let's see it after dinner."

LIX

It was just past eight in the evening when the convoy stopped in front of a small, clean, fairly new hotel on the perimeter of the city of Parma. The name of the hotel, Maria Luigia, Italian for "Maria Louise," was indicative of the atmosphere of the city, very Franco-phile, very Stendhalian.

Their incognito was successful: there were no *paparazzi* on the horizon. Still, Michael thought it wiser to eat in the salon of their hotel apartment. He ordered everything that Parma was famous for—the rosy Parma ham, linguini with fresh Parmesan cheese, and he even managed to purchase two large bouquets of Parma violets. The head waiter recommended the sparkling version of the local red Lambrusco, which was cold and delicious.

Neither their mood nor their conversation was sparkling; the coming events of the next forty-eight hours weighed heavily on them. Gladys worried about Patrick and how he was managing in Washington without her.

Through the connecting door, Phyllis went to Michael's room to spend the night. Her father's abrupt change of plans had upset her terribly, and Michael ached to confide in her and ease her mind. Michael could still not confess how Phyllis's eyeglasses were being used. This bothered him. Perhaps tómorrow he would be rid of the secret.

They left fairly early in the morning and arrived at the Villa d'Este in Como before lunch. The impressively large rooms all looked out on the lake through tall, heavily curtained French windows. The parquet floors, spotlessly clean, had an inlaid geometric design that showed the wear and tear of many feet. The pastoral paintings on the walls, the Venetian chandeliers, the Mediterranean-green–painted doors and cabinets all contributed to the pure baroque ambiance.

Michael parted the curtains, took Phyllis by the arm, and led her out on the terrace. Under the pale-blue sky, all was green—the lake, the surrounding evergreens and deciduous trees. Here, the promise of *primavera*, the long awaited spring that they had felt hopefully in Rome became a reality. This was spring in its most riotous form—cascades of rhododendron, azaleas, magnolia trees, camellias—all in full bloom.

Like two children on the threshold of Paradise, Phyllis and Michael inhaled the view and the heady scent of the flowers.

"Let's not think of tomorrow," Phyllis said. "Can you force yourself to blot out the CIA just for this one night?"

"I will and I can," Michael assured her.

"Where is that noise coming from?" Phyllis asked. There was the sound of hammering from one of the buildings.

"I'll have a look." Michael crossed a large reception room and arrived at either a salon or dining room. Here, all feeling of the decorative baroque was gone. The room was bare except for small tables and chairs to accommodate a large television set in the middle of the room.

"Mr. Burren, sir?" asked the tall, black technical sergeant.

"Yes, Sergeant Nichols?"

"We are setting up this television operation for you. It will be ready in an hour. You won't be needing it until early tomorrow morning." He looked at his watch. "It is noon in New York now."

"Will I be able to handle this monster myself?" Michael asked, pointing at the oversized television set.

"Very easy, sir. Let me show you." They both approached the set. "This is the on-and-off button. Only five channels will be visible here," the sergeant explained. "Four American, and the fifth, the BBC in London. The right screw is for sound, the left for the image. Okay?"

"Fine. Well, we will be through in an hour. If you need me, just press this buzzer, sir."

Michael explained to Phyllis what the noise was about.

"Is it that important for us to have television?" Phyllis asked.

"Yes. The President is expected to make a speech on television tomorrow."

"From Rome?"

"Yes. About the results of his trip to Europe," Michael said, unhappy about being compelled to lie to her. The bug was still in her glasses, and although Castor could not monitor, there must be others. It will all end tomorrow when we destroy the devil's device and replace her glasses. Just one more day.

He remembered his promise to Phyllis and shook off all thoughts of political strategy. "Come on, let's find out how great this caravansary is on Italian food. Where is Gladys?"

"Waiting in the so-called Blue Room. They set up a cozy table there with candlelights."

"You know, Gladys is the best-behaved mother I know. The way she tolerates and even encourages our sordid affair is admirable."

"What is so sordid about our 'affair'?"

"All affairs are sordid until they become legitimate. A question of timing."

"Well, her timing is perfect. In Gladys's book we are already married. She is dreaming of the future. Names for our kids and the possibilities of a distant divorce."

"Not from me, my love. I am allergic to divorce from you."

After an extended and fervent embrace, Phyllis disentangled herself. "Let's go and eat."

They went into the Blue Room.

LX

Donovan had never felt so alone, so lonely, as on the dawn of this fateful day. For the first time he saw himself sitting, literally, on the top of the world, a top like a wind-swept moonscape, a desert without shrubs or flowers. He was shivering.

Holt's security was so tight that he was not permitted to call Gladys, not even on the scrambler. He had spent a miserable night, full of ugly specters, ghastly half dreams. I would not experience another night like this, not even to buy a world of eternally happy days, he thought. He had not undressed, but walked in shirt sleeves through the rooms of the White House. In and out of his bedroom, to the Oval Office, the blue salon, the white reception room. The anxious and sympathetic faces of the servants and of the Marine guards all reflected his own anxiety. He could not touch his dinner, but he gave in to hunger when the Marine sergeant handed him a tray at two in the morning with a chicken sandwich and a pint of champagne on it.

His conscience was clear. He had begun the meeting of his own Security Council comprised of generals, admirals, and the secretaries of state and defense, with the words, "If any of you can convince me that I am not thinking or acting correctly, I will gladly change my mind. I need to be absolutely sure that we are doing the right thing." No one disagreed. Surprisingly,

he received no flak from either London or Rome.
Bonn, as always, was on his side, and even Paris, after
some cartesian and self-serving reservations, came
through positively.

As he walked the long corridors, he rehearsed his
forthcoming speech. It needed to be brief and simple.
He was tempted to start with a quotation from Dante's
"Inferno," so aptly describing his own mental pains:
"In the middle of the journey of our life I came to
myself in a dark wood, where the straight way was
lost," but he discarded this as too intellectual and too
pessimistic. Instead, he substituted a quotation by Plu-
tarch that reflected his own reaction to the Kremlin's
deviltry: "No beast is more savage than man when pos-
sessed with power answerable to his rage." He had the
power but wanted to explain that he had mastered his
rage.

As a background for the television speech, he had
selected the white salon. The room had a large working fireplace, with the Stuart portrait of George Washington's unpretty face hanging over it. This was the
room from which Roosevelt had made his famous fire-
side chats, later emulated by President Carter. The
room's informal, cozy atmosphere helped to dispel the
effect of the grave and heavy oratory.

He could hardly wait for the sun to rise. He ordered
an unusually big breakfast at six thirty, for he felt he
would need sustenance. There were many meetings
scheduled with the Chiefs of Staff, and he wanted to
divert himself by plunging into technical details, red
telephones, yellow alert signals, electronics, and questions both strategic and tactical. All of these, while important, did not compare with the major problem.

The day went by fast and furiously. There was no
time for private soul-searching.

At five thirty Fred Elkins, the television director,

called him, and they went to the white salon. He
drank a glass of milk and sat down in the armchair in
front of the fireplace in which big hickory logs were
burning. He started talking at seven sharp.

In Como, Gladys, Phyllis, and Michael tried to kill
time until the President's talk. Early evening in Washington meant the wee hours of the morning at the
Villa d'Este. They listened to records or played scrab-
ble, their minds five thousand miles away in Washington.

A face bruised with adversity, Michael thought
when he saw Donovan's image on the screen. Perhaps
adversity was too strong, maybe only concern.

Donovan spoke easily, with natural simplicity. Michael appreciated his exposé of facts. "The United Nations Charter assures self-determination, and we will
do all to help all peoples to determine their own fate.
But not with the aid of mercenaries or hired assassins."
He hinted at Machiavellian machinations of what he
called a "small fraction" of the Soviet Politburo and
indicated that his own actions would help the realistic
and pacifistic leaders of the Kremlin get rid of that
political section of hawks and hotheads.

"I have been asked by the majority leader of the
temporary government in South Africa to assist them
in making the final transition to majority rule. I
agreed to their demands for credits and for materials. I
also agreed to their request to have our Seventh Fleet
visit their shores and to keep company with the Soviet
Indian Ocean Fleet." He paused. When he continued,
his face showed forceful determination. "Therefore,
with the consent of the Security Council of our nation
and the approval of our allies, I have given orders to
Admiral of the Fleet Fletcher to sail into Cape Town
harbor and . . ."

Michael wondered at what time the order had been given. By now the Seventh Fleet should be either right at the harbor or very close to it.

When Donovan concluded his speech with a prayer for peace, Gladys turned to Michael with a very worried look. "Does this mean war?"

"We don't think so," Michael answered. "The State Department, the CIA, and the British all believe that they will back down, just like they did in Cuba."

"And what if they are mistaken?" Phyllis asked.

"Tell you in a minute," Michael said. "But first, please lend me your glasses for a second."

Puzzled, Phyllis handed him her eyeglasses. Michael took the plastic frames, put them down gently on the parquet floor and stepped on them.

He has gone crazy, Phyllis thought. Terrified, she shouted, "What are you doing?"

"Destroying the enemy. I don't want the Kremlin to listen to this conversation."

"The Kremlin? Are you mad?"

"Not quite. Please sit down and let's have another glass of champagne. It's going to be a long story, and if you decide at the end of it that you're marrying a congenital liar and an unrepentant conspirator, you'll be right."

He rang the bell and asked the sleepy waiter for more champagne.

LXI

Houndsworth had no time for the checkup in Rome. He sat, day and night, in the Communications Room, listening to the buzz of the telephones, picking up coded messages on the ticker, looking at both the Italian television and the BBC.

The food they brought in to the room was not bad, and the coffee was excellent. He had one short meal with Castor, who seemed very cocksure of himself.

It was on the second day when things started to go sour.

As the day progressed, the news worsened. Houndsworth could not make up his mind whether he was watching a Greek tragedy or a Feydeau farce.

The structure, a well-conceived scheme of imagination and planning, was collapsing. The real Pope was back in the Vatican, and nobody would ever know that Monticelli had been replacing him for many months. South Africa was going into the Western camp, perhaps forever.

After Donovan's speech, Houndsworth waited for instructions from Moscow. There weren't any. Italian radio and television, along with the BBC, was announcing over and over again—and repeating the "red line," the "good news" telephone conversation between the heads of the United States and the Soviet Union.

He lay down on the cot and tried to sleep. He must

have just dozed off when he heard a not-too-friendly voice say, "Comrade Houndsworth."

"Yes?" he answered, still half asleep.

The man read the message from a yellow piece of paper. "You are to fly to Moscow this afternoon at six thirty."

Houndsworth repeated automatically, "Fly to Moscow at six thirty. Thanks, Comrade."

He got up and took a swig of vodka. Not good for his liver, but he knew helpful for his morale.

"I have to make a decision," he thought, but he knew that this was not the moment to make one. He compromised on an intermediate solution. He would take a brisk walk in the city, down the beautiful Spanish stairs to the Via Condotti, then to the park of the Villa Borghese. And after that?

He put on his heavy coat but left the fur hat. The sun was out, and spring was definitely in the air.

He inhaled that air, trying to disregard the gasoline fumes. Leaving the embassy was easy, although the guard at the desk in the entrance eyed him suspiciously. So did the two swarthy Italians across the street, secret police written all over them. Okay with me, Houndsworth thought, as he descended the graceful steps on the Piazza di Spagna.

He overtaxed his strength. He ordered an espresso in an outside café on the Via Condotti and enjoyed himself thoroughly. Another planet, he thought, as he watched the chic, young, gay, attractive females, chattering and window-shopping.

He wanted to go to the garden of the Villa Medici for reasons still half buried in his subconscious, but he felt too tired to walk all the way. The cabstand on the corner was empty, and he tried to hail a passing cab, but it was occupied. He succeeded on his third attempt.

Houndsworth sat down on a comfortable bench by a fountain and turned his face up toward the still chilly sun. It gave him physical pleasure to look at the ever-green trees, the well-kept lawn. His thoughts turned to the icy, snow-covered streets of Moscow. Occasionally he stooped to pick up some small, whitewashed pebbles and throw them into the basin of the fountain.

He was not aware at first of the dapper little man who sat down discreetly on the far end of the bench.

"My God, Alan, a long time it's been," Romanelli said. "Roughly thirty years."

Houndsworth turned and looked at him.

"You haven't changed much. More prosperous-looking. Well, in 1944, you were just a boy trying to learn the secrets of the secret service. Have I changed?"

"Well, you look a few years older. Are you keeping well?"

"Moderately. When we used to sit on this bench in the middle of the war I felt somewhat younger."

"Can I buy you a drink? Or dinner?"

"You can. But let us sit here for a moment. It is so peaceful. A meeting of old friends and colleagues. On two different sides of the barricade."

"Alan, this thing with the Pope. It has your imprint. Was it your idea?"

Houndsworth sighed. "I confess I'm the copyright owner. Of a not-very-successful book."

"Well, we all have our setbacks. You can't win them all."

Sadly, Houndsworth said, "But you can lose them all."

"Look, Alan, I have no intention of putting the bloodhounds on your trail. Are you going back to Moscow?"

"They want me back. Today."

"And?"

" 'And?' is a good question. I did not know what I wanted when I started on this little excursion. When I saw your goons in front of our embassy, the idea crossed my mind that we would meet here. Now, talking to you, I know what I don't want. I don't want to go to Siberia. It is nicer here—and warmer."

"Well, I don't know how long we can keep you here. M16 in London will insist on seeing you again."

"I know. Still, the prison hospitals are not too bad there. In any case, better than in Khabarovsk."

"Hospitals?"

"Yes. I have a bad liver. They call it cirrhosis. Too much vodka, I guess."

"Well, our hospitals aren't bad. In the meantime you can pay your bill by giving us some KGB gossip."

"I am not ready for that yet. Perhaps. Perhaps later."

"Guess you can risk one more drink, Alan—a grappa. My car is around the corner."

LXII

When the Foreign Office let Cholmondley know that the President of the United States was to make an unscheduled speech in half an hour in Washington, he did not understand. Wasn't Donovan in Italy? Was the speech prerecorded? What kind of mystery was this? He made a quick call to their men in Como, but could not get through.

He did not need a road map. When he heard the first word of Donovan's speech, he said to Colvin, "Gentleman, Comrade, boy, we've been had."

Like Gladys, Colvin asked, as Gladys had, "Does this mean war?"

"Don't be silly," Cholmondley said. "They'll back down."

"Wait a minute." Colvin saw the blinking red light. "Signal from the President's daughter." He pressed a button. They heard Michael's voice, "Please lend me your glasses for a second . . ."

"To use a cheap Yankee vulgarism, the jig is up," Cholmondley said.

"Khabarov."

"Or Barushnya."

"Can't get our tobacco, Baby's Bottom or Dunhill's 74 Downfall there."

"All is possible if you play your cards right."

"Like what?"

"Lean a little on Maximus."

"He can lean back quite easily."

"Well," Colvin started to say when the intercom rang. A deep baritone voice said something without any warmth. Colvin put the receiver down. "They want us over there. Komsomolskaya. Right away. Take your pipe and tobacco in any case."

In the black limousine, Cholmondley asked, mostly just to make conversation, "Where did we make our mistakes?"

Colvin shrugged. "We talked about this before. So-called human errors. We didn't know that Clemens knew how to handle electric equipment, and we thought that an atheist is immune to faith, religion, or whatever you call that shit. Here we are."

"Will we see Alan again?"

"I guess not."

LXIII

Admiral Vladimir Rokosowski sat on the poop deck of the aircraft carrier *Gorki*. He held a tall glass of vodka with crushed ice. He had acquired the taste of iced vodka at a reception at the American embassy in Moscow. Captain Ilya Zubow, drinking uniced vodka, sat next to him.

Both men with mild interest occasionally focused their binoculars on the harbor. It was much too hot for Rokosowski, a big, heavy man. He had inherited his height from his father, a giant from Kiev, and his girth from his Georgian mother. He put down his binoculars and said to the captain, "All blacks." It was a rhetorical statement of no meaning and no importance. They were in Africa, and the dark color of the population could surprise nobody.

What Rokosowski probably thought unconsciously was simply, "I am here with my fleet on account of these blacks." As a born Ukrainian, the most racist of all Russian tribes, he had strong conceptions of the superiority of white races, especially the blond ones. He never expressed these thoughts in words, and actually, if somebody had accused him of racism, he would have violently protested in angry surprise.

He stood up, and with the glass of vodka in his hand, he walked around the deck of his carrier. He looked with real pride at his fleet—the new, light, and speedy atom-powered cruisers, the slender destroyers that carried more power and destruction than a Second World War dreadnought. And the second light carrier, the wolf pack of submarines. All clean, neat, and very functional.

The thought of advertising all this hardware to the population of South Africa did not displease him. But the thought that did frighten him, even disgusted him, was a possible confrontation with the Yankee Seventh Fleet. Rokosowski simply could not face the idea of sending his fine fleet into battle. The purpose of the makeup of this fleet, the composition and the buildup, was to show that it existed, a deterrent against imperial aggression.

To send this fine, expensive material into war action would be criminal, and the admiral categorically refused the thought that this could actually happen. Thank God, the Americans were playing it wise. No trace of their Seventh Fleet, which was cruising somewhere in the Indian Ocean, not far from Lorenzo Marques. They will probably sight them on their way back to their new Indian Ocean bases. No, there was no reason to be disturbed. He walked back to the poop deck.

LXIV

Bwato stood in the center of a small group of men. Like a flag on a lead tank, his tall, thin figure protruded over the heads of the group. Most of the men carried binoculars of all makes and sizes. That of Bwato was a gift from his friend and mentor Kenyere, and it was an expensive one.

They stood on the very end of the *molo* in Cape Town harbor and looked out on the ocean to the horizon where the line of prehistoric sea monsters—ugly, gray steel structures—were clearly visible. The glasses were not needed to see the red hammer and sickle on the flags of the Soviet Indian Fleet.

Bwato was glad that Kenyere had not lived to see the superspectacle. Perhaps he would have refused to come out to this jetty and look at the display of Soviet power. He might have been right. What was the use? He looked back at the inside harbor and the crowd gathered there to view the fleet. Not a large crowd, and Bwato knew the quality of it. A few members of the really poorest classes with legitimate aspirations, misguided, according to Kenyere, by the hirelings, coming from all parts of Africa, of the all-promising Marxist religion.

Would there be any change on the horizon tomorrow? Did the good President of the mighty United States receive Kenyere's letter? And the news of his assassination? Would these things change the President's attitude? America was so far away and President Donovan had other worries on his agenda. Not that this one was less important. Bwato, who had studied in Cambridge, had a good global comprehension, and he knew how important this local election was, not only for South Africa, but for the whole world.

Bwato was not a very firm believer in the dogma of religion, but if Bishop Kwa were still alive, he would spend the whole night praying in Kwa's "kirk." He consoled himself with the thought that prayers are accepted from everywhere, even from the little native café where he intended to spend the night drinking beer and praying secretly.

LXV

It was three o'clock in the morning when Admiral Tamarov burst into his commander's bedchamber. Vladimir Rokosowski, admiral of the fleet, snoring peacefully, did not react to sound. Respectfully, Tamarov touched his left shoulder. No result. He grabbed both shoulders of his commander and started shaking him.

Suddenly, Rokosowski came to life. He sat up straight and uttered a fancy curse, involving Tamarov's mother and the mother of all whores, the Virgin of Kazan. Finally, making more sense, he asked, "Where is the explosion?"

"No explosion, Admiral. Perhaps worse. Our radar is going crazy. A fleet of three aircraft carriers, six cruisers, twenty-two destroyers, is coming in fast from the east."

"Damnation. The American Seventh Fleet. They must be crazy. No announcement on the radio?"

"None, Comrade Admiral. Total radio silence. What are your orders?"

"My order is for a pot of coffee. I have to call the boss. Tell the operator to put me through to the emergency navy desk in Moscow."

By now he was completely awake. He dressed quickly and gulped down the hot coffee.

Moscow was just as astonished as he. "We will call you back." It was the voice of the secretary of the navy. "Way above our jurisdiction. The Kremlin will decide."

Rokosowski ordered the red alert. Bugles sounded, whistles shrieked. "Battle stations. How far are they?"

"Here is the latest radar report. Sixty nautical miles."

"This means that if they keep the speed of twenty-nine knots, they should be here a little after five A.M."

A lieutenant commander rushed up the bridge and saluted smartly. "Moscow is on the red line, Admiral," he said.

Rokosowski went to the Communications Room. He could not believe that "this was it." He hoped to hear the voice of reason.

He was not disappointed. The "superboss" was calm. He instructed him not to move, to wait and see. The Kremlin was contacting President Donovan.

At 5:42 A.M. they received the first signal from the admiral of the Seventh Fleet, now abreast of their own. "Admiral of the Fleet Fletcher sends his compliments and warm greetings to his Russian colleague. The American fleet is on a peaceful maneuver exercise, just paying a friendly visit to the port of Cape Town." Rokosowski's cryptic answer was, "Message received."

The Seventh Fleet moved slowly, closer to the shore, the Stars and Stripes waving in the breeze, while the guns thundered the twenty-one obligatory rounds of salute.

Admiral Fletcher saw through his field glasses the crowds on the jetty and in the harbor. The crowd was increasing rapidly. His aide-de-camp reported that the Cape Town radio and television had canceled all programs and were featuring the news of the arrival of the American fleet.

Just before six A.M., Rokosowski held a longer talk

with Moscow. He was told that President Donovan had announced on television that he was sending the Seventh Fleet into Cape Town harbor. In the middle of the conversation, he was told to hold. The boss was on the red line to the American President. His hands trembling, Rokosowski spilled half the vodka on his trousers while waiting.

Then, at last, the voice came back. "No confrontation," it said. "Stay as you are. Be prepared to return to the Lorenzo Marques base at noon. Over."

With a tremendous sigh of relief Rokosowski downed what was left of the vodka. Being alone, he could risk a *boze moi*, a "Thank you, God," for His intervention.

LXVI

When the call came in the late afternoon, Donovan said hoarsely, "Darling . . ."

Gladys tried to disguise her teary voice and repeated, "Darling . . ."

For a few seconds neither spoke. Finally, Donovan continued. "It's all over. I won't say thank God—all over but the shooting. There won't be any shooting. Ivor called me on the red line, and he spoke, surprisingly, in English. In his deepest baritone, he assured me, quoting what I said, that I had helped him demolish the few hawkish elements in his entourage. He used the French word *entourage*."

"Pat, dearest, I'm so relieved—you pulled it off."

"No need to tell you what a weight has fallen off me. Now to important things. I want you to take the helicopter to Verona and fly back here as fast as possible. I cannot sleep another night on your side of the bed, smelling your perfume. And breakfast without your nagging me for spreading too much butter on my toast is terribly dull."

Gladys laughed. "Okay, funny one. Michael has checked and found that it would be faster to drive to Malpensa airport and take the scheduled Milano–New York TWA flight. I am all packed. How about that?"

"I leave it to Michael. He will see about security. And Phyllis?"

"Yes, Phyllis. She would like to stay here a couple of days with Michael. A sort of prehoneymoon vacation. Okay?"

"Fine. I expect General Holt will explain to him that illegitimate honeymoons don't figure in the CIA budget. When is the wedding?"

"The minute I get back we will start the preparations. Well, I'll have to start packing. In ten hours I'll be with you. One last question. When you delivered your message about the Seventh Fleet, what were your thoughts about us?"

"I confess I was glad that you and Phyllis were on Lake Como and not in Washington; that you are safer there than here crossed my mind. Especially when Holt suggested after the speech that I board the doomsday plane and wait in it, cruising at an altitude of forty thousand feet, for the Soviet reaction. I refused because I was even then convinced that they wouldn't start anything drastic."

"Next time, you sonofabitch, we cruise in the doomsday plane together."

"There won't be a next time. Just get back fast."

Phyllis and Michael had entered and heard the last words of the conversation.

"What is that doomsday plane? Sounds terrifying."

"Your CIA expert can explain it to you."

"Well, it's a supersonic plane that costs about two hundred million dollars. It's equipped with all the electronic devices, a radar tail five miles long, food for ninety hours. The President, with the commanding general of the army, the heads of the navy and air force, can direct all operations in case of an enemy attack."

"Thank you, Michael," said Phyllis. "Now I want you to listen to me very seriously. I hope that this is the last CIA operation you're mixed up with. As I told you, I've forgiven you for using me as bait in an international intrigue, though it wasn't easy when I found out that we were making love in public—a Russian public, at that. But I kept in mind that it was very important for national defense. But I'm addicted to privacy, and I don't like voyeurism. And I hate the secret service and your being involved in their dirty methods. Also, I have a sneaking suspicion that it began to intrigue you: the reality was becoming more exciting than the fantasies in your books."

"Now wait a minute . . ."

Phyllis continued. "No, Michael. I am not going to wait a minute. I want your promise that you will resign, now. I don't want Murgatroyd to be heckled in school because his father is a spy."

"Who is Murgatroyd?"

"Our first son. If you continue to work for the CIA, I'll baptise him Murgatroyd."

"That frightens the bejesus out of me. I give you my solemn promise that on the day of our return, I'll hand in my badge and replace it with my favorite fountain pen."

Gladys read the paper on the flight back to Washington. The headlines and the front page editorial under the caption of EPILOGUE dealt with the conversation between Donovan and the Russian premier. Another item dealt with the victory of the moderate group of Kwa in South Africa, and a third spoke of the defeat of a Communist attempt at taking over the Portuguese government. These events were linked together as a compliment to President Donovan's strategy and the *Post* called it "the epilogue of an era."

Two lesser items interested Gladys. One was Pope Clemens's obituary at the funeral of an unknown priest killed in the line of duty, and the second spoke of the arrest of a Russian superspy, whose identity would be difficult to establish. He was to be deported to the United States.

Epilogue, Gladys thought. I hope it is. The end of a nightmare. She raised her champagne glass, and with tears of joy in her eyes, toasted her own Patrick Donovan.